FELICIA C. SULLIVAN

FOLLOW ME INTO THE DARK

FEMINIST PRESS
AT THE CITY UNIVERSITY
OF NEW YORK
NEW YORK CITY

Published in 2017 by the Feminist Press
at the City University of New York
The Graduate Center
365 Fifth Avenue, Suite 5406
New York, NY 10016

feministpress.org

First Feminist Press edition 2017

Copyright © 2017 by Felicia C. Sullivan

All rights reserved.

 This book was made possible thanks to a grant from New York State Council on the Arts with the support of Governor Andrew Cuomo and the New York State Legislature.

 This book is supported in part by an award from the National Endowment for the Arts.

No part of this book may be reproduced, used, or stored in any information retrieval system or transmitted in any form or by any means, electronic, mechanical, photocopying, recording, or otherwise, without prior written permission from the Feminist Press at the City University of New York, except in the case of brief quotations embodied in critical articles and reviews.

First printing March 2017

Cover design by Drew Stevens
Text design by Suki Boynton

Library of Congress Cataloging-in-Publication Data
Names: Sullivan, Felicia C., author.
Title: Follow me into the dark / Felicia C. Sullivan.
Description: New York City : Feminist Press, [2017]
Identifiers: LCCN 2016034355| ISBN 9781558619456 (softcover) | ISBN 9781558614109 (ebook)
Subjects: LCSH: Stepsisters--Fiction. | Brothers and sisters--Fiction. | Psychological fiction. | BISAC: FICTION / Suspense. | FICTION / Contemporary Women. | FICTION / Psychological. | GSAFD: Suspense fiction.
Classification: LCC PS3619.U425 F65 2017 | DDC 813/.6--dc23
LC record available at https://lccn.loc.gov/2016034355

"Within the first words you'll find yourself pulled into something rich, luminous, and unsparing. I'm reminded of contemporaries like Merritt Tierce and Ottessa Moshfegh, but Ms. Sullivan achieves an emotional intensity and pacing that is simultaneously seductive and blistering. *Follow Me into the Dark* is both an invitation and a dare. Accept both. You'll be glad you did."

—JOE McGINNISS JR., *Carousel Court*

"I really did not want to recognize myself in Felicia C. Sullivan's murderers and victims, her deranged children of deranged parents. But she beckoned to me with her blunt poetry—which is to say, with truth—and I followed her into the dark. This is one demented and brilliant book." **—MATTHEW SHARPE,** *Jamestown*

"From the first sentence, *Follow Me into the Dark* plunged me into a storm of family, secrecy, madness, and murder so intoxicating I had to remind myself to breathe. Felicia C. Sullivan has crafted a haunting and wholly engrossing story of uncommon moral complexity, her prose bright and swift as lightning. I could not put this novel down." **—LAURA VAN DEN BERG,** *Find Me*

"Elegant and brutal, stunningly imagined and frighteningly real, *Follow Me into the Dark* takes you on a journey through the darkest sides of human nature, with unforgettable characters that grip you from the first line and don't let go."

—LIZA MONROY, *Seeing as Your Shoes Are Soon to Be on Fire*

"The novel draws you into its twisted web with lyrical, luminous prose. A gripping exploration of pain, anger, and revenge, this story will stay with you long past the last page."

—KELLY BRAFFET, *Save Yourself*

CALGARY PUBLIC LIBRARY

AUG   2017

"I could hear my heart beating. I could hear everyone's heart. I could hear the human noise we sat there making, not one of us moving, not even when the room went dark." —RAYMOND CARVER

"THERE IS A woman on a hotel bed, and her hair is on fire," I shout into a pay phone. The operator asks me whether I saw actual flames, was there actual fire? Maybe I saw a woman smoking a cigarette, because this is California and that's what people are prone to do. "No, you don't understand, I'm talking a fire here. I'm talking about a burning, a smell."

Come to think of it, the woman, Gillian, was smoking or, rather, swallowing a lit cigarette that burned down her throat. I know this because I put the cigarette in her mouth, struck a match, and said, "All you have to do is breathe. I'll take care of the rest." I bound her wrists and ankles with rope, dialed up the thermostat to ninety (because why not?), and drew the curtains. The woman writhed and thrashed; her face was a river—a flood of tears and black kohl.

I waited for the heat.

You should know that I'd come for the hair. The hair that is a constellation of stars, a map of red curls tumbling down the woman's back. The hair I saw James, my step-father, run his fingers through. The hair he tucked behind a pierced ear. The hair he took in his mouth. The hair that replaced the clumps that fell out of my mother's head.

"Tell me why you did it. Why you came into our home and broke things," I had said to Gillian. "Actually, forget it. I don't want to know."

The operator makes inquiries about the location and coordinates, room numbers and facial descriptions. "To be honest," the operator confesses, "I'm finding this hard to believe. Who goes and sets their hair on fire? You swallow pills. Or turn on the gas. It's easier that way. Quick." Nobody wants a problem suicide, a complicated death by one's own hand.

From the pay phone I've a terrific view of the room I booked and paid for with a credit card that belonged to James. While the flames devour the curtains, I clutch a lock of Gillian's hair, tight. Later I'll place it in a small box, next to my mother's ashes.

The hotel manager arrives in a pickup, surveys the fire, and calls the police. "Murray, you're never going to believe this, but my goddamn place is on fire. Again." By then I'm in the car. Gone.

I imagine my mother's suffocation: her love strangled in her body in life, and her regret, rage, and hurt contained in a small box carrying her to the afterlife.

CALIFORNIA ISN'T HOME. It's not Nevada. Death in California comes without warning; the land never stills.

Quit it with the story no one wants to hear, says everyone, always, whenever I complain about Gillian, the home-wrecking whore who's stealing the breath right out of my mother's mouth by prying my stepfather's warm body out of bed. All my friends want me on mute because they've heard this story before, and the story is never new. Wife becomes a somnambulant. She's expired, beyond her best-by date. Husband lifts the sheets and checks for signs of life but there is no movement, only the warmth of the sheets. Wife removes her ring and places it on one of her toes, and then kicks it off the bed. Husband raises the sheet over her head as if she's already one of the departed. Wife still breathes but no one bothers to check for a pulse. See the chalk outline of her body. Feel the sheets cool. Husband drives down to the beach to collect his head and meets a girl listening to *Tosca*. Her name is Gillian, and she's a photocopy of me, which sickens and comforts him all at once. I think about the bed and the beach as crime scenes, and I tell my friends this but everyone stops caring. Hurt becomes a constant state.

It's an affair, Kate. They'll likely divorce, Kate, they say. Until my mother becomes terminal, is delivered a death sentence in an oncologist's office, and then they don't say anything at all.

The day my mother is diagnosed with advanced lung cancer, James drives us home, lets the motor run until we're inside the house, and then hits the gas. Hours later, I find him and the whore in a hotel room and I watch my stepfather wrap a scarf around Gillian's neck. She nearly blacks out; her eyes roll to white. Coughing out sentences in starts and stops, the whore speaks in staccato. It gets to the point in the game where it seems like she can't breathe. James makes out the word *love*, and he pauses and says, "Let's get something straight. That's not a hand I'm playing."

Gillian says, "Okay, fine," her mouth all dry and scabbing. Her pain registers—the physicality of her face coming undone, as if it were an abandoned house with rotting stairs, a flood rising up through the floorboards, and a Closed for Renovations sign swinging like a pendulum (although this is the kind of house no one will take on, gut, clean, and repair)—and I can tell that this makes my stepfather want her more.

After six minutes of the old in-and-out in a room they've rented, after their bodies come together and untangle like live wires, they eat ceviche with their hands and talk about Cubans—cigars, not people. On the television a man shifts uncomfortably in his seat as he regales a now-infamous story about a former employee who didn't quite work out. *A perfectly normal individual,* he says. *Two barrels of a shotgun*, he says. *Stacked neatly in one of the hotel rooms*, he says. From my secret vantage point, I watch them nod, their bodies covered in fuck, letting the scene play out.

Lately I've been thinking about the old, deaf artist who painted savagery on his walls. He felt a need to correct the serene and sublime, to undo the harm done by portraits of refined gentry, and the artist was something of a fakir drawing out the barbaric. A still-beating heart held in one hand and a scissor in the other. He made a mural of the macabre, replete with Viejas conjuring, a Sabbath, and a mad Greek devouring the limbs of his newborn. The child was rendered in a chilling white, but all I can remember is the cavern that was the father's mouth.

Gillian sits naked in a chair, crossing and uncrossing her legs. "You know what I like about us, James? We're just two tools that fit well together," she says, James's tie a tourniquet on her wrist. Her lips barely move when she says, "Just a hammer and a nail. What keeps this interesting is that we're never in the same role; sometimes I'm beaten and other times I'm beating."

"Ellie's dying," he says, referring to my mother. The woman he once loved, who's now nothing more than a mess of patchy blond hair, bleached skin, and bone. "She's got no more than a few months left and I'm fucking you. Don't be a lesser version of her. Ellie mastered the game of not caring, of crawling through the dark and coming up empty. Improvise for me, at least. Give me a new play on an old trick. Don't just sit there and pass off all her best plays as your own."

"I'm not a fucking *dog*. I don't heel on cue."

"Is that right?" he says slyly.

"And besides, Ellie's been dying."

"I don't know why I fuck you," James says.

I watch him reach for the watch my mother gave him. I watch him clasp it around his wrist. I watch him register the time. I watch him glance at Gillian and then at the door with a longing that resembles love. He wants out, I can feel it, but why bother? The damage is done. On the upside, he'll squeeze in a few last lays before he has to play the role of mourning the departed.

"You fuck me because it feels good," Gillian says.

James buries his head in his knees, like what you do in the event of a plane crash. Four-color brochures depict the serenity of the *leaving*: the dramatic gasps for oxygen and bodies folded in half. Perhaps we're instructed to do this, not because we have a desire to breathe (what's the point, really?), but because we've an innate need to return to what we believe to be the beginning. To close our eyes and humbly crawl back to the warm and familiar dark, because although this is the one thing we don't remember (that one head pushing out, those eyes that opened wide to the first light, and the mouth that screamed so valiantly, the terror of being born), it brings us an unexplainable comfort. James once asked Ellie, why him? Of all the men, why did she choose him? She paused, leaned over, and smoothed his hair out of his eyes—no one had done that, gotten so close, touched the skin above his brow—and said that she liked men who had been through war and would spend the rest of their days dressing their wounds. Who could predict then that the wounds would stay open, never heal? This is how James feels when he's with Gillian—a walking wound.

"You gonna bake me a cake, James? Like the old days? Buttercream frosting with a cherry on top?" Gillian says. "You know of my affection for ovens."

"These aren't the old days," he says, weary.

"You used to have some fight in you. Stop acting like *you* have cancer."

"We're not talking about my wife. We're not permitted to have that conversation. You want me to draw you a fucking map of where you can and cannot go?"

"Maybe I was wrong," Gillian says. "Maybe there's some fight in you left."

I watch her eat fish. Is there no end to how much this woman will devour? The chewing, the picking out of flesh from her teeth, the swallowing—it makes me dizzy, but I have to keep it together. I need to see. I've got to gather the evidence, do the math, and make the case. All of them will invariably beg for a reason, and I will hand over that whore of a woman's hair and say, *Do you understand I had no choice?*

Things had to be done. This woman had to be burned.

THE DAY MY mother dies, but before she does, I make her toast. Palming a hot cup of coffee, I feel the steam rise and warm my hand. "We can talk about it, if you want. Or not, if that's what you want, too," I say.

"Men are always ready to trade you for a younger version of you. It's still you, but with lighter hair and a tighter face. A passport with no stamps," my mother says, slathering cold butter onto toast. She doesn't seem to notice the bread tearing, the crumbs scattering the counter.

"You're breaking the toast," I say.

"*That's* what concerns you," my mother says, "a mess in the kitchen." Sometimes when Ellie speaks she sounds like me, or me like her. I can't tell which.

"Mother, of course not." But I don't register. I might as well have not been in the room.

"I spend my days, my life, reconciling the woman I once was, all my wants and desires, with the woman I became, and the wants become needs, necessities, and there comes a moment when desire extinguishes. So here I am, holding the ashes of my former self, mourning. Marriage made me selfish—don't do it, Kate. Don't get married. Become allergic to the thought of it. Because you'll keep asking yourself if what you have, who you are, is ever enough. And one day you'll wake and realize this is your life, all of it. Your life has become an inventory of all the things you've accumulated over the course of a marriage, and you wonder if it was all worth it. You're not a wife or a husband—you're an accountant, a taxpayer, and a divider of property. I made a mistake; I asked for too much, loved too little. I thought I could get away with giving only the minimum. But in the end you're left with so much less than what you started with, and no one can solve that. Maybe my love should have been a tidal wave—all-consuming, a love that swallows you whole. Or maybe I shouldn't have bothered to love at all. Look where it got me. Look at you, sweet Kate, aching for what I can't give you."

My mother's wrist shakes. She holds a knife in her hands. Butters toast as if her life depends on it.

"Please. Stop. This isn't your fault," I say. "You didn't make him fuck that woman. Mom, can you stop buttering the fucking toast?"

"I did this to you. I allowed this to happen, and for what? We're none the happier because of it, in spite of it."

Ellie balls up the obliterated toast. Stands there, feels the crumbs rain down from the spaces between her fingers. She's gone, now. Never coming back, now. All the life drained, now. Sessile, now. Finally in love, now. But there's only room enough in her heart for James; I get the scraps, the never enough, the remains of what James will inevitably abandon.

My mother says, "I did this to you."

I'm not going to talk about what it was like to find my mother when I came home that evening. Cold cheeks, hair shorn with the scissors in her drawer (no one will understand why she cut her hair to the nape), lips parted from when the contents of the bottle pulled the last vestige of air out. Traces of crumbs in her palm. The toast remnants, buttered now. Cold remains on a plate.

At the wake, I observe the people in black, our friends and family, and think: keep moving. Go on, there's nothing to see. The motley lot slouches past, with their popcorn and binoculars, their suppositions and theories. *Now* my friends want to talk to me so they can fill in the blanks. *Now* my friends are in the business of concern with their thin lips and sympathy symphonies.

The Chinchorro were unique in their dedication to preserving the dead. Embalmers excised the skin and the flesh, replacing it with clay. Precious organs were removed and pickled before they were returned, tissue wrapped, to the body. Only the heart remained, lying still among the pickles and animal hair. I admire this ritual, the Chinchorro's fastidious connection to the departed, and the nearly two months of care devoted to the remains.

The curtain closes. It's the end of the show, folks. The coffin glides in.

After everyone leaves, watch me scream.

I READ A book where the author replaced the word *die* with *complete*. As if to say, we're done with that now, let's move on to something else. Let's change topics. Let's move to the next item on the agenda. Let's muffle the tears of the grieving with a word that is at turns gruesome and elegant. Why don't we all gather over *here* and whisper because there's no need to go out and create a massacre on the street?

Childhood Is the Kingdom Where Nobody Dies, a pro-life billboard reads. What if you were never a child? What if you sprung as an adult out of the womb and spent your life in constant repair? Where does everyone go when they complete?

There is no nobility in a body shuddering its last breath, of a heart slouching forth to its final beat, of a mother's hand that has grown cold and inert, like unworn cashmere. There is only a full bottle of prescription pills and an empty one. There are knuckles in my mouth in the middle of the night smothering screams; I hear her voice. It's Christmas morning and she tells me that when she dies she wants to be burned. None of this below-the-ground business with worms in her eyes. *Burn me up and spread me out in the water.* I am fifteen and I nod, taking note of a time when I'll have to endure a burning. There are only the sentences *My mother is alive* and *My mother is dead.*

Excuse us. *Complete.* Let's be careful not to make a disturbance.

After the wake, James sits in a car and cuts the engine. His face is a mess of pain. He wraps his hands around his neck and begins to choke himself, but stops because he can't handle the pressure. From the window above I shake my head. Fucking amateur. You can't die that way. I want to tap the window and say, *Give me the keys. Let me turn on the engine. Let me let it run.*

In the kitchen where I remember a wadded-up ball of bread in my shaking mother's hand, James makes an attempt at familial love by squeezing my shoulder. My body is a house that collapses inward, caves in. No survivors. Just a slice of light from the window above, a dam of water breaking, and the rush of waves careening in. "You're touching me," I say.

"I just wanted to see how you are," James says.

"Complete," I say.

The following day, I hear them.

"The body isn't even cold," James says.

"I thought the body was burned," Gillian says.

"So now you want to be touched."

Something in me seizes.

AT DAWN, I wake and select an outfit from one of eight shirts, ten pants, fifteen socks, forty-two pairs of underwear, two bras, and two pairs of shoes. I launder and fold my clothes neatly into drawers with sachets separating the layers. Mostly, I wear blue.

It takes me forty-five minutes to walk the 2.22 miles to the bakery, where I tie a white apron over my blue outfit and make cakes in the shape of eighties cartoon characters. I make and pipe the cakes by hand even though every shop in town now uses industrial mixers—giant machines that sift and mix ingredients. It terrifies me to think of a mass production of buttercream Smurfs, tubs of multicolored dye for Rainbow Brite's hair, and I indulge in this lamentation with my boss, Minnie, daily.

Minnie makes her rounds about town, sniffing out her competitors and reporting back all the sordid tales of their mediocrity in excruciating detail. "Bunny Blake's got an apple-pie display in the window. That low-rent charlatan was making a butter crust before she met me. She's gone fat, you know. Got high on the supply. Don't get like her, Kate. Fat in all the wrong places."

I'll keep that in mind. Sifting flour, creaming butter, and making vanilla extract from scratch, the precision of baking cakes comforts me. Right now I need to follow an outline. I need to color in the lines. This is how I get through my days without screaming. At night, I bite into my pillows and swallow some of the feathers.

In a small voice Minnie says, "You know I'd kill her. I would. With my hands. I've never met the woman but I heard the stories. That's not right what she's doing, feeding on a dead woman's leftovers. I made the cake for your mother's wedding, you know. She was a terrible baker, bless her heart, but she had good taste. Ellie was exacting about the things she loved."

I nod, crack eggs, and mix in the dry ingredients.

"Funny how she wanted it blue," Minnie says. "She wanted the whole charade blue, right down to the napkins and frosting. Look at you now, all freckles and red hair dyed blond. You look just like her."

This is how I mourn my mother: I wear the color she was burned in. Let my hair grow to my waist. Refuse to cut it. I grip the counter with my hands. Don't cry. Don't eliminate. Never conceive of a love so deep it threatens to complete.

My grief has yet to take form or shape; it's a wound that never closes or heals. It's mammoth. Every day I wake to that word and at night collapse into bed with it. Grief comes like swallows. That's what it's like to love someone more than yourself, when what you can feel can only be described as mammoth. Even then, the word doesn't fit. This is why I can't be around people. They make my grief small, reduce it to less than the sum of its parts—who gives a *fuck* about wedding cakes and blue napkins—when it should be sweeping, large, and as dark as the ocean. This is why I cry in cemeteries—the only place where it's acceptable to be a wreck. It hasn't been a month and people ask me if I'm *better* yet. In response, I tell them about this article I read. Charles Manson is getting old and he's worried about the environment. The scar of the cross on his head has healed and he's just like the rest of us, frightened of climate change.

Minnie wonders aloud if she's gone too far? Said too much? "I know how you love, but I also know how you grieve."

I steady myself. "No, this is good. I need to hear this."

Minnie lays a hand on my shoulder and says, "You don't need to be here, kid. You can go home."

I consider a playlist, music for torching. "No, I need this."

Sometimes I feel like a vampire.

Come nightfall, I visit the barnacles. They've set up shop on the surface of a giant rock in front of the ocean, and this is where I stand most evenings, watching. I run down to the shore and the trees shake from my velocity, never quite resuming their former shape. Don't ask me to explain why I do this; something about uneven surfaces and permanent attachments pleases me.

The sun settles into the horizon, painting the waves red. Once, I spent an hour watching a public television special on the feeding habits of barnacles. They're tricky, sessile, set on feeding on anything in motion with their spindly, sticky legs grabbing at things. Determined to drain every bit of life from their host.

Observe the multiplication.

Consider this: Imagine trying to make a life for yourself and there's some faux mollusk trying to leech it away. Survival is now predicated on discipline—how you notice the drift and cleave, and how fast you're able to cut it off and push it away. If you don't, you'll become lost, unable to locate any semblance of your former self.

A seduction based on legs wrapped around a body, tight. A life boxed in, a constant suffocation, and a realization that there's no way out—this is what Ellie's marriage must have been like.

The air is cold now. As I fall asleep I see her body framed in a box. A column of flames swallows her home.

A man waves to me from the lawn. He stands there, one hand patting the side of his thigh while the other is cupped, slowly twisting and turning from the wrist, a wave that reminds me of beauty pageants and tiaras. I open the window and lean out, stare back.

"I think you have the wrong house," I shout, although something in me knows he doesn't. He's exactly where he's meant to be. From my window I can see that he's a scruffy, beautiful boy with a mop of blue-black curls trailing down his neck, and an alabaster face.

"We have a lot in common," he says. "Why don't you come down and we'll talk about it."

"I'm sorry. Do I know you?"

"Let's say we have a common interest," he says. Bicycles fly down the sidewalk, mail is being delivered, and weeds are yanked from flower beds. He smiles and says, "It's the middle of the day, Kate. Public place, lots of witnesses."

"How do you know my name?" I open the window wider, so wide that the possibility of me falling out of it becomes real.

"My friend Lionel, he's good with names; he helps me keep track. He's my table of contents. Aren't you even the least bit curious why I'm here? What I've got to tell you? Because if it were me . . . I'd be interested. I'd already be down here, asking what's what. Because Kate, I have a lot to tell you. I know things, things about your father. Your real father."

I run downstairs, almost fall down them.

Closer up, he's beautiful in a way that's disturbing. Something about his face, the symmetry of it, reminds me of an unfinished painting. Bushy eyebrows, curls falling over his eyes, wide and blue—his is a face that commands one to stare, to get lost in it. Sometimes I wish I carried that kind of beauty.

"Who are you?"

"You have knees like my sister. Bruised. But I know you're not like her," he says. "I'm Jonah. I came a long way to set things right. To clean."

"I don't understand."

"Let me tell you about my sister, Gillian," he says. "The woman fucking your stepfather."

"Your hair," I say.

"Is familiar," Jonah says.

I TOOK THAT woman, my stepfather's whore, from her home while she lay sleeping. The thermostat was set to eighty degrees, yet she cocooned herself with a pile of wool blankets, the kind that makes your skin itch. Wasn't she hot, even in the slightest? Didn't her underclothes cling in all the wrong places? Didn't she want to claw and scratch her calves in the middle of the night? I got sick just looking at her, all moth-like and rapid eye movement. I spent an hour watching Gillian sleep. I monitored the steady rise and fall of her chest under those blankets, and how she rarely shifted from a fixed position. I observed, with disgust, the wrinkled dresses and balled-up T-shirts covering the floor of her closet. How she allowed bits of food to settle into the carpet, to the point that her room smelled of sweet rotting fruit, is something I'll never comprehend. She owned garbage bags, bins, and cleaning products (bleach! ammonia! hydrogen peroxide!), but it was clear that she never used them. Dust collected around the caps, and the childproof plastic remained intact. Were these products for show, an act of mockery to those who believed in an unsullied home?

Believe me when I say that I considered dumping her in a Hefty bag with a bottle of bleach, a pack of matches, and some rope. She got me so mad! But I've learned it's important to stay the course, see things through, as it were. So I pulled that shiny needle out of my coat pocket, and, with a prick, I made her all mine.

"Do you hear that, James?" I said aloud. "She's *mine*."

WHEN I WAS ten, James told me that teeth were accidental stars God drilled into my mouth. Thanks, God.

When I was eleven, I walked in on my mother punching the Orion's belt out of James's mouth. The surgery was painful. The recovery was riddled with obligatory blow jobs, about which my mother complained to a woman who was not her friend.

When I was fourteen, James purchased a wire cage for those stars. My mouth was suddenly a chicken coop.

When I was twenty-five, I watched a pigeon nip at its wing until it could no longer fly.

When I was twenty-nine, I thought I felt something that the books described as love, but it wasn't. Instead, it was a pain I hadn't yet registered or recognized.

When I turned thirty-seven, I leaned into Gillian's hair, took a bite of it, and said, *It's my birthday! Make a wish! I'm about to light all the candles.*

I leave a room blazing.

THE WOMAN ON THE HOTEL BED

2013, 1985–1989

MEN PREFERRED ME blond, rich, and on the verge of expiration. I was someone before my hair caught on fire: a woman with a pedigree who glamorously slummed it, the owner of black diamond earrings and forever-bruised knees. A daughter whose heart once broke in four places when my mother called me *an expensive parking lot, trash taken out on Wednesdays.* Even after that strange woman with the butter breath and wild eyes tied my ankles so tight the slightest movement made my skin scrape and burn, even after the flames singed my hair charcoal—even then, I never considered an apology, a final cinematic plea for forgiveness.

I wasn't the woman who barged into that house and rearranged the furniture. The house was run-down and flashing No Vacancy long before I pulled up in the driveway and made my demands.

When that woman yanked the sock out of my mouth and said, "Tell me why you did it," I coughed through tears, "I . . ." Mind changed, sock shoved all the way in, lights out, door locked, and the woman soft-knuckling the window, waving her goodbyes.

Somehow I managed to escape before any real damage was done.

I wasn't always this way. I wasn't always the lightbulb hanging over a man's bed.

WE COULD START the story with me, Gillian. That's one way to go about it. The story of the home-wrecking whore who got her hair caught on fire and managed to survive. Managed to shake free from the ropes and jump out of a window. Do you know what it's like to feel your skin burn like paper, to see glass cling to your body? I heard the sirens and smelled the smoke, but you should know that my story begins and ends with my brother, Jonah.

Jonah's not a man, not yet. In the literal sense of the word, of course, *of course*, with his license to buy booze he'll never drink and rent cars he'll never drive because he walks. But to me he's a thirty-five-year-old boy with uneven arms from a car accident we don't talk about. Holes in his arms that are slowly closing up, needle marks everyone wishes they could drywall. *Points of entry*, Jonah once called them.

In his sleep he talks about a girl called Lucia. In his sleep he's always talking about girls.

WHEN JONAH WAS eleven he told me that he drew circles around his body with chalk, marker, whatever he could get his hands on, and he'd ask me why people traced outlines around dead bodies. "That's a myth," I said. "Chalk upsets the integrity of the scene. Cops take pictures."

One night after our father came home drunk, Jonah snuck into our parents' bedroom, and, with string, made an outline of our father's body. He took all the paring knives out of the kitchen drawer and arranged them around the body, the blades pointing toward his sleeping father. Mother smiled, smoothed his hair in all the right places, and said, "Look at you, saving me."

"Take pictures," I said. Sometimes I wrote stories about small children murdering their parents. Sometimes I read these stories to Jonah out loud. But they were just stories—words stranded on a page.

Back then, Mother held Jonah longer than she should. She was always grasping at things, and he seemed to be the one constant, the one thing that would allow for her fierce attachment. Theirs was a love that made him grow and forced her to retreat. When he wandered off, which he was prone to do, she would trail behind, tidying up. When he caught a bird by the legs and squeezed it, hard, Mother begged him to let it go. There was tetanus, rabies, and multisyllabic illnesses to consider, treat, and manage. "Sixteen shots to the stomach," she said. "Needles as long as your arm," she said. But he didn't acquiesce, rather he stared at her with eyes that were a chilling blue, and said, "Do you think it can feel me?" The bird thrashed and Jonah's arms were clawed but still he held on. Mother later told me she was awestruck, admired Jonah (*so fearless!*), but I never understood it—how Mother didn't shake the crazy out of Jonah and lock him in his room. But that was our mother: always wanting to be the thing she created, never what she was.

After a few moments, Jonah let the bird go. Said, "I'm bored with this. Do we need to go to the hospital now? Should we go in the car? But wait, you can't drive."

When I was sixteen and back from a short stint at a boarding school out east, Jonah said, "You're adopted." Over the past year I had whittled down to bone and was horrified by the prospect of this smooth, buttery cake adding a layer over my slight frame. Was it possible to gain weight by proximity, by standing next to the thing one was desperate to avoid? I felt old. But I was small, like sonnets, and I believed this to be a good thing. Woman as integer. The kitchen was quiet save for Jonah's steady breathing. Our father was on a plane to who knows where, coming from who knows what, and Mother was in the bedroom, buying skirts from catalogs.

"It's not my fault you're a loser," I said.

"Try putting something in your mouth, give it a new sensation. I'm talking about things that are edible, although that's debatable." Jonah reached for a muffin, a blueberry one, which was cruel and calculating because blueberry muffins were my absolute and unequivocal downfall, the one thing that could bring this elimination game down, tip the scales as it were, and he knew this. Look at that fucker tearing into the muffin like some barn animal. It wasn't even a muffin-top tease—it was a full-on assault, down to the burned ends and crumbs on his plate! As he reached for another muffin I realized I hated him. This was more than the normal sort of hate that transpires between siblings who, say, dodge one another between classes and deny each other's existence in the confines of fluorescent hallways and cafeterias. Rather, this was a body gone numb, a loathing that rises up your throat, the kind that makes you feral, where I could imagine stabbing my brother with a fork because he devoured what I desired. Look at his mouth, all gruesome and covered in crumbs!

"At least Mom didn't catch me getting off. Oh wait, that was you," I said, sipping hot water.

"She probably liked it. Probably the most skin she's seen in months. Now I get why Dad put the clamp on porn. Looking through people's windows and barging into their rooms is far more interesting. You get the unscripted version of things."

"You're totally sick."

"I'm not sick and stop saying *totally*."

Upstairs a door creaked. Mother shouted: "What's with all the yelling?"

"You're adopted. We picked you from among the children in an orphanage in the Dakotas. You know they had children in cages back then? You were filthy and ate your hair but we took pity on you, loved you anyway. Or that's what Mom told me. No one told you until now because we didn't want to hurt your feelings, but someone has to put an end to it. Someone needs to wipe the tears. Come on, make with it, Gillian. Show me sad."

"Shut up. Shut your mouth." He'd been on this kick for weeks, talking about bloodlines and lineage, and Mother had said, *Well of course you're not adopted. Who would tell you such a story?* Behind me Jonah stood with his finger over his lips. I knew how far he could go, which secrets to reveal and which to keep, so I shook my head and had said, *Never mind, never more.* Jonah had a way of crawling under your skin and settling there. Altering the way you felt things.

"You're not our kind," Jonah whispered to me while he thought I slept. "But maybe that's a good thing."

A decade later I reminded him about the argument, to which he replied, "Of course you're our kind. What does that even mean, *our kind*? Who else's would you be?"

"WERE YOUR KNEES always like that? Bruised?" Jonah says, leaning into me in a way that feels like an intrusion. It's a month after the hotel room incident and I cut my hair short to hide the fact that parts were burned. What right did he have to my knees? Jonah continues, "It's a good thing that Ellie's dead. It's good. She's gone one-way while we're still scrambling for our round-trip tickets."

"What are you talking about, Jonah?"

"I think you mean *who*. By the way, what happened to your hair?"

"My hair is none of your business. Tell me you're not skipping pills. Didn't the doctor tell you about the pills? How you needed to keep taking them?"

"Why would I take pills that stop me from seeing things as they really are?"

"Tell me about your life, about the friends you're making," I say, desperate to change the subject.

"Friends? I never figured you one for banalities. Should we make small talk then? Talk about the weather, the book I just read, or the five-year-old girl that was fucked in India and forced to marry her rapist? No, I thought we'd talk about you. About the *friend* you've made."

The way Jonah says *friend*.

And then: "About the car he drives, that house he lives in with that dead wife and the daughter in the window. Never thought you'd be a woman who goes in for stucco. I used to like to watch her sometimes—the daughter, not the wife. Although I suppose I could go visit her if I knew where she was buried. Mainly, I wonder how the story about my sister, and the man who sleeps on top of her sheets instead of between them, will play out."

"She wasn't buried, she was burned," I say. "Quit playing Nancy Drew. It doesn't suit you. Remember, you live in New York."

"You brought me back, dear sister, remember? They say after your body is cremated, they grind the remains of you. Imagine a body in a blender," Jonah says. "But I'll tell you about Lionel. He's smart. He's been teaching me about evil. How to find it, carve it out, and make the necessary calibrations and corrections." Jonah talks in a way that's foreign, in a voice that doesn't belong to my brother. Or possibly this was him all along.

"Jonah, you're scaring me."

"Have you met her?" Jonah says. He's lying on the floor, staring up at the ceiling.

"Met who?"

"Kate. She's a piece of work, that one. Sometimes I follow her to the ravine just to see her stare at the rocks."

"What are you talking about?"

"I'm talking about the sad girl who still watches you sleep. By the way, why haven't you gone to the police? Press charges."

"I want to be a person who turns over leaves."

"News flash: leaves look the same on both sides."

Jonah's room is blue. He needs it that way, clean. Jonah rents a building under construction, a building still being renovated, and his room was once a laboratory where doctors in the business of elimination would perform procedures on rich pregnant women. Floor painted black, walls the color of certain skies—he needs space to move because he's become dormant, like barnacles affixed to the undersides of large ships and fat whales. He's become attached to pain, so much so that Lionel has to put the shake in him, has to shove him in front of the mirror so Jonah can see the barnacles. They cover his face. There's no way to get clean. "They know their own kind," Lionel says, handing him a knife. "Get to scraping," Lionel urges. "There's no way of getting clean otherwise." His words are a blinding sunrise Jonah doesn't want to see, a note held for too long (needle lifted, placed back on the record, again, again) to a point where the music becomes unbearable. Jonah's face hurts, feels smothered, this is why he needs the blue. The river will loosen the grip and cool him down.

"Through me you go into a city of weeping; through me you go into eternal pain; through me you go among the lost people," says Lionel, whispering in Jonah's ear like resuscitation.

"I don't need your CPR," Jonah says. "And I don't need you to clean up my mess. I need my sister back."

"You keep holding on to that," Lionel laughs.

A head lifts, a word holds and plays out the scene, looks for places to hide but there are none. And the cold, "No." The word is a note folded into itself, a wave carrying his voice out into the ocean, and he finds himself grabbing for a mouthful of air, wants to shut Lionel the fuck up ("Dude, can you just quit the shit?"), but there's no quitting of the shit. There is only Lionel, whose voice, with the passage of each day, only seems to get louder.

Behind him, Lionel breathes down his neck and whispers, "We need to talk about your sister. We need to talk about what should be done with her."

"What should be done with her?" Jonah says.

"I think you know."

WHEN JONAH WAS twelve, he was tall, angular, but soft, the sort of boy who didn't shoot guns like the rest of them. He kept close to our mother, hid behind the folds of her dresses, and our father hated him for it. Hated that his son was allowed access to his wife's heart, permitted to touch the skin underneath her clothes. Once Jonah was in the picture, Mother swatted our father away.

When our father arrived home from a village that cartographers failed to diagram, raw from a deal that fell through—a botched investment that would require us to move to a garden apartment, hock all the finery, and use the old dishes with the flowers rubbed off—he was drunk on gin and sore beneath his clothes from a disagreement regarding the failed deal. Later, Mother affixed ice packs to blankets to wrap around his thighs and shins, which had swollen and bruised black. Later, they packed the whole of our lives into boxes they stole from the super-market. Later, Mother shrilled at her husband, "You are lesser than." Mother's fury gave her the kind of temporary apoplexy that prevented her from completing sentences, but her fragments and half thoughts were just as ruinous.

But in his room at that particular moment were just Jonah, age twelve, and our father's anger.

I also remember blood, my own, how it soaked through my pants and stained the sheets. I spent two days each month in the bathroom, and on that Saturday I heard our father stomp up the stairs and reprimand Jonah for something that we won't remember.

A scuffle, chairs knocked over, and a succession of screams. Father bolted, fled into the street. I found Jonah on the floor, one blue eye bleeding. I pried open his fist to find a pair of tweezers, wet with blood. Smiling he said, "I tried to be good, but being good does you no good so what else is there?"

"What did you do?" I asked.

"I didn't like how he kicked open my door like that. I didn't like his *tone*. So I taught him manners. It's sad when you have to teach adults things they should already know."

We ran to the car. How hard could it be to drive, I thought. Shove the key into the ignition, hit the gas pedal, and steer the wheel. I was fifteen, swerving a car down the street.

The road shows us how close to the edge we are.

31

Jonah stared out the car window, seeing through it, beyond it, to the houses down the drive. "You know what I did, but we can pretend if that's how you want to play it."

"Jonah, what did you *do*?"

"I don't like mittens, or people who wear them. That poor thumb is left to fend for itself, while all the other fingers point and laugh."

"Tell me what you did with the tweezers."

"You saw. Lionel cut things," Jonah said. "He told me to sleep. Told me he was going to play doctor and Dad's role was the victim. So I went to sleep. Where are we going?"

"We're running away."

"You're driving. I'm sitting. No one's running."

"We can't talk about Lionel. You know the rules."

"Yes, *sir*," Jonah said. "Let's play a game."

"What kind of game?"

"To play it, we'll need the tree."

His hand jerked the wheel. My foot pumped the gas instead of the brake. The smell of steel and smoke perfumed. Glass raked through our hair. His collarbone shattered. My knees were scraped and battered.

At the hospital, Mother hissed at me, "What were you thinking? What did you do?"

"I'm bleeding," I said.

"You're good for nothing," she said, but she was already gone, scurrying away with her little address book to the pay phone.

"Don't listen to her," my father said. "Your mother's trying to calm down after the thought of losing you kids."

"How? By acting like an asshole?"

Father walked like a man past his prime, already put out to pasture; a man who knew that his wife changed the sheets on their bed before he pulled into the driveway because he couldn't bear the thought of sleeping on something used. Once I overheard him say to Mother, "Keep it clean and quiet." To which she responded, "What kind of woman do you take me for? I've been clean; it's been quiet."

All those years, Mother gave him the gift of clean sheets.

Even in the waiting room, with its air conditioning and too-bright lights, they could feel the heat. The hot wind came down from the desert, determined to scorch the earth clean. Twenty days a year they suffered the kind of heat that made sane men wild, rabid, prone to killing garden snakes and black rabbits with machetes. The kind of heat that made women push their husbands out of moving cars while their newborns were strapped in the back seat. Teenagers jumped off the tallest buildings they could find, but only ended up cracking ribs and breaking a few bones. The streets stunk of carrion, cigarette smoke, and bad luck.

Mother stood against a pay phone, loading it up with change, punching the keys, and wailing into the receiver at whoever was on the other side. When I approached her, placed a nervous hand on her shoulder, she whirled around and hissed, "You just couldn't keep it together, could you? Always have to be the star of your own show."

My lip trembled. I fought back tears. And then I saw my father watching us. Pity washed across his face and I momentarily hated him for the luxury of being loved more than me. "It must hurt to have another man in your house. Fucking Mom. On your bed," I said. Men in our town were buying up real estate in Mother's heart and only two could fit—the man on current rotation in her bed and Jonah, asleep by her knee. The rest were the remains: renters who dared to shove their way in if there was a vacancy. I was fifteen and I knew this. Our father was thirty-eight and still thinking he had a claim by way of a marriage certificate, but that wasn't a deed and no one told him the rules of the game or how it was played. He withdrew, maybe realizing the graft of love he tried to stick wouldn't take. He was molting, and the one person he loved didn't care.

"Why would you do that? What have I ever done to hurt you?" he said.

Jonah shook his head. "You got it all wrong. It was Lionel."

CITY OF GIRLS

1990–1991

AFTER THE TWEEZERS incident, I was sent away to a boarding school where I subsisted on rice cakes and cocaine. "Everyone's got it figured out but you, Gillian," Alice said, as I left my bags unpacked. Lying in bed, my roommate wore a pink sombrero and a T-shirt that read, "Chick Buffet: All You Can Fuck." The room smelled of the clove cigarettes Alice smoked.

Surveying the Guns N' Roses and Linda Evangelista posters tacked onto the walls, the flannels and tight T-shirts balled up by the door, the oatmeal packets and empty Cup O' Noodles cartons littering the floor underneath Alice's bed, I considered calling my parents collect, asking *what in the fuck* had I done to deserve this. I mean, seriously. I wasn't the one who got creative with the tweezers, took the wheel, and slammed into a tree.

"This is temporary," I said, regarding the one lone sweater I'd begrudgingly hung in the closet. "I'll be home in a few weeks. They just need time to chill out."

"Can I be honest with you? Your parents aren't coming back. They never come back. This is last call, last exit, and no Kodak reunion is in sight. Welcome to Hotel California. They check you in and you can never leave," Alice said, pinching her smoke with her thumb and forefinger, turning up the volume to Radiohead's "Where I End and You Begin." "This is the part where you accept the reality of the situation. So I suggest you unpack your bags before I decide what I really need is your half of the closet."

Before I knew it, it was twilight and then dawn. After two weeks of answering machines and unreturned calls, I quietly folded sweaters into drawers and hung shirts and dresses in the closet.

"Welcome to the jungle," Alice whispered from under the covers.

"How do we undo the horrors of our history?" Mr. Pratt scrawled on the chalkboard. We had just spent two hours watching *The Pawnbroker*, a film about a man haunted by the concentration camps of decades past. I'd seen films on public television, uniformed men dragging bodies from the gas showers, tossing them into open pits, and setting them aflame. Even after death the Jews were a petrified frieze of suffering with their gaped mouths and eyes bulging and wide. The way their brittle bones broke; their legs rotted to tree stumps. They knew they would suffer because they were Jews, but never like this. No one had ever imagined this: an end that is the smell of sweet gas.

When Mr. Pratt flipped on the lights and removed the tape from the VCR, I could still see hundreds of erect hands reaching over a barricade and how the uniformed men with their hard consonants, barking, growling from the other side, removed gold rings from fingers. Removed glasses from faces. Drilled out silver from the insides of teeth. The iron chill of Germanic typewriters, of metal striking paper, and the ledgers accounting for the accumulation of hair and teeth in a bold, elegant cursive—yet I only came undone when I saw the removal of rings. My face reworked itself so that it caved inward, a series of dots converging into a singular, small blackness.

"The Nazis were people who believed that the annihilation of the Jews would cleanse the earth. In the Final Solution, the world would finally be pure," Mr. Pratt said.

Out of some persistent sense of large-scale ruin, we kept inventing hope.

I felt my hand rise, heard my voice say, "If we think about purity in terms of color, we think of white, which is essentially all color—all people equal along the spectrum. Then we consider black, the absence of color, a single person on a spectrum, so I wonder, Mr. Pratt, how would the Germans think that all this death would get them pure?"

Everyone turned and stared at me like they always

stared. Alice laughed, aimed a balled-up wad of loose-leaf paper at the back of my head. "What the fuck are you talking about?" she said.

"Settle down, Socrates," someone said.

"*Class.*" Mr. Pratt sighed.

"What are you going to do to us, Mr. Pratt? Ship us off to prison?" Alice said. "News flash, we're already there."

"Yes, Alice. Only you would think that a boarding school that costs $8,000 a year is a prison."

Melanie Clegg raised her hand. "I don't understand why the Jews didn't fight back. There were, like, millions of them. They could've totally taken the Nazis. Wasn't Hitler a coke addict with Parkinson's? Hardly scary."

"You're a fucking moron," Kevin Flynn said. "Stick to what you know best. Blow jobs and Benetton."

"Bitches be trippin'," Simon Marx said.

"Stop acting like you're black. Your dad builds malls in Long Island."

"My great uncle was Native American, which is practically black. And who says a black man can't build a mall? That's straight up oppression right there."

"Sometimes your generation makes me want to shoot myself," Mr. Pratt said.

"That really hot guy in *Dead Poets Society* shot himself in the head."

"Ethan Hawke was certifiable in that movie," Melanie said.

"Are we having a quiz on this? Because I fell asleep during the movie."

I heaved, closed my eyes. I imagined a man going about his day buying and selling junk to people, and all he can think about is a hand punching through glass and reaching for his wife. All he can see is the gold ring removed from her finger. He curses to himself in Yiddish, furious that he can't erase the German language. He feels the burden of the compound words on his tongue. He wasn't a Jew; he was a *Juden. Judas.*

In the hallway after class, the girls planned their weekly *90210* viewing party. Someone smuggled in booze and smokes, and everyone was freaking out over the fact that the Walsh family might move back to Minnesota. Everyone agreed that this episode was pivotal. What would become of Dylan and Brenda if the cruel world put geography between the Romeo and Juliet of our time?

Who gives a fuck about some rich kids in the West when there are massacres, fucking *holocausts*, in the East played out in Technicolor?

Alice's mother was called Lullaby, Lulu for short, and she was the kind of woman men passed around. She wore suede fringe and tight leather—dead animals were her camouflage—and imparted boarding school survival tactics like she was one of us. *Only swallow after a boy buys you dinner at the best restaurants four times in a row. Don't you dare eat the food, not one bite. Just order the courses and let the meal go cold.* Lulu sustained herself through multiple divorces, trading up rock stars for biotech millionaires. She lived off the remains of other people.

Regarding me she said, "Watch out for this one. Gillian's the sentimental type. She's the kind of girl who would give it all away for free if a boy asked her to. Pluck out her heart, if she had to. Alice, you have to teach her the rules."

Alice dragged a paddle brush through her hair.

"I'm right here, you know," I said.

Through a face full of smoke, Lulu said, "Let me guess, you've spent your whole life waiting for your mother's love. Not having a mother's love makes you do crazy things like fuck boys in basements without rubbers and take drugs sold on the street."

"We don't buy drugs off the street, Mother." Alice rolled her eyes. "We have pager numbers, connections."

"You don't know anything about my mother," I snapped.

"Oh, honey. You got *desperate for love* written all over your face."

"Never love so much it makes you vulnerable. Never cry. If you hurt, never let them see you bleed. Cover the bruises with powder. Always say no, especially if you mean yes." Alice announced her mother's rules in singsong.

"A flower doesn't choose its color, but it controls how

it blooms," Lulu said. Turning to Alice, she demurred, "There's hope for you yet."

"Did you think about what we talked about last time? About me coming home?" Alice said, burying herself between the pelts of her mother's rabbit coat. "I want to come home, Mom. I miss you."

"Silly goose. What home? What house?" Lulu lifted her dress to show legs bare and unshaven. An old joke between mother and daughter, a minor recompense. "Is it here, this house? Sweet child, there is no home to go home to."

Alice lunged for her mother's calf. Drew squares on her mother's bare leg with her fingers. "This is home to me. You. You. Let me in. Let me in."

Lulu's sighs were extravagant. "We talked about this a million times, baby."

"A million and one. Refresh my memory about why I'm still here. What kind of family is a family you can't go home to?"

"I don't have it in me, Alice. Don't make this any more difficult than it is. I'm here now, right? I come and visit you a few times a month, right? What else is there?"

Alice pulled away, pressed a pillow over her face, and screamed, "FUCKING LEAVE, THEN."

Lulu gathered her things and said to me, "I don't know why she insists on acting like a child."

"Because we are children," I said.

It looked as if Lulu were on the brink of apology when she said, "You were never children."

After Lulu left, Alice sat up in bed and said, "See what I mean, G? We can never leave."

"We're home now," I said, feeling a kind of love for her.

Alice's shoulders quaked. "I fucking hate her. What kind of mother disappears for months at a time and comes back with a new language and a guru? Promise her a payday and she'll spread like peanut butter."

I held her tight, as if my pressure would ease out the pain so I could absorb it. Just like Jonah used to do when we were small. *Squeeze my hand so hard it hurts*, he used to say. *I want your pain. All of it.*

Over a telephone line I whispered to Jonah, "I love her. You can't have her. She's mine. Do you hear me? *Mine.*"

"When has anything ever been yours?"

"How are they? Mom and Dad?"

"Here's a lesson for you: don't worry about snakes in the garden when you've got spiders in your bed."

That night I dreamed of oleander stained yellow, of a belt behind a woman's neck. Hair that resembled the insides of trees, and bodies that assumed the shape of branches spreading outward.

In the spring, we tore off our T-shirts, rose up from our mattresses, and fled into the night. We took the train into the city, drank pitchers of beer, and feasted on french fries at Jackson Hole and wings slathered in ranch at Brother Jimmy's. We'd saved up our stomachs for weeks for tonight, and no wing was left abandoned. Alice and I stomped our feet to bad rock songs from the seventies, because this is what we thought we should do. We blew boys in Kelly's Kitchen, and when we saw Telly and Casper in *Kids* drink forties out of paper bags in front of Kelly's, we jumped up, pointed, and said, "I know that place!"

No one ever thought to ask for names. We gave boys numbers of the take-out places we knew from memory.

That night I lost Alice in the Zoo Bar, after one too many bowls of mixed drinks the color of skies. Stumbling out of the bar, I collapsed into bodega flowers and ended up falling asleep on a stoop on Amsterdam Avenue. The next morning, inside a bodega, I asked to use a phone, and ignored the diverted eyes of the family working the register. "No phone," they said. "This is America," I said. "Everyone has a fucking phone." Outside I lay down on the ground and made a snow angel.

There was no snow, only sadness.

I hailed a taxi and asked the driver to take me to the train station. "Which one? You got a station on every block."

"The big one," I said. "The one with all the lights."

Before the taxi driver shook his head, rolled up his

window, and sped down the street, he said, "Your face is bleeding."

It took me four hours to make it back to the dorm, and Alice, who was eating ramen from a hot bowl, said only, "Welcome to the jungle."

LATE ONE NIGHT, Alice said, "Your brother called. How old is he? He sounds hot."

Another time, early: "Jonah had me on for an hour. What's up with his obsession with knees? Kind of pervy, but I like it."

Today, right now: "Can your brother not call here anymore?"

THERE WAS A piano in the room and I was dancing on top of it. I was on the verge of sixteen and remember someone telling me that I already had the look of a woman whose lipstick had been kissed off one too many times. I remembered Lulu: *You got "desperate for love" written all over your face.* But I didn't care (why care?) because cocaine made me feel nothing and everything all at once. I swiveled my hips, knocked my knees, and lifted my skirt until—*Stop. That was just the preview, boys. You need to pay for the show.*

Alice and I were in the city, in an apartment that

spanned a whole floor. We heard about a party in a building outfitted with thick rugs in the lobby and men dressed in crisp navy who once joked with the kids who tracked in mud from soccer practice. The kind of building where, over the years, doormen overlooked those same uptown boys who now sported backpacks filled with glassine bags, riding the elevators until dawn. The dealers made deliveries to the kids who'd grown into smug replicas of their parents, aware of how much money they had and what it could buy.

Someone at the party told me that my legs were oars, and I laughed and said termites had plagued my sticks. "Oh, the fucking itch," I cried from on top of the piano, and Alice shouted, "Coke bugs." Scotch was our varnish of choice. My heels left claw marks on the lid.

From a window I saw a woman pushing a cart filled with shopping bags, groceries, and this put me to thinking about home. It was two thirty in the morning when I called Mother, and she answered, all breathy, mouth full of sleep, "Hello, hello," and I bit down so hard on my lip that it bled, put down the phone, and said, "Goodbye, goodbye."

A couple soft-knuckled the door, tumbled in. "We need the room," Kevin Flynn said. As I left, Kevin grabbed my arm and said, "You're the girl from the piano. There's room on the bed."

"I'm the girl from your history class," I corrected.

"I won't go down on you," the girl slurred.

"Who are you kidding? You'll go down on anyone," Kevin said. To me: "Let's make some history, then."

"I'm good, thanks."

Kevin shrugged his shoulders and kicked the door shut.

In the hallway a girl pointed to an Ellsworth Kelly drawing and asked, "Is that real?"

A boy responded, "Depends on your point of view."

The girl wondered if she could take it, if anyone would notice, and her best friend said, "Isn't your dad, like, a collector?"

"Yeah, but I don't know what he collects."

"Accurate," the boy said.

In another bedroom a bunch of girls with knives said, "Let's play doctor and nurse. You play the victim." I thought about Jonah and his pretend friend, Lionel.

In the hallway Alice tapped me on the shoulder and said, "I need to hit the ATM. I'll be right back."

Four hours later morning broke, and Alice walked through the door as if no time had passed. Everyone had gone home except for a few girls from downtown who had snuck into the party and spent the night earning a place to put down their heads and rest. Alice opened the fridge and cabinets and stuffed her duffel bag with sturgeon, beef fillets, and jars of imported pesto sauce.

"Why are you taking food?" I asked.

"Bonus payment for tonight's party favors," Alice replied, waving me toward the bathroom. "Get some of the lotions. Smell them first. The expensive ones always smell like real flowers."

"Your dealer owns a Mercedes."

"My dealer lives in Spanish Harlem," Alice corrected. "They can buy all the cars they want, but they could never live here. They've never been on a plane. This is what we're giving them. The feeling of being *here*."

So I stole shea body butters imported from Africa, French perfume encased in Baccarat crystal, hairbrushes with leather handles and clumps of fine hair snared between the delicate bristles. I even pinched an ivory canister that held Crest toothpaste.

As we were leaving the apartment, the host walked out of the bedroom. "I'm going to need payment for all that," he said coolly. "Did you think you could just raid my place and get away with it?"

Alice turned to me and ordered, "On your knees, soldier."

Over a telephone line I whispered to Jonah, "I hate her."

"What did I tell you about spiders in your bed?"

"I want some of her hair."

Lionel: "Now we're talking."

IT WAS LATE, or early, depending on how you looked at the situation, but when Jonah phoned I begged, "Please come."

Alice had gone missing.

"I hear your school is the kind of place where everyone's stomach looks the same. Is that true?" he said.

"Please come."

"Are the girls as hot as the brochures say they are?"

"Jonah, please come." My eyes couldn't adjust to the light.

"How's that roommate of yours? The one who smells like yogurt? Don't get like her," Jonah said. "Picked clean."

When Jonah arrived that weekend they'd found Alice, or parts of her, in an apartment in Spanish Harlem. She'd been strangled by what police believed to be a women's belt. I had no doubt that the police took away the men in their silver cars and kept the money and coke for themselves. *Pretty good work for a day's pay*, I imagined them saying. Lulu was somewhere in upstate New York, adjusting her levels.

Outside, the grass that had once dried to straw was now verdant and damp. The evening sky burned gold and violet, while the fireflies and hummingbirds flittered through the trees pregnant with bloom, determined to puncture the pollinated air and fly through it. That year, we plucked lilacs off the trees and plugged them into glass iced tea bottles, ignoring the withering. Ducks journeyed up the lawn from the nearby ravine, only to be rebuffed by the scuttling footfalls of the boys playing lacrosse. The boys waved their sticks, creating wind while the birds lowered their beaks and skittered to a run. On the lawn us girls hawked, puffed our cheeks, and curled our hair around our fingertips when we said, "You guys are so mean."

Outside and in, our world revolved around the boys.

The way that Jonah leaned, stood, sat, filled the room with what I didn't know or couldn't articulate. But it was cold, desolate, and precise. He picked up objects and placed them down without even looking at them, as if he were taking inventory instead of observing. As if he were counting. As if he made the room his, in the way that he made everything his.

That bird in his hand, thrashing. The tweezers tucked under a thigh.

Jonah smelled of lilacs. The lotion, not the flowers, but it was hard to tell.

Before he left, he said, "I'll get you home, I promise."

"What about Mom? Won't she be pissed? She still blames me for the accident. And Dad . . ." I said.

"What about him?" Jonah said.

A week later Jonah held me too close. "I missed your hair, the wreck of it," he said. To our father, he said, "Tell your daughter how much you missed her."

"I'm sorry to hear about your friend," our father said. His voice was a soft stutter. "What they did to her. I heard they found parts . . ."

"Didn't I warn you?" Jonah said.

"It was one measly murder. Not enough to justify pulling her out of school and wasting a semester of tuition," my mother snapped.

"That place was no home for her," our father said. Not once did he glance at Jonah.

"That girl was a room with no windows, only walls," Jonah said.

I think of Lulu, her animal skins, gold bracelets, and rules. "That girl's name was Alice."

WOMEN, DON'T BREAK
2013, 2003–2005

WHEN I WAS small I wanted a pony but never got one. Instead, my mother purchased a horse head attached to a long stick and told me to *ride*: "Wild animals you can't control, but this toy, this, you can hold in your hands. You can make it go anywhere you want it to. Do you hear me, Gillian?"

"I see," I'd said.

A teacher once told me that my handwriting was almost confident.

I've kept that pony for over twenty-five years. Hid it in my dorm-room closet behind a stack of empty shoeboxes. There are stores that sell designer shoeboxes to give the suggestion of a kind of life. Now the pony is under my bed. A lover once found it while he was tying a shoe. "Whatever gets you off," he said. I mean, this was a man who once confided to me that he made love to an inflatable doll on three separate occasions. Sober. We fucked for a year.

I've never been good at letting things go.

When I moved to California, I had problems with the

water. I started to miss hurricanes; I cried out for storms. I only watched television shows that promised hard rain. I fell asleep to videos of hail and wondered why all the famous storms are named after women. An air robbed of moisture does things to you. A constellation of red, blistery bumps covered my chest, arms, and back. The insides of my mouth tasted of rusted pipes. I brushed my teeth with tap water and my lover laughed and said, "You're just moving the metal around, baby."

My brother Jonah laughs. He lives in New York but he comes here often. "You're worried about water when you live in a place where the ground sometimes rearranges itself?"

"Don't you find it strange that everyone talks about the water?" Even the act of drinking water requires a plan, a filtration system.

"There are worse things."

After six months my skin returned to its normal state.

"In New York you can drink water right out of the faucet," Jonah says.

"I like it here," I say. "Everything, including your freedom, requires a plan."

WE MAKE LOVE, quietly, while his wife lies unconscious in the next room. The meds have seized her, and she drifts in between life and a darkness that resembles death. Some days she's lucid; others, like this one, she keeps calling me

Kate. Keeps telling me to leave. *Let me sleep. Go away, I never loved you. I did this. I did this to you. It's my fault. I hate you. I know what you do while I sleep. I maybe loved you once.*

I shake my head. Poor woman. You don't know me. You don't know about the horse head I've hidden under your bed.

While James is fucking me, I hum a lullaby my mother once sang to me when I was a child. "Mommy's home," I say. My fingers spider down his back—real slow like, so he can feel it. He puts his hand over my mouth. I'm loud. I bite him. Wild animals you can't control.

"You're not making this easy."

"Your dying wife is in the other room. You made this what it is. Suddenly you're too cheap to afford a hotel room?"

"It's not like you have a home we can go to," James snaps.

After, I pull on a T-shirt that reads, "Future Corpse."

"I'm worried about you," he says. "You look like you never sleep. When do you sleep? You're out all night for days at a time, and during the day . . ."

"Since when are you concerned about my health? I'm fine, just fine. You need to be focusing on your wife and your daughter. How is your daughter? The one who bakes the cakes—what's her name again?"

"I'm too tired to play this game. Why are you doing this to her?"

"The cancer patient in the other room? I don't know her any more than you do, James. But hey, if you want me to go back to playing Kate, the dutiful daughter, I can do that. That's a game I can play. I know how much you miss her."

Whatever gets you off.

I get up and walk across the room and out the door in nothing but my T-shirt. I bring his wife a glass of water because that's what I assume a good daughter does—brings a dying woman something to drink. I fill the glass directly from the tap because why bother? It's not as if she's straight enough to notice a little fluoride. If I were her I'd drink the whole glass because when you're about to die why not live dangerously?

I go into his stepdaughter's room. Sometimes I like being in here when she's not. The sadness is palpable; I feel like I'm not alone, like she's here with me. There's not much here in terms of decoration: a blue curtain, a fringe rug, and stacks of books written by dead men. I flip through photo albums and I notice there are no pictures of her from when she was a baby. It was as if all the years before ten ceased to exist, as if she just appeared in California, aged ten, wearing a twinset.

On the windowsill leans a frame: it's a photo of Kate and Ellie when they were younger. A mother and daughter at the beach, but Kate is out of focus—it was as if the photographer wanted to blur her out of the frame. I remove the photo from the frame and, on the back, written in small script, a name: *Tim*. Underneath: *Remember him*. I curl the photograph in my hand.

James is dressed and in the kitchen. A man on the television warns of a tsunami, aftershocks from an earthquake in Chile. Afterward, a woman recounts a study that reveals that within the next thirty years an earthquake will swallow us whole. I laugh because we've heard this before. Brush fires in the canyons, the blustery Santa Anas blowing hot from the desert, and tectonic plates rearranging themselves like some sort of jigsaw puzzle—the story of our impending catastrophic ruin is common. When I press the photo into James's hand, he looks at it as if it's far more terrifying than the images projected onto a television screen.

"I'll play Kate. I'll play nice, if that's what you want me to do."

"Why are you doing this? You're acting like a child again. You're not fifteen and this is not that house."

Massaging the inside of his leg I say, "Kate, Gillian, who do you want? Who do you want me to be?"

Another time: I tell James I watched *The Shining* when I was five. He rents us a room on the far part of town and we feast on raw fish while a madman wields an axe. On the news we learn that the inhabitants of a small California town have vanished. Reporters scour the remains. Bowls filled with soggy, half-eaten cereal. Televisions tuned to soap operas, game shows, and the local news. Cigarettes burned down to the filter. It was as if five hundred people woke one morning, started their day and then . . . disappeared. There are forensic experts, state troopers, and investigators on the scene—all dressed up in astonishment. Everyone is mystified. Evangelists dial in to local radio shows and talk about the rapture, that this is the first step of our punishment for not being what He had intended. This disappearance was phase one of The Plan.

"Of course Jesus has a project manager," I say. I smoke a cigarette with the eerie feeling of being watched. I once drove through a town near the Sierras where everything remained in a state of arrested decay. Soup tins lined supermarket shelves, bullet holes sprayed Shell signs, and abandoned tractors and pickups were strewn across wheat fields. Structures were maintained, but only enough so they remained standing. I remember that town was the last place I could hear the sound of my own breath. I took a man then, and the only things we had in common were our inability to love and our proficiency at fucking. We wondered aloud, how does one attach oneself to someone else? We'd lived our childhoods as if we were phantom limbs crying out for the familial love we were deprived of. When you're in the desert, you're thankful for even a thimble of water—so this sex, these two bodies forming a temporary attachment, was our thimble.

"Pets, people—all gone. Even the plants, all signs of

life, vanished. Where did they all go?" James says, massaging his forehead with his fingertips. He seems to be in pain. We sit in silence for several minutes. I continue to eat the fish. My mother hated fish, couldn't stand the taste of it.

"I wonder if I can go to where they went," says James.

Did Kate appear the way this town disappeared?

"I feel like we're being watched," I say. I pace the room and look out the windows. I open and close the door. There is a piece of paper on the floor. In bold, slanting script the note reads: *This has been your warning.*

"WHAT DID YOU do today?" Jonah said.

My brother hated small talk. Exchanges involving weather reports sent him into a blind rage. Celebrity gossip made him lethal. Jonah preferred to start in the middle of things. On a checkout line, he'd once threatened a cashier by saying, *If you ask how I am today, I will end you.* When he told me the story, I asked him why he went to Costco; I didn't figure him for being into multiples. Subtraction was his game. He said he needed duct tape. Lots of it. No one thought to ask a man why he needed twenty rolls of tape. Perhaps people assumed that he had much to fix.

"The same thing I did yesterday. Maybe more of it?" I was watching a comedy show without laughing.

"Sixty percent chance of thundersnow tomorrow.

Winds are coming in from the north. Buffalo is already covered in eight feet of powder."

"You called me with a weather report? Are you dying or is someone dead?"

"What's the forecast? Be descriptive. Spare nothing."

"It's seventy-five and sunny. It's always seventy-five and sunny."

"And the barometric pressure? The humidity? I need you to talk to me about pressure." Jonah was in a panic. He spoke like a skipping record.

"Jonah, are you taking your pills?"

"I think I might love someone."

"Far worse than I imagined."

"This is serious business. I love Lucia and I think she's going to leave me."

"So how's she different than the rest?" My eyelashes hurt. I was jealous in a way that was less about sex and more about possession. Jonah belonged to me. Jonah was my property. I thought about an interview with Ted Bundy I once saw: *The ultimate possession was, in fact, the taking of the life. And then . . . the physical possession of the remains.*

"She's worse off than both of us and trying to climb out of it. Why does she get a free pass?"

"You want me on a plane? I can be there in the morning."

Jonah sighed. "I want you to listen to weather reports."

"THERE ARE NO pictures of her before she was ten," I say. I hold Kate's photo album in my hands.

"You know why."

"I wasn't asking a question."

"I spoke with Jonah yesterday."

"Why the fuck would you speak to my brother? How did you get his number? What could you possibly have to say?"

"I called him because it's starting again. I called him because I'm worried about you and he's the only one who's able to get through to you."

In a voice I don't recognize I say, "You'll be sorry you did that."

WHEN THE WIFE dies, I remove the pony from under my bed and wrap it neatly in two white trash bags before I return it to my closet. I weep because I accidentally purchased scented bags, the kind that remove stubborn odors. Everything that has come before has been removed. The past twenty-five years—gone. When no one can see, I clench the stick between my legs and run. My legs chafe and burn. The horse's hair matted with tears.

A few days later I enter the house when no one's home. I am a hurricane. Kate's room is tidy, neat, and I take all the clothes out of her drawers and throw them on the floor. I spit on them. I remove dresses—why is everything blue?—from the racks and rub them all over my body, even the dirty parts. I walk into the kitchen and make a sandwich and get crumbs all over the carpet because why not? I pull socks over my hands and play pretend like my brother and I used to do when we were small, before my mother called me trash taken out on Wednesdays, when we all knew it was collected on Fridays. I was what you left to rot.

I have the picture of Kate and Ellie in my hand. At least you had a mother.

"SOMETIMES YOU GO too far," Jonah says. We are in the same place, seventy-five and sunny.

EVERYTHING WAS BEAUTIFUL
AND NOTHING HURT
2003–2005

JONAH KEPT THE best girls in boxes, crates, and cabinets—anything with four walls and a lid. He wrapped
them in linen, and, with a litany of chemicals, he pre-
served them as best he could. Everyone thought he was
a taxidermist, with all the skull bleaching, skin tanning,
and preservatives he routinely carted into the house—*a
man should have a hobby*—but he was an artist who kept
the murdered girls in chain-wrapped boxes, and locks in
the shape of hearts. Jonah loved his miniature dolls, and
sometimes he'd open the crates and smooth their hair,
tend to their cotton and silk dresses, finger their lashes,
and imagine a life where all his creatures played house.
Their collective murmur drowning out Lionel's angry
voice in his head, for Lionel was a shouter.

"You're too weak for this kind of work," Lionel said
after the last girl, baring rows of gleaming white teeth.
If you looked closer, you could see his incisors, chiseled
bone. Lionel was the kind who liked to linger; he wanted
to spend time with the girls long after they were gone.

This was important because each of them had to know they were among the chosen. They were special. After a while he got ravenous—one doll would be fresh in a bag while he whispered to Jonah about the next hunt. When it came to their projects Lionel sometimes regarded Jonah, and his care of the prey, with disgust. "I'll leave you with the lady parts. You dress them up and put on that glitter nail polish while I do the real work."

Lionel was good at cleaning the scene.

Jonah was a coward; this was true. He couldn't even bring himself to say the word "murder" out loud; it was far too coarse and cold for conversation, so instead he called their kills "excavations" or "projects." Responsible for scouting, Jonah would find girls standing alongside empty roads and highways, thumbs outstretched, or in the parking lots of bars after they locked their keys in the car, or alone at the bus stop, shivering, knowing the local would never come. All of them wanted to go home, and as soon as they slid in the passenger seat Jonah promised them this. It wasn't a complete lie; he'd just neglect to clarify whose home he'd take them to, or whether they'd make it to the front door intact. That's when Lionel stepped in and took over. He never appeared like an apparition, rather he was a constant mutter, a sonata rising from the side of Jonah's mouth.

In the car, the girls always pleaded for their lives. Always with the tears and wet, matted hair. The guttural feline cries for mercy rising up from their stomachs, gurgling. Jonah loved their flushed faces and wide eyes; they were alive. Invariably, they'd cry out for their families: the children who expected them home and the boyfriends who missed tracing the shapes of their faces.

Many of the dolls smelled of wild flowers and cotton, and Jonah often imagined the boxes coming to bloom, bleeding arms reaching out of the dead land and mouths catching their first breaths.

They'll come looking for me was their constant refrain, and this was true, too. Men always hunted for women killed by other men. Pressing a knife or a gun to their cheeks, Jonah would nod and make promises that their lives would be spared if they didn't scream, if they drove a few more miles. He knew it was cruel to dole out hope like foil-wrapped sweets, but he was a coward. How do you tell someone that you're about to kill them? Snuff out their life like some cold, cruel thief in the night?

"You always leave me with the dirty work," Lionel said. "How do you think that makes me feel? Always the bad guy left to snap their pretty necks. Washing the blood off my hands. Blood stains, you know. Bullets leave holes in windows and car seats."

"I clean up. I do my share," Jonah said.

"You gotta take some responsibility. Own some of the work. We've been at this for years and you're acting like they're all Lucia." No more knives or guns, Lionel decided. Stick to belts or our hands. It's neat that way. Close.

"Can we not talk about Lucia, please?" Looking

down at Lionel's hands and then at the marks on the doll's neck, he continued, "Leave that one's face alone. I want her eyes intact." This creature was special. When he picked her up in Roanoke, hitchhiking, she called herself Victoria, but he'd change that soon enough. Give her a new name like the rest of them. Her skin was bruised and blue, and for a second he could remember the way her teeth cracked. He could hear his voice telling her that this was the moment her life would begin. Tonguing the word *extinguished*, Jonah played around with the syllables, allowed them to linger. Words had more power than hands around a woman's neck.

After the first time, Jonah got sick for three days. He hadn't anticipated all the blood, the mess of it under his nails and on his face. This was before he learned how to manage the details and be clean about it. This was before he'd feel the thrill of bones cracking.

Jonah wanted to stop, he did, but the urge to kill was always greater than the urge to stop. Then Lionel: "You're in this. Deep. There's no going back. Mop up those tears; I don't give a shit about those people and you shouldn't either." After the first time, Lionel had quoted someone he'd heard on television: "You learn what you need to kill and take care of the details. It's like changing a tire. The first time you're careful. By the thirtieth time, you can't remember where you left the lug wrench."

Jonah pressed his eyes shut. No, no, no, that wasn't

him. Those weren't his hands laboring that last breath out. That wasn't his voice humming a lullaby as her chest fell quiet. That was all Lionel's doing. Jonah's work was afterward, dressing up the remains.

This one he'd bury in his wall, standing upright, one hand waving. First, he'd have Lionel skin her lips.

"No one gets out of this," Lionel said, stepping over the body with a paring knife. "You get it one way or another."

HE'D MET LUCIA on a plane two years ago. She was on her second flask when she leaned over and offered a swig, by way of introduction. "I hate flying. They say you're more likely to get killed in a car accident than on a plane, but I don't buy it. Every single time I get on a plane I feel like I'll soon be barbeque."

"They have pills for that," Jonah said. Shaking a packet of sugar, he poured it into tepid coffee.

"Drinking's cheaper, and I don't have to spend an hour of my life that I won't get back lying to some doctor just to get a scrip."

Midway through a flight from Los Angeles, and this woman threw up four times. Every time she returned to her seat, she proceeded to drink some more. Even flagged down a nervous flight attendant for backup miniature bottles of Merlot. "We could hit turbulence," was her excuse. She was something out of a film noir, with her black hair bordering on blue, lips painted red, and a crooked nose, as if she were built to break the surface of things. Dressed in sheer black crepe with only a cashmere shawl to lend modesty, she was beautiful in a way that made you think she'd cut open your face with her mouth, and pry her fingers in.

She also smelled of vomit.

Jonah made a dramatic showing of opening his manila folder and examining the photographs. Fixated on the construct of home, he was an artist who spent his life deconstructing its meaning. His photos were of his latest canvas installation, *The Kingdom of Limbs*, where he superimposed daguerreotypes onto blueprints of California mansions. Vermont barns and New England Tudors collided with cool Spanish tiles, billowing palm fronds, and floor-to-ceiling glass windows. On top of the photos, he drew Victorian figures swimming in indoor infinity pools and cooking frankfurters over hot pots. The women wore corsets while the men stood stalwart in their wool coats and expensive hats. The children were styled as Kurt Cobains in miniature, with their sweeping blond hair, dour mouths, and track marks. Jonah loved this carefully composed mess of image, time, and texture, and apparently the woman did too. He felt her sour breath on his cheek.

"It's straight out of a Buñuel movie. I'm waiting for a

mother to start waving raw meat in a kid's face. I'm Lucia, and I'm drunk."

"Telly," Jonah said.

"Like the virgin hunter in *Kids*. You must get that a lot."

"No, mostly I get Telly Savalas."

"The bald guy with the lollipop? Which generation are you rolling with? Just how old are you?" Lucia laughed.

Something in Jonah curdled. This woman set his teeth on edge. He had this sudden urge to choke her. "The kind of generation that has a name for the amount of drinking you do."

Lucia snorted. "Alcoholics go to meetings. I'm a catalog girl. Well, former girl. I'm twenty-eight and I've already been put out to pasture. Replaced by some teenager with implants and a hollow throat. I imagine they'll make glue out of me. You know what's hard about getting old? People look at you and find fewer ways to use you."

"Do you always speak this way to strangers?" He noticed that her teeth, like her nose, were crooked.

"Do you always flaunt art that makes you look like a mental patient?" After what seemed like an extraordinary amount of time had elapsed between her last word and her next, Lucia said, "You have sturdy hair."

Jonah looked at her and felt the whole of his world invert. Cars tumbled out of the ocean, the sky birthed trees, and everyone tiptoed on their heads. Lucia was a blind nymph, some sort of black star that, having collapsed into an airplane, found her way to the seat next to his.

"You show me yours and I'll show you mine," she said, tapping his folder with a blue fingernail.

When they arrived at JFK, Jonah had to carry Lucia to his car. Later, she'd joke and say that he liked his women narcoleptic and his bed cold, like the inside of a grave.

Lucia made a habit of breaking into empty apartments. Maybe because it was the only place where she could really hear the records she still played with the volume turned up, or perhaps she was comforted by what had been abandoned; she liked to imagine the lives of people left behind. Sometimes she'd find small dresses in large closets, tags stapled to the sleeve. Other times, she'd thumb through secondhand books filled with pictures of couples who were once blinded by their love. And now, these pictures—a catalog of them through the seasons—were shoved into the books you read as a teenager: Salinger, Cheever, and Faulkner. Lucia imagined the division of a home and the business of leaving, and she'd text Jonah, "Come." Come. And he did, and he kissed her ten times on her nose and told her, "You can't eliminate what you don't own." They would never have to suffer through the mess of math; "There will never be an end," Jonah promised. There would never be a leaving.

Always she came before the paint, before the crew of men lumbered in and whitewashed the previous owners, and their lives, away. She came before the women who swept and scrubbed floors, the women who woke before dawn and took two buses and a train to neighborhoods where men spent hours watering sidewalks, carrying their sons and daughters on their backs. Lucia came when the place was dirty, when the scent of the departed—wet leather and something rotting and sweet—still lingered.

Jonah always followed, even when she didn't know he was behind her. He watched other men stare at her parts. He understood her loneliness, which was a mirror of his own, and when she called, and she always called, he made a show of running up the stairs, climbing through the windows, and holding her close when she sat on the floor with an old record player and a stack of 45s.

"We're going to get caught," he said, once. They were on the first floor of a Park Slope brownstone. Lucia told him she picked this one because of the bay windows, and how she felt when the light came through the wooden blinds. *Look at the children play.* She played Sade's "Smooth Operator": *Jewel box life, diamond nights and ruby lights, high in the sky / Heaven help him, when he falls. / His heart is cold.*

"No, we're not. I've cased this place for a week. Do you know the people here pass one another in the lobby without even saying a word? Collect their mail without so much as a *hello*? For all they know, I could be the new neighbor."

"But you're not."

Lucia shook her head, as if she were speaking a language Jonah didn't understand. "We're always someone's neighbor. You think a number on a door decides that?"

"You brought me here to pick apart the etiquette of stroller moms and banker husbands?"

"I have two Italian sandwiches and a sad song playing, and I thought you might want to share them with me."

"You know, we have an apartment where we can do that. Eat sandwiches." Jonah kissed her ear, bit it. He loved her because she was the kind of woman who would eat a pork sandwich without faking it. She'd see the whole thing through.

"I know." Lucia nodded, taking a bite of her sandwich. She tore the bread with her teeth in a way that was savage. "I like it better here. I like us in the in-betweens. There's never a beginning or an end."

Jonah handed her a letter. "This came for you today."

She eased open the envelope and laughed at the check, a final payment from her former agent for work in her former life. "No, I don't want to talk about it. I don't like endings."

He took her hand in his and felt the coolness of her. She had pastry hands, and for a moment this reminded him of his sister. "You don't have to worry about money."

"Do you think that's why I'm with you? For the money?"

"If only you were that simple," Jonah said.

Lucia handed him a sandwich and purred into his neck. "Eat before it gets dark."

The record skipped. They permitted the stutter.

Lucia gave him her pickle because she knew he liked it. "So, where were you last night?"

"We're here again?" Jonah sighed in the dark. He picked up *Death in the Afternoon* and flipped through the photographs. "There's only so much of this I can take."

"It's a simple question."

"Out. I was out."

"Out where?"

"I was out *not* fucking another woman."

How do you keep a wave away from the sand? How do you hold it back from grabbing at the one thing it desires? Lucia slid her underwear down her legs and let it rest at her ankles. "I'd like you to fuck me now," she said.

Afterward, in the dark, Jonah traced three words on her back. *Three blind mice.*

In the city, the former catalog girl traded her bejeweled corsets and Chantilly lace for crepe suits and tweed jackets. Four days a week Lucia was the telephone girl at Mc-Cann Harrison, responsible for managing the carousel of phone lights, the sprucing of conference rooms (sprucing was included in the fourteen-bullet job description), the watering of plants, the rearrangement of lobby magazines, and the doe-like fawning over the male executives who strode past her on their way to close deals. Lucia didn't know what actually transpired at McCann Harrison beyond the cackling of *We're on a deadline! We're not selling a bar of soap, people—we're promising a lifestyle! We ran out of coffee filters! Someone stole my yogurt! WHERE IS MY DAIRY-FREE, LOW-FAT, GLUTEN-FREE BLUEBERRY YOGURT?*

Sometimes it was Lucia's job to procure yogurt, even though she was the one who stole it. During one of her three allotted bathroom breaks, she'd sneak the tubs in and devour the insides. Flaxseed and whipped lemon meringue and cherry crème, she'd wrap the evidence in tissue. No one ever noticed the evidence on her upper lip or cheek because Lucia was the front-desk girl, the girl who transferred calls—she was universally invisible and routinely ignored.

Pilfering the supply closet was the work of low-rent clock-watchers, but food theft was primal. Only a former catalog girl, whose fame had been eclipsed by a knock-kneed teenager with tits the size of Kentucky, would opt for the more dubious art of snack theft. No one would dare suspect the girl whose sinewy hips once tumbled out of their mailboxes of hoarding string cheese, frozen grapes, and Lean Cuisine meals. Models, even former ones, didn't eat the food relegated to the plebian, peanut-crunching lot. They hired Lucia to set a mood, project an image, although they never thought that the mood would be one of rampant distrust and the image of paranoia. Coworkers started labeling their food with notes that read, *I may not know which one of you animals stole my salad dressing, but God does. Jesus is watching.*

Tensions were high; interns went ballistic over the theft of their carefully budgeted and packed lunches. They booked a conference room and spent two hours deliberating a desk-to-desk search, but knew HR would never comply for fear of lawsuits and vigilante recriminations. "This is bullshit," Ryan, the experience guru intern, lamented. "My sandwiches cost my parents a lot of money. Multigrain isn't cheap, people."

Lucia made it her mission to eat all of his sandwiches.

"I SAW THE devil last night," Lucia said. This time, they were in their home with all the lights turned off except for a tangle of Christmas lights she'd strung up. She liked how they winked at her.

"Come again?" Jonah said. He picked out all of the pork from his pork fried rice because he knew how much she liked it, and how much the Chinese joint on the corner overcooked it. Lucia liked her meat either raw or well-done. In life she needed the middle, but when it came to meat, she couldn't tolerate the suggestion of something undone. It either had to be bruised or burned. "You saw the *devil*. Like Damien in *The Omen* devil?"

"Damien was the Antichrist," she corrected. "And no, I didn't actually see the devil; I saw a movie. About a man so consumed by his grief, you end up wondering who's the predator or the prey. I thought of you and me. I'm wondering if I'm the predator in all of this. Am I what will undo you?"

"Why are you talking nonsense?"

"I just wonder if I'm keeping you from . . ."

"From what?"

"From living your life?" Lucia said. Under the pink and blue lights, her cheeks were flushed and her eyes appeared dark and gray.

"What life? No life of mine," Jonah said, quoting a line from a Grace Paley story his sister had once sent him. He couldn't remember the story, but it began with, *Hello, my life*. "There was no life before you." And this was true. What Jonah had, *has* to a certain extent, is a like life. A suggestion of something real, something just in the periphery, and it was only when he was around Lucia and all her sadness—he loved his walking wound, he did—that Jonah felt as if he understood the quality of his breath: the involuntary inhalations and exhalations, the taking in of new life and the letting go of waste. He only understood love through the act of sacrifice, and in Lucia he saw mouth-to-mouth personified in the way she would involuntarily give up her breath for his.

"There was life. You just weren't there for it."

"Maybe you're right. But all I remember from this life is you on a plane trying to play hotel instead of house," Jonah said, and kissed her collarbone and allowed his mouth to settle in the delicate space between bone and skin. They were quiet for a time, until Jonah asked, "Tell me, what's with the lights? It's July."

"I had in my contract that all of my sets and hotel rooms had to be filled with Christmas lights. Even when the men with their cameras told me that I was as *cute as kittens*, I wouldn't come out until I saw the blinking lights. Only then did I give them a hundred watts and a thumb inching a bikini down low. God, my ass used to be *epic*. Feel free to forward your bereavement cards to this address; you're looking at a widow mourning her former life."

Jonah went into the other room and got his camera. "I'll take your picture," he said. She was beautiful in parts, and Jonah photographed her that way, limb by limb, with the flash on. Lucia was a face full of high beams: jumping up and down on the couch, she posed, preened, and gave him a light that blared a little too bright, and he saw something in her that resembled happiness. In the pictures, she looked bone white and the Christmas lights resembled tears, but in life, *oh in life*, she looked terribly, terribly happy.

"Don't stop," she gasped. "Don't ever stop taking my picture."

"IF YOU WERE going to die and you knew you were going to die, and you could choose how . . . what would you choose?" The road ahead of them unfurled a blanket of varying shades of gray: paved to gravel to dirt to gravel and paved again. They barreled down the back roads of Virginia; Jonah pressed a steak knife into Victoria's neck as she drove. He watched the symphony of her body—the quick rise and fall of her chest, the uneven breath and quivering lips—and he found comfort in her terror. He liked this disquiet.

"Please let me go. I'll be good. I won't tell anyone, I promise," Victoria said.

"This isn't about being *good*, Victoria. This is about *choice*," Jonah said, suddenly impatient. "Not many women in your situation have options. Someday we're going to die, because everybody dies. I haven't seen anybody yet that didn't die. And I'd like to choose my own kind of death for a change. I'm tired of being tormented to hell, that's what I'm tired of. Tired of people's lives in my hands, and I certainly don't want your life in my hands, and I'm going to tell you, Victoria, without me, life has no meaning. But if it were me, I'd choose a midair plane collision. There's poetry in that—a burning body falling to the ground like some sort of star."

"I have money. We can go to an ATM, and you can have it. I'll give you my pin, account number—anything you want. Just let me go."

"You think this is about money?"

"They'll come looking for me."

"I don't doubt that. Tell me, are you the slit-wrists-in-the-bathtub kind of girl, or the hail-of-bullets kind of woman?" Jonah tossed her a napkin. "Fix your face."

Victoria wiped her mouth, crumbled the napkin in her lap. "Pills," she said. "A bottle of sleeping pills."

"It's like you're a fifties housewife, chewing tranquilizers and burning steaks. Folding before the first hand is even played. Maybe we should talk about all those bags in the trunk and where you're going."

"Why are you doing this?" she cried, gripping the steering wheel. Veering the car outside the lines. "Please take me home. Take me *home.*"

It took everything in him not to jam the knife all the way in, Lionel or no Lionel. Always with the shelter they're privileged to have, but inevitably abandon. Always with the family they complain about, and secretly hate. Always with the men with whom they lie frozen between undisturbed sheets. They all begged for the life they didn't have, but thought they could if they had the chance. Jonah's job wasn't to help them live up to their fiction; his work was excavation and preservation.

Why didn't they understand that?

Why is it that we miss what we've always taken for granted at the very moment we're on the verge of losing it? Nearing death, we cry out for our rotting floorboards, the oven that burns all the cakes, and the lovers who crawl into our beds stinking of someone else's happiness. But what we really mourn is our own loss; we lament the time that exists just beyond our last breath, when a shovel presses cold earth on top of a wooden box. How do you mourn this loss when you're on the precipice of it? We're unable to say its name or define its shape, it's so elusive; instead we call out the things that compose this minor life, in hopes that the sum will take form from its ramshackle parts. We are nothing if not children who regard a manual with terror when we see the words *some assembly required*.

Jonah's sister went to the crazies; his mother became a light in a house that had blown out, and his father, well, he'd never loved his father to begin with. And for all of it, Jonah felt nothing. So why should these women make a case for a miserable life they're so desperate to save? Be honorable. Lay a blanket down over your sadness because the only way around pain is through it. These women were fucking lucky to receive the gifts that Jonah gave; Lionel wouldn't stand for release; he would never allow Jonah to go quietly.

Lionel's here, and it's about time.

Lionel reached for Victoria's hair, petted it. It was no use, though; she couldn't hear or feel him. She was only a repository in which their pain could be placed. Lately, he'd been getting these nightmares of a girl in a white lamb's mask, wearing a Crazy Eddie's T-shirt and ripped dungarees. The girl, who couldn't have been older than ten, stood in the middle of the street with a snake in her hand, and in the snake's mouth you could see a mouse trying to claw its way out, only to be swallowed whole. Lionel remembered the claws that took on the appearance of tweezers. The girl held the snake to the sky like some kind of victory, and then Lionel woke up.

Lionel woke to another car speeding down a back road, another woman pleading for her life who would invariably become another doll stuffed in a box or buried under the floorboards.

"Took you long enough," Jonah said. "We need to have a discussion about punctuality. Quit it with the snakes; you know how I hate them."

"You're not the one dreaming about them," Lionel said.

"What snakes?" Victoria cried.

"Seems to me that you're on the run," Jonah said. "All those clothes folded up neat and tidy. Pictures of your kids shoved into books. Tell me about the home you so desperately want to go back to, but when you picked me up it was the one thing you seemed intent on leaving." A thin line of blood trickled down her neck from where Jonah pressed the knife a touch too deep.

"Easy, soldier," Lionel said. "Look at you, cutting up her neck. Making a mess. Are you looking for a one-way ticket to a needle in the arm? What did I tell you about the belts? They're clean, honest. But no, you got to be the kid throwing sand outside the sandbox."

Jonah peered over his shoulder. "Put on the gloves." To Victoria, "Pull over. Park."

"What are you going to do to me?"

"We're going for a walk. See those trees over there? I'm going to leave you there and take the car. All your talking's giving me a headache."

"I told you to gag them. I told you to take the wheel, but you never listen. Sometimes I think you're suited for back office, because you're starting to fuck up the basics," Lionel said.

"You're going to let me go," Victoria said. This was the part Jonah secretly loved most—the walk from the car to the tree, and the hope occupying the small space between the two.

She cut the engine and Jonah tied her hands with rope. Behind him, Lionel shook his head and said, "The gloves, you moron." But Jonah didn't listen. Skin on skin excited him.

They walked into the forest and stood under a canopy of trees and purple sky. He told Victoria to get down on her knees, that he had to blindfold her before he drove off. Security measures, he called it. Then he told her that he wanted to give her a hug before he left. He was sentimental like that. She nodded, thinking this was the end, and it was.

Her jaw, in particular, was probably broken. Jaws tended to break around him.

He pressed her face into his chest and stood still as she writhed and screamed. Choked on her cracking teeth. "Everything's okay," he assured her. *Be assured that the choice is not ours now. Children, it will not hurt if you'll be quiet.* When she collapsed into him, he started to hum a lullaby about buttons and lambs—the kind of song his mother used to sing. Slack and beautiful, Victoria was a blond version of his Lucia. Two dolls, two hearts ceasing to beat.

ON MONDAY, LUCIA got caught. She'd gotten sloppy with the merchandise, stuffing granola bars and rotting bananas and half-eaten apples in all of her drawers, until the flies came with their multiplication. She hardly noticed when they formed a halo around her desk because she was drunk. Yvonne and the interns huddled in the kitchen, whispering about the tragedy that was Lucia.

Banding together, the militant clock-watchers dissected the events of the past month: the botched call transfers, dead plants, and conference rooms littered with trays of picked-over muffins, and melon and cantaloupe, second-class fruit. Lucia used to send email alerts detailing the bounty up for grabs. Now, she just let the trays pile up. Deal makers clicked through their PowerPoint presentations with one eye on a lone pineapple congealing in its own juice and the other at the glare from their computer screens.

Everyone at McCann Harrison was apoplectic; Lucia colonized. Last week, she stole a pile of printouts and set them on fire in the bathroom. Watching them burn in the basin gave her a certain kind of calm. Lucia hungered for the days of Sancerre lunches and lace thong shoots. In Biarritz, her body was a ticker tape of ivory along the shoreline. Surfers strode past with their wetsuits and boards, murmuring to her in clumsy Basque. Come nightfall, she'd eat steak with her hands and let the meat slip through her fingers. Back then they called her carnivorous—the girl with the twenty-inch waist who could devour you down to gristle and bone. The threat of Lucia sold millions of bikinis and mesh tanks. When the famous catalog fired her, they promised her a lifetime supply of terry shorts, to which she replied, "Fuck the shorts. I want the million-dollar bra."

Lately, she'd taken to measuring her waist, thighs, and hips, and couldn't stop them from expanding. The gap between her thighs closed up, and she felt that her thirties were one long, steady march to the grave. At home, she'd press the tape measure into Jonah's palm and beg him to strangle her with it while they fucked, because her neck was the one area of her body that did not multiply. *String me up like tinsel,* she'd plead, and after a time she saw something ferocious in Jonah, as if this were the one thing he desired all along.

"Black me out," she'd scream.

When Lucia returned from her lunch, which consisted of her coworkers' half-eaten snacks, Debbie from HR and Yvonne hovered from behind Lucia's desk. Debbie said, "We need to talk about the granola bars, Lucia."

"And my fucking *yogurt*," Yvonne said.

Lucia could've fought it, could've said that the items were planted, that she had been framed, but all she wanted to do was inch home, crawl under her bed, and stare at photographs of herself in silk and vinyl. "So, let's talk about it."

Lucia already saw her replacement: a pert blond with berry-stained lips and red-soled stilettos. Lucia noticed the subtraction of years and pigment, and understood that she was being replaced again. On a long enough timeline, everyone will expire. There were no second acts, no revivals—there was only a tawny blond on the cover of a magazine, or a temp sitting behind a desk cooing, "McCann Harrison. How may I direct your call?"

Lucia calmly collected her things in a small brown

box and carried it to the elevator, down twenty-two floors, and beyond a glass revolving door. In the street she dumped her box on the ground, kicked it, and walked home in heels that tore at her ankles. She wouldn't cry; she wouldn't allow herself that privilege, so instead she laughed. Laughed so hard it hurt. She stopped in a store and loaded up on Entenmann's cakes, donuts, and pies. One by one, she took a bite and hurled the desserts, piece by piece, to the pavement, as if leaving a trail.

People stopped and stared, but not like they used to. It didn't matter though, because they were staring, and Lucia felt good, calm, and right.

At home, Jonah's face was so complicated it would take days to describe it. "How was your day?" he asked in a perfunctory way, in a way lovers were supposed to do. But on Jonah it felt wrong, scripted, as if he were trying on normal for size, not realizing the pants were too tight and the buttons had come undone.

"A day is a day like any other day. There's a food thief in the office," she said, extending her legs as Jonah removed one shoe, then the other, and pressed his hands against the arches of her feet. Closing her eyes, she murmured, "That feels good."

"Did you call the FBI?" Jonah brushed crumbs from her face; he never made inquiries.

"Funny guy. I've a far more dangerous weapon in my arsenal: Human Resources."

Jonah laughed.

"What did you do all day?" Lucia said, moving his hair out of his eyes.

"Waited for you to come home."

"And at night? Tell me, what do you do at night while you think I'm asleep?"

"I know you're awake," he said and paused. "You know what I do. I drive around. Take fares. Make money. Mostly I drive around the city waiting for you to wake up." He rattled a DVD in his hand, some Korean horror movie where everyone is haunted by their past and ends up dying from the guilt. "I got us a video, some takeout. Chinese. Remember *Lost Boys*? The scene where Kiefer Sutherland's character makes Jason Patric think he's eating maggots? *You're eating maggots, Michael.*" Jonah bared his teeth.

"Come on. It's not like you have to work."

"So I should just sit around and count my money? Is that what you'd like me to do, Lucia?" An edge creeps into Jonah's voice and he closes his eyes, prays that his anger won't awaken Lionel.

"I'm asking you to be honest. Is this about *her*, your sister? You know she keeps calling in the middle of the night when we're supposed to be sleeping. Maybe she knows you're not home and this is why she calls when she does. Maybe she knows you've trained me to disable the voice mail, to never pick up. Tell me, Jonah. Does she know something about you that I don't?"

"I know what you're doing. You're trying to get a rise out of me," Jonah said. "We can keep at this all night if you'd like."

"Why won't you take her calls? What did she do?"

"What makes you think *she* did something?" Jonah said.

Lying in the dark, Lucia said, "That day you met me on the plane, you told me your name was Telly. Why did you lie about your name?"

"Because everyone lies. That's the foundation of every relationship," Jonah replied. "No one wants to know the truth, otherwise I would've asked you again how your day was. Because the bloody feet—and what is this, chocolate on your chin—tell a different story."

"I quit my job today," she said, closing her eyes, drifting to sleep. "That's the ten o'clock news. Maybe this'll get a rise out of you." She delivered the words as if they were barbed wire intended to keep Jonah from getting closer.

Jonah regarded her as a doll with two cracked eyes and a sewn-up mouth. He shook it away, desperate to retrieve the image of the woman he loved—the woman who was breaking, was broken—as she was at that moment: real, human. Doll parts, beating heart, doll hair, knotted ropes—Jonah's eyes were a shutter that slowly edged out the human part of Lucia. The one thing he had been wedded to.

He stood over her sleeping body and pressed a box

cutter against her cheek. Over and over he said, "I love you, I love you, please, please let me love you . . ."

Lucia went to meetings in basements. Sometimes she'd get a call about a location change—a high school auditorium on the Lower East Side or a Baptist church in Washington Heights—but mostly she met in basements crowded with picked-over pastries, Styrofoam cups, and men who smoked Camels under No Smoking signs.

For the first weeks she couldn't speak. Instead, she'd hold up evidence from her former life, which was unnecessary since half the men recognized her from the junk mail piled up in their mailboxes (her catalog was the lone piece of mail that would survive the avalanche of Final Notices) and the rest didn't care. It didn't matter that Lucia had once been "that famous catalog model" because in this room everyone had been something once. This room was the Last Exit—no seriously, this was the end of the road, the final Final Notice before the repo man or undertaker took it all away.

But still, Lucia held up the pair of jewel-encrusted underwear she'd stolen and said, "This was me."

From the back of the room, a woman laughed. Her name was Asia and her shrill was the loudest sound. "*Girl*, that ain't even *you*."

"Lucia is sharing," the counselor said in a voice that made you crave powdered, arsenic-laced donuts.

"She's not sharing, it's self-pity." To Lucia she said, "You need to stop carrying around your panties like you're Linus or something. Holding on to them won't bring your life back. You white women are always crying over some bullshit. You're not a model . . . you're not a millionaire. Try living with your mom in East New York and having to ride the A train for a fucking hour because this is the only meeting you can make before you have to work the night shift. Now that's some sad shit right there. Now that's a story."

"I'm feeling a lot of hostility in your voice," a man said.

Lucia balled up the diamonds in her hands. Everything was ugly and everything hurt.

"You about to feel my fist, old man," Asia snapped. To Lucia, "Say *something*!"

The counselor asked Asia if she wanted to take a break or go outside, as if the words were a code for Asia to cool it, because as soon as she heard them she leaned back in her chair, crossed her arms, and remained quiet for the remainder of the session.

When the group broke, Lucia wrapped her scarf around her neck and walked out into the cold night. Asia followed.

"That was me trying to help you back there; that was me paying you a compliment," Asia said.

"You're right," Lucia said. "I don't know what it's like to live with your mother in East New York. But I do know what it's like to feel like you're nothing before, during, and after you were something, and having to live with a man who only loves you because he knows you know you're nothing."

Asia nodded and said, "Let me get your phone."

"What?"

"Your phone, your phone. I want to give you my cell, you know, in case you want to talk. You may be fucked-up, but you're not nothing."

Lucia watched Asia in her white puffy coat race down the subway steps.

From a parked car Jonah watched Lucia, his dark, fallen star. Over the coming weeks, he'd remain here, bearing witness to her slow ascension and his steady, frightening decline.

When Lucia phoned and asked him to meet her in a house, he thought it was like old times, but when he arrived he found a second-floor apartment half-filled with boxes and a cat weaving through them.

"What the fuck is this? What's with the cat?"

"Calm down. She's gone off to work. She won't be home until morning." Regarding the cat, she said, "Oh, that's Felix."

"We're not taking the cat," Jonah said. He was a fuse ready to blow at any minute. "Our building doesn't allow pets."

"Our building doesn't allow heroin, but you don't seem to have a problem with that, do you?" Lucia snapped. Today, there were no sandwiches, but there were bags of groceries on the counter and boxes of food on the floor. "Don't bother with the fridge. She doesn't even drink real milk."

"Do you want me to take your picture?" Jonah touched her hair but she turned away.

"No, the last thing I want you to do is take my picture. But I guess you already knew that since you've been following me to my meetings."

"Maybe I wouldn't follow you if you were honest with me."

"Honest? Do you even hear yourself? You stalk me at my AA meetings. The same man who disappears for hours at a time at night, and don't even start that nonsense about being a cab driver. You hate people. The last thing you'd ever do is drive them."

"Let's talk about this at home," Jonah said.

"I am home."

Jonah surveyed the apartment, opened the boxes, and saw piles of Lucia's things. Her life, their former life, dismembered: books in one box, clothes in the other. He moved from box to box and saw none of her lingerie, photographs, or even the bejeweled panties she treasured. But he did see another woman's clothes. This woman was larger (XL) and wore cheap polyester, knockoff bags, and a sweatshirt that read, "I like my Michael Coors, Light!"

Pointing to the cat, Lucia said, "I'm spending tonight in your home but then I'm leaving you. I'm so sorry, Jonah. I don't love you."

"You don't love me," he said quietly.

"Right now I need to love myself, and Asia is helping me with that."

"You're moving in with a woman named after a continent?"

"It's better than a man who stockpiles chloroform in his closet."

Jonah laughed. "Come home."

"For tonight, I will."

Lucia woke with a headache. Her skin hurt. Jonah sat on the edge of their bed, his hands steadying the mattress. In the corner of the room was a wooden crate. How did it get there?

"I know you're awake," he said. "I just didn't know for how long."

"Come back to bed," Lucia said, reaching for him, but all he could do was stare at the wall as if he were looking through it, already clawing his way to the other side. "One last time before I go."

"I wanted to give you everything. I wanted to give you all of it. But now I realize I can't."

"I don't understand."

"Remember that winter we went to Utah and you wore that red hat and we realized we didn't know how to ski and drank instead?"

"I remember the bourbon." She also recalled the sex, and how Jonah tied his belt around her throat and pulled so hard she feared her neck would snap, but she kept on and closed her eyes.

"How the old man who ran the inn nearly kicked us out for getting booze on the floor and all over the sheets? And then you got naked in the snow, rolled around in it, and yelled at anyone who would listen that you were in camouflage?"

"I did blend beautifully into the scenery. We had a time." Lucia sat up and drew her knees to her chest, waiting for the searing pain in the front of her head to move to the back, to wane. She was confused. She didn't remember drinking. All she could feel now was the pain, the sharpness of it. All she could see were parts of their room, pieces of their furniture, through a fog.

"I don't think there was a moment when we weren't drowning. When we weren't anesthetized."

"I want to learn Arabic," Lucia said. "Maybe I can take some classes. Go back to school."

"Arabic? Christ, Lucia. Do you hear yourself?" Jonah said.

Lucia palmed the sheets and slipped her fingers between her legs and felt only warmth. She looked at the sheets and then at her hands, not noticing the cuts down her leg that Jonah had made while she slept, and said, "Why is there blood on the bed?"

"I tried to give it to you," Jonah smiled and gave her a white dress he'd been holding. Told her to put it on. "I tried to give it to you. I've practically laid down my life. I've practically died every day to give you peace. And you still don't have any peace. You look better than I've seen you in a long while, but it's still not the peace I want to give you."

"Jonah, you're starting to freak me the fuck out." Lucia eyed the door, the window, any means of escape. "Stop this."

"I know about you and my sister. I know everything."

"Your sister? What are you talking about?"

Jonah drew her close and kissed the place on her head where her hair was the thickest, the unruliest. This is sacrifice, he thought, swallowing his love for Lucia because he knew that she wasn't fit to survive this life. On that plane he'd thought she was just like him, but he'd come to realize that Lucia, his great love, was nothing like him. She was ordinary, just like the rest, and he hated her for it.

"Jonah, I can't breathe," she said.

There's a figure at the door, watching. The figure advances. "Let me take care of this."

"What? I don't hear you," he said.

"This is me *making other arrangements*," Lionel said, pressing down on Lucia's mouth.

When it was over, when their work was done, Jonah said in a small voice, "I wish I had the strength to kill you."

JONAH SAID TO his sister, "Fine, you won. I'm coming home."

THE MUSIC OUR TEETH MAKE

1985, 2013

I'M LONELY. DOES it hurt? Yes. Does it stain? Yes. It takes time to wash the blood off your hands, longer than you think. I used to say that I was alone, never *lonely*, and there was a difference between the two, but now, right now, I'm the loneliest I've ever been. This is my small life and I'm smothered by the weight of what I've done, my constant trembling forms another layer of skin.

What have I *done*?

My mother died, killed herself. Pills spilled out of a bottle, and a note on the bed. I set a woman's hair on fire, and then my stepfather disappeared, picked up that woman—I can barely say her name, Gillian—right out of the emergency room, dumped her in another hotel, and then drove farther west. He told her that he needed some time, a break, but he'd come for her. "Don't worry," he said. "This isn't me leaving." They say that a mother can feel every inch of her child's pain, down to the tenderness of aches, but does that apply to a father at the wheel with a girl in a seat once warmed by my mother, by me? Can the man cutting through lights feel his daughter's hurt, even if the daughter isn't technically his? Or does another wounded bird, whose wings are wrapped up in gauze, and whose scalp is stitched up tight, infatuate James?

The man I blame for it all is in a car with the top down, sitting next to a woman who is the image of me. Not my mother, *me*. Kate. Sweet Kate. Down to the blush on her round cheeks and the blue eyes that any man would dare tumble into.

I mourn her by dyeing my red hair blond. I no longer look like Norah, Ellie's mother. Hair and history are the only things that distinguish me from Norah.

I select her final outfit, something cashmere and blue.

I put on a shirt, James's, and say, "My mother is dead."

I slam the phone down, crawl under the bed, and rest there. I'm safe here. I remember a show where arctic polar bears practiced "still-hunting," the act of paralyzing one's body, perched over a spotted sea lion's breathing hole, waiting for the moment when the hunted emerges to breathe. That's when the polar bear pounces, comes down on top of the ice with all of his weight to shatter, grab, and devour.

Underneath the bed I wonder, which am I? Bear or seal?

Later, I hear Jonah on my lawn. "Kate, come out and play."

That night I catch a news report about an investigation gone wrong. The local police have teamed up with the FBI to hunt down a serial killer, whom they've been calling the "Doll Collector." A man (why must they always assume it's a man?) who sews his victims' mouths and eyes shut, like some rag doll, and disposes of them precisely three months after they've been murdered. Since killers tend to return to the scene of a crime, the police have replaced one victim's body with a department store mannequin fitted with a hidden camera behind its eyes, but the only action they've witnessed from the footage is a bunch of drunken teenagers humping the doll and slathering her face with pizza. *Run of the mill action*, they say. *Boys will be boys*, they say.

I wonder this: Who would be brazen enough to return?

It's when I shut off the television that I realize all the victims resemble *that woman*. Gillian. And since I look just like her, someone out there is killing versions of me.

Now all I have left are the Smurf cakes, and I don't even have them anymore because one of those fancy organic markets just opened up, and they make cakes faster and cheaper than two hands ever could. And then my boss's nemesis, Bunny Blake, swans in with her offer nobody can refuse and smiles for days. Minnie says, "Maybe this is the time when we fold, kid. Leave the table." I know

Minnie's not just talking about shuttering her shop; she's talking about me.

What did I do? My mother: *I did this to you.*

I still make the cakes because it's what I know. Having baked for the greater part of my life, why should I stop because a sow of a woman kicked me out of the shop I considered a home? Because the one woman I trusted found her midlife crisis twenty years too late? We are all in our prisons, our man-made spaces of confinement. Some boxes have windows, some have doors, but they're merely mirages in the sand, illusions that give us hope of escape. So I erect a room of buttercream and white flour walls, with bars of butter serving as window grates. Sometimes I try to claw my way out, only to see the scratch marks on my face.

Over a telephone line Minnie says, "I drove by the Tower of David today. All that mirrored glass reflecting the scabs down below, and I thought of your father. Too much?"

"Never enough," I say.

"What you run to, what you escape from, never ends up as good as you want it to be," Minnie says.

I've graduated from My Little Pony, Glo Worms, and Strawberry Shortcake to nineties teen melodramas. Cakes decorated with scrunchies and Baja shirts remind me of *90210*, of R.E.M. and Paradise Cove. Banana cream pies in the shape of a swan are a nod to *Swans Crossing*, the ill-fated morning soap that starred a young and cunning Sarah Michelle Gellar. I hide the cakes in my kitchen and take small, measured bites before I leave in the morning.

It's like heroin, only cheaper.

But I let Jonah in, and watch as his hands rove the photos on the walls and the books in the bookcases. He listens to me. From sundown to sunrise, I tell him stories. That, for a time, it was just me and my mother, and I wanted to hold on to that happiness for as long as I possibly could, but Ellie was always distracted. Always looking beyond me, she was determined to see what was on the other side. I tell Jonah that James taught me to bake. How I tended to my cakes as if they were children, exercising patience, restraint, and a love that was missing from our cold and very beautiful home. Baking gave me a family, and for years I remained like that, a woman alone, living with machinery.

I regard the windowsill as if it's a place where tears could be deposited.

Jonah gestures at the barren walls and bookcases, places where framed photos would reveal the history that is one's life. He says, "There are no photos. Anywhere. Do you have a family?"

"We're not exactly the pose-for-pictures kind." I remember a time when the local paper wanted to take our picture. I had a minor part in a play and we closed on a good run. An old man with a camera signaled for all of us to huddle, get closer, *closer*. Ellie walked out of the frame, James trailed her, and I stood alone, staring at the ground. The old man snapped the picture anyway but it never made the paper. Weeks later, we received the stills in the mail, and there's me, tormented, and a boy about my age—his face all blurred out—resting his hand on my shoulder. "And the ones I did have are gone."

"My father . . ." Jonah says, and falls quiet—his father will always be a sentence he struggles to complete. "He loved my sister, completely, and she didn't even know it. Gillian threw it away because she felt entitled to a love that's easy, and never got the simple fact that love is something you earn."

"Do you love her?" I ask.

"That's an interesting question," Jonah says.

"A simple one."

"There was a time I'd do anything to protect her, but she makes it difficult for me. I noticed all these people around her get hurt, but she's the one who survives, and it occurred to me that she didn't need my help. If anything, I needed her. I suppose, in some way, I'll always need her."

"Need isn't the same as love."

Jonah stares at me in a way that feels like I've intruded in his private space, trespassed where I'm not supposed to go. "My sister makes it impossible for me to love her."

I wonder aloud about work, how it's possible that Jonah is ensconced in my home in the middle of the day. Jonah was an artist once, but now just lives off a bit of money put away. Now he takes pleasure in watching other people go to work.

"You don't have a job?" I say.

"I have a kind of work," he says.

"I don't understand."

"I have projects that occupy my time."

The phone rings. It's Minnie and she's breathless. "I'm with some Colombians," she says. "A singer and an exporter who tell me I'm the perfect cover."

"Where are you?" I shout.

"Cartagena. I had to dump the caftans. I got me some Jackie O sunglasses and boleros. The girl sings me to sleep, Spanish lullabies. The man is always on the phone. Mostly they ball in the other room while I watch TV. We're about to take down a score."

"Speak English, Minnie. You're not making any sense."

A rustling of paper, a radio turned up high. "I'll call you when it's safe."

When I hang up the phone, I fail to notice the tremors.

"What's wrong?" Jonah says.

"I don't know when it'll be safe."

I wonder what my mother would have done, had she not had the cancer, had she not stopped caring. I'd like to think that Ellie would have reverted back to a semblance of her former self. She'd meet Gillian head on, interrupt the fucking, and say, "Do you really think he'll ever leave me?" While my mother may have taken James Kelleher's last name, that man belonged to her; James was her property, and no way was she going to allow some red-haired, boarding-school whore of a woman trespass to her life.

BEFORE THE SICKNESS, before my mother's body was burned, she was slick with baby oil. I was thirteen and we went to the beach to celebrate her birthday. She was a woman who always had to be near water. Hair pulled back tight, Ellie's skin was fragile, the color of parchment, but she never feared the sun. She didn't cower from the inevitable burning; rather, she sought it out, took it like sacrament. The years were an overcoat she was desperate to shed, and now all she wanted was to feel *something*. Later, I would spend an hour slathering Noxzema on my mother's back (*you feel this?*), but now, right now, my mother smoked Virginia Slims down to the filter and dove into the water. Left her clothes, and her thirteen-year-old daughter, behind. The fathers gawked through their sunglasses, wiping froth from above their lips, while the mothers held their children close, pulled their skirts over their knees, as far down as they could go.

The sky was cloudless. The waves advanced.

The ticker tape of wet sand divided me from the water. That summer, I watched all the bodies emerging from the surf, and they looked as if they'd returned from war or a night cruising the strip: hair all webbed and matted, eyes red, the cold snaking their limbs with bumps. Why would I crawl, so willingly, into a coffin? But Ellie was at home in the water, setting up shop, ready to do business. Sometimes, when she didn't think I could hear her, she pretended to be talking to someone named Cassidy. Telling Cassidy to cool it with the black beauties. Those pills will kill you.

Hours later, the sun settled into the waves that had turned black. The fathers took swigs from beers with tears raining down the bottle while the mothers folded everything into squares. Where are you? I wondered, scanning the shoreline.

A man slept behind the rocks. Curled up against the moss, the flies arranged themselves around his body in the shape of a halo. The rocks were a muted gray, drilled with holes that gave the appearance of eyes, from which ants traveled in and out. I wanted to lean in and check for signs of life, but my mother had warned me about the men. Always sleeping. Always jerking off. Don't get too close.

It's not like I hadn't seen a dead body before.

"Let's go," my mother said. "Now." I threw my books, towels, and beach pail into my book bag while my mother made a break for the boardwalk. Our footfalls caused a pigeon riot; they scattered and abandoned the remains of half-eaten hot dogs and tepid cheese fries.

On the boardwalk, I heard a familiar voice call out my mother's name. "You're going to ignore me now? Is that any way to treat me after all that I've done? The thing with Delilah, the thing about your grandfather, I mean, how could I tell you? I thought you already knew. Don't you turn your back to me!" The seagulls came like swallows.

Under her breath I heard Ellie whisper, "You knew for years. You knew everything and didn't tell me." To me she said, "Come the fuck *on*."

How is it that she'd managed to light a cigarette and smoke it?

In the car my mother said, "That was close." We were stone on the ride home. In the driveway she said, "Don't tell James. Our secret, okay?"

"That was my real father, wasn't it? Tim. How could you just run away?"

"What do you mean, real? You act as if James were imaginary. *Real* is what's in front of you, not what you've left behind. Promise me you won't say anything. Promise me you won't ruin this."

"I barely remember what he looks like. Do you know what it's like to forget your father's face?"

Ellie sat quiet, covered her mouth with her hand as

if she could catch the words coming out of her mouth and prevent my hearing them. "I do know what it's like. I never knew my father; he died when I was three. Actually, to be specific, he got killed right in front of me, in a car accident, although I can't remember any of it. Sometimes I wake at night and see glass and a camera and that's it, that's all I have of him—a few broken objects. Do you see me crying? Do you see me whimpering for Daddy like a fucking baby who's shit her diaper? Consider yourself lucky that you had this time with Tim because this is life, and we bear it. We take our losses, and we don't act like children stomping our feet when we don't get what we want."

"I am a child," I said. "And it's not wrong to want your father."

"How many times do I have to explain this to you? You have a father," Ellie said, exasperated. She cut the engine, opened the car door, and walked into the house.

Later that night I heard the familiar creak of my mother's bed. Ellie was sobbing through the sex, and afterward, James promised her that he'd rub it all away.

"Why didn't you tell me you saw him?" James said.

"What was I going to say? The man who beat my head in and fucked my daughter found me? Things have been so quiet. Now Tim's back and it won't take him long to find us. We have to go, James. We have to sell the house."

"No, we have to call the police," James said, firmly. "We don't have to run from that monster; we'll have his ass in jail."

"You know we can't do that," Ellie said.

Monster? Beat my head in? Fucked my daughter? What was she talking about? My father wasn't a monster. He wasn't the one who strapped me into a car in the middle of the night and drove for two days until we arrived at the house owned by a man she met in the personals. He wasn't the one who put a lock on the phone so I couldn't dial out. He wasn't the one who told my guidance counselor, *My daughter is troubled, prone to telling lies, and can you call me if my daughter exhibits any unusual behavior?*

If anyone was the monster it was Ellie.

I STRAIN TO recall the Tim who called out to Ellie on the beach all those years ago. All I can see are his aviators. But I remember the hurt on his face, how it washed his cheeks salty and white, and the heartbreak in his voice. When my mother used to talk about sacrifice, I wondered why money and comfort were what you earned when you traded in love.

In the mirror I notice my eyes. Were they always this blue? I seem to remember them being green. I have to put on some clothes—and that is the moment when I realize it's over. My mother has been reduced to a pile of bone matter and fragments, gray sand that I can collect and hold in my palm, while my real father is forever waving from a boardwalk.

NO ONE EVER talks about what you do with a dead person's things. Somehow we're led to believe that after a funeral we'll come home to boxes stacked neatly, a whole of someone's life packed up and ready for the next place. We tell ourselves we do the right thing by donating the clothes where the scent of her soap lingers the most, and the library books she neglected to return (*Spring Snow* was the last book she read). We are not selfish; we keep only that which is necessary—a handful of things that bring us closer to the dead.

Ellie owned nothing personal. She had everything you'd expect a woman to have and nothing more, nothing that would allow you to lift up the folds of her skin and peer inside her beating heart—rather she was shut down, a closed-up cavity. Her life was a wiped-down crime scene: impeccable (and baffling) in the way that she left no fingerprints or impressions in the carpet. My mother wrote no letters, played no records, returned books to the library after she had read them (except for that last book, curiously), bathed with Ivory soap and water, and refused to have candid photographs taken. A life lived in perpetual reconstruction, Ellie torched all remnants of her history before James, before this home in which I now ghost, and this unremarkable life they once lived; so I end up taking a toothbrush rinsed clean and a hairbrush with strands of hair already discarded.

"Why couldn't you leave me anything that would remind me of you?" I say, out loud, in the middle of the street, to no one in particular. I mourn my mother by brushing my hair, my teeth.

"You're not alone in this," Jonah says. He's in my house now, eating a blueberry muffin. He's in my house. How did he get in my house? I don't remember letting him in. Did I let him in? These headaches; I keep getting these headaches. I've been having these dreams where a woman with red hair sprints past me. Her movements are so sharp and swift I feel her cut into my skin. Sometimes I wake and there are marks on my body.

"How did you get in here?" I say, reaching for the phone on the wall, but he intervenes.

"Call the cops? Now why do you want to go and do a thing like that?"

"The fact that you broke into my house in the middle of the night to eat a muffin. That's not even my muffin. Where did you get that muffin?" I say.

"I didn't break in, *Kate*. You let me in. Five minutes ago. Don't you remember?"

"No, I don't remember."

"It's the headaches, right? They're always worse at night."

How did he . . . ?

Jonah's holding up the muffin for inspection, plucking out blueberries. "With you there are always surprises."

"We barely know each other," I say, and the headache, the rush of it, hurtles back, and for a moment I see a pair of tweezers falling to the ground. Tweezers, a boy with a bloody blue eye, a car hitting a tree, a hospital—the images come in waves, but they come swiftly, careening in front of me, and for a moment I feel suffocated by pictures moving.

"When I was five, my father told me that a dog in the neighborhood had mange. The kind of disease where mites burrow under the skin, and the poor dog had to claw at something he couldn't get to, but how could he know that? The dog was a skinny thing with crusts up and down his flank. So my father shows me a pup that was part of the litter, and tells me that the pup's got the sickness. We drive home, and later that night I get out of bed. I leave the house through the front door. I find a rock. I find the dog. I hit him with it. So hard that the puppy squeals and a man runs out of his house and kicks the shit out of me because his dog is fine. Turns out, he didn't have mange. No dog in our neighborhood did.

That's just a story my father liked to tell," Jonah says. "My father isn't as innocent as he makes himself out to be. He has motives."

Jonah lowers his eyes, chuckles, as if conjuring a scene from memory, one that he'd give anything to project onto a screen, onto the sky.

I reach for the muffin. Jonah tears off a piece. We chew.

"I killed because my father told me to. The knowledge of that does things to you, changes you."

"Your father didn't tell you to hurt that dog. That was a decision *you* made on your own. Why didn't you take it to a shelter or a vet? You're acting as if death was the solution when it was only an option. I'm not saying your father's not a dick, but you had a choice. You do see that, don't you? You chose to kill that animal instead of seeing if it could survive."

Jonah laughs; bitterness gives it edge. "Where did you learn that from?"

"Learn what?"

"Compassion, empathy."

"You don't learn it. You have it. Everyone has it. So I have it."

"You think children have the luxury of choice."

"We're not children, Jonah."

"You can't afford to be this blind, Kate. Not now." Jonah sighs. He looks impatient, like a clock's ticking in his hand and time's running out. He paces the room, asks,

"Where the fuck is Lionel when you need him?" (How convenient for Lionel to take a pass on this, to finally let Jonah do the dirty work.)

Who is Lionel, and why is Jonah acting as if he's a person who should be in the room with them?

"Why are you telling me this?" I say.

"Consider it a motivational speech. You're not going to let them get away with your mother's death, are you?"

"What I did was wrong."

"What you did was incomplete," Jonah corrects. "Because in this story, right now, you've got the dog with mange. Now it's up to you to put it out of its misery."

"This is your *sister* you're talking about. The woman I took from her home and tried to burn alive in a hotel room. The woman who could've had me arrested and in jail right now, but didn't. This is the same woman, right? I'm not crazy, right? Because all I want to do now is go back to normal. Back to my life."

"Tell me about this life. Where you get up every morning to walk to a job you're about to lose. Where you come home every night and sit in silence, thinking of new ways to make yourself more like your mother. How is this a life? I want you to think back to that day, how you saw what you were about to do as a way out, because it was. So finish this."

"Have you been watching me all this time?" I rise.

"Kind of like how you've been stalking my sister and

your father fucking for months? Like that? The guilt must be killing you."

"That was different. What I did was in self-defense."

"Is that a fact? I think your mother was pretty resourceful. It wasn't like she didn't know; it was more like she didn't care. But for some reason, you do. You cared enough to make up for how much your mother didn't."

"You don't know my mother."

"I know my sister better than you think. In the end, she will fight and weep, but she will thank me. They always do."

I notice a shift in his voice, a reverberation. How, when he started to speak, it was from the center of his mouth, and gradually it morphed off to the side, as if someone else was speaking, sitting right here, occupying the space between them.

"Pop quiz. Tell me who said this: 'You learn what you need to kill and take care of the details. It's like changing a tire. The first time you're careful. By the thirtieth time, you can't remember where you left the lug wrench.'"

"How did you get in my house?"

Jonah shakes his head. He starts to whistle, letting the air make music with his teeth. "You're not hearing me. You let me in. You've never been alone; it's always been us."

Later, Jonah says, "I need you to finish this, Kate."

SOME ASSEMBLY REQUIRED
1968

"TODAY YOU ARE Ingrid," says Norah, my mother. I don't even have time to rub the sleep from my eyes because Norah's already put the finishing touches on the mask I'll wear this month. I feel my hair and notice that clumps of it are missing—she must've cut it in the middle of the night again. My mother tells me that Ingrid wears tight clothes and blue loafers that pinch her feet. Her hair is short because she was angry once, and took the scissors and started cutting until there was no more hair to cut. Norah locks up all the sharp objects in the safe. Precautions, she tells me. Norah clips pink barrettes into the places where she cut. I tell her that it's 1968 and I'm fifteen not five. I tell her that I hate pink and I hate barrettes, but she never listens.

"We'll write notes to one another in crayon because pens are dangerous," she instructs. I shake my head. My neck is so cold. I bite back tears. Not again. I'm tired of playing other people.

"Why are you so angry?" Norah says.

"You keep changing my story. I can't keep all the girls, and that one boy, straight. Why can't I just be myself, Ellie? Your daughter. Aren't I good enough?"

Norah says, "Because Ellie, my dear, is boring. Ellie doesn't amuse me."

There is a boy. We'll call him Tim. We sit across from one another in band class, and since he can't play the saxophone, Mr. Harmon has him practicing scales. During class, Tim moves his fingers over the keys, *tap tap*, but no sound comes out. Mr. Harmon says Tim doesn't know how to breathe. But I can breathe, too much for my own good. When it's my turn to go off register, Mr. Harmon taps his baton and warns me that I'm *so damn close* to blowing my clarinet straight across the room and he sure as hell isn't getting sued because some wise kid can't keep her air in check. "Must you always glare, Ellie?" Mr. Harmon sighs after class, and I remind him that this month my name is Ingrid.

"Right," Mr. Harmon says, rolling his eyes, walking out. "Ingrid."

Tim remains, breaking down his instrument. I notice red marks on his wrists. When he sees me see them, he covers them with his sleeves. "You know what everyone says about you?"

I cock my head. Raise an eyebrow. "Tell me. What do they say?"

"In the third movement you're slurring your notes instead of hitting a staccato." For a moment Tim stares out the window, looks through it.

"This coming from a guy who isn't even allowed to play," I say, licking my reed for no reason. Mother tells me that there are only a few places where a tongue is allowed to go. Wood isn't one of them, so it feels good to risk it. To hope for a mouthful of splinters.

"Just because I can't breathe doesn't mean I can't read the music."

"Tell me what *they* say. They talk a lot, don't they?"

Tim laughs. "They do."

"They say I'm weird. I'm desperate for attention, right?"

"I don't think you're desperate; I think you're lonely." Tim says this softly, quietly. He says this in a way that makes you want to take off your coat after a long walk home and sit in front of a table, knowing that he's made you something to eat. You hold on to his words while he packs up his saxophone, clips his case shut, and you know that home is a place where you make your own meals because Norah can't be bothered with something as trivial as slapping cold meat onto two pieces of white bread, or boiling macaroni until the noodles become soft and tender. Because Grandfather will bring home a half-eaten steak from his dinner or hand you a wad of bills and tell you to run down to the diner and get yourself something to eat. *Make it an adventure*, but you're tired of adventures, and for once you'd like to play it straight. Be normal. Eat a frozen Salisbury steak with a fork and a knife at the kitchen table.

"I'm alone, not lonely," I say.

Tim comes closer, says, "I liked your hair longer."

By then, I'm gone. Out of the races and onto the track.

There is a girl, too. My neighbor, Delilah Martin, sits in the window yet rarely leaves the house. She was born funny, not ha-ha funny, but not-quite-right funny. Parts of her body are bigger than they should be: eyes bulge out of her sockets, protruding teeth beg for escape from the prison that is her mouth, and her arms flail. Everything is too big or too small on Delilah, so she's often screaming because her clothes never fit or from the pain she feels from the boys who hurl small rocks at her back. One night I overheard my mother talk about what a shame it is that we can put down lame horses yet poor Delilah is confined to a window. Another night my mother's friend lamented how there should be a law against putting that poor retarded girl on display like some mutant mannequin— *She's not retarded*, my mother corrected—scaring all the perfectly normal children who want to walk to school without getting a freak show. *We have a right to peace*, my mother's friend whispered, to which my mother responded, *Send Joan some curtains then. She'll get the picture.*

Delilah taps at the window, *tap tap*, whenever I pass by, and I sometimes bring her chips or suckers because she lives in a Christian house and sugar and salt are sins. Delilah opens her window just wide enough for me to slip a bag through. She'll make one of her loud grunting sounds as a distraction. One time I asked her why she sits in front of the window all the time. "Are you kidding me?" she says. "This is better than the television. People do all sorts of queer things when they think you're stupid." Delilah's big thing is tracking the goings-on of the neighborhood whores: cheating husbands and Catholic girls giving blow jobs in parked cars. Friday's a big night in the neighborhood as men tend to splurge on their mistresses, and all the girls knew their fathers wouldn't be home until dawn. "I should sell tickets and popcorn," Delilah says one Friday as we pass a smoke between us.

"Your sister would flip if she saw us."

Delilah exhales. Her eyes bulge wider if you can believe. "Joan's at Bible group praying for my soul. You'd think it was yesterday that my mother died since she keeps crying those crocodile tears. I swear that woman's capable of making her own river. I don't know why she's still so torn up. My mother was an asshole."

Two years ago, some kids messing around found Mrs. Martin facedown in the ravine. Local gossip pronounced Farah Martin's death a suicide, but the local church wouldn't hear of it. The coroner registered Farah's passing as an accidental drowning. It didn't matter that she was an excellent swimmer who taught at the YMCA, or that two boys found her in shallow water. What mattered is that the days pressed on, folded into one another, and soon the shock of Farah Martin's death became a story the kids would embellish and tell—*She bled out of her hands, she did!*—until the Farah we all knew became a story we conjured, a figment of our imagination. After Delilah's mother's death, her older sister, Joan, moved home and took up with the Bible where Farah had left off.

"Do you pray?" I ask.

"Fuck Jesus. What's Jesus ever done for me?" Delilah says.

"Good point," I say. Norah waves from the window and I stub out my smoke.

"What's she got you playing this month?"

"A poor Swedish girl, Ingrid."

"If you ask me, your mother's missing a couple of buttons."

"Lately I've been waking to this beeping. It's constant, loud, like a howl. It never goes away; it only gets louder. So I fall back asleep and in the morning my mother tells me that this month I'm Swedish. Today, I'm Ingrid. Soon the beeping goes away, and after a while I start to believe I'm Ingrid because maybe that's the one thing that will stop the loudest sound."

"You could get her arrested, you know."

As if that'll happen. When an amusement park is named after your family, people tend to ignore it if you're a weird kid who changes her name every couple of months, because God forbid anyone raise their voice for fear of losing the jobs that your family so generously gave them. "Rich people don't go to jail. Rich people get buildings named after them; they get to cut the butcher line for the Sunday roast. My mother wears diamonds, not handcuffs." Right on cue, my mother opens the window and yells that it's time for dinner, which is bullshit because it's four o'clock and the only dinner in my future is a piece of bread and grape jelly. Who's she trying to kid?

Delilah lifts the screen and grabs my hand. Her hands are cold, enormous; they remind me of oven mitts. She says, "I'm scared that she's going to make you crazy."

"Oh, baby. I'm already there."

When I'm Ingrid, I'm dangerous. Knives and sharp objects must be hidden and all mirrors covered. Reflections are reminders of lives past and I can't be reminded of all the horror in the camps. My mother and I communicate by crayon and whisper under bedcovers because that's the only way. Sometimes my grandfather visits and his hellos are a fistful of coins he pours into my hand like gravel and rock, and he tells my mother, sotto voce, that having a child is the biggest mistake she's ever made. *You're not built for it, Norah. Perhaps you should have acquired a nice*

German shepherd from the local pound? In response, my mother tells Grandfather that no way in hell was she going to bring a mongrel into her home. Besides, a dog is no fun. A child, well, a child is a great deal of fun.

Scanning our home, I consider the sharpness of objects. Ellie would never have dared, but Ingrid. Ingrid is a whole other country. Try to remember where Norah hid the scissors.

Delilah tells me about a new girl named Cassidy. There are too many people in the picture, I think, too many names to keep track of. Just when I think I've got the town covered, just when I can finally manage all the people my mother wants me to be, there's Cassidy.

"This one's different," Delilah says. "Cassidy lived in Europe. Her parents flew to Burma and dumped her in that large house on Barrow Drive, you know, the haunted one, with a colored cleaning lady and a pile of cash. Imagine that. Living on your own. I'd gladly send my sister and her stack of Bibles on a one-way ticket to anywhere if it meant I could drink pop all day." Delilah plays with her new coke-bottle glasses.

"Your eyes look weird in those things," I say.

"My eyes *are* weird."

"Have you met her?" I say. "Cassidy."

"No, but I've seen her."

"I think you're spending too much time with Delilah. What will people think?" my mother says. Today she's cleared out the cabinets and the food in the fridge.

"Unless, it's part of your plan," she continues.

"I'm hungry," I say. "When am I eating?" It occurs to me that I've never actually seen my mother take a bite of food. If she eats, I'd never know it. Once I snuck into my mother's room to find tins of peach pies under her bed, and, as punishment, my mother padlocked my hands together and poured salt on my tongue. I was seven.

"Ingrid is always hungry. That's what it was like in the camps—the hunger was palpable. It got such that people regarded one another's skin and hair as a meal. Can you imagine pouring a little hot sauce on a French braid?" Laughing, my mother grabs my arm and drags me to the basement. It'll only be a few days, she promises. Then I'll be rescued and fed and everyone will call me a survivor. When I scream my mother tells me it's no good. No one will hear you. She cuts all the lights and turns off the heat; her eyes are black pools. "Don't you see? I'm merciful. I got rid of all the traps so there's plenty of food to eat. Just like in the camps. Be brave, my Ingrid. Be resourceful."

In the basement there are no windows, only doors.

A week later I've lost five pounds and it feels as if there's charcoal under my eyes, but I have to keep my cellar secret. Before I leave for school, my mother holds up a roll of duct tape and asks, "Is this the way Ingrid wants to sleep? Does Ingrid want to lose all feeling from her lips? Besides, who would believe you? Just the other day I was telling Margaret that I ought to have you checked out on account of me being concerned—teenager making up names and stories and the like. You kids aren't like us. We were proud of our lineage. Why is it you hate Ellie so much? Such a pretty name, it was my mother's."

I hold my book bag to my chest, as if a piece of nylon could shield me. "I'll be late for school."

My mother runs her fingers through my hair. "We'll need to get this trimmed."

We learn about the Industrial Revolution, how man went from toiling land to building great steel machines. The people who once churned butter by hand now purchased rectangular bars wrapped in wax paper. Peasant coats were traded in for sensible slacks and caps lowered down to the eyes. Tim sits in front of me as Mr. Haddock regales us with tales of the mass migrations and the promise of a living wage. No longer would farmers be beholden to their crops, the inflated seed prices, and land rents. Now they would sleep near factories and risk their limbs working massive machines. Exhaustion is a constant, no matter how you play it, and in my mind's eye I draw constellations from the freckles on the back of Tim's neck until my head finds the desk. Until I wake to the sound of a bell ringing and Tim shaking my shoulders. Sometimes I'm guilty of feeling too much.

"You're lucky Haddock was half-asleep himself. You would've been toast had he gotten up from his chair," Tim says.

"He never gets up. Haddock's the only man I know capable of sleeping while standing up," I say, rubbing my eyes. It's nearly three but it feels like midnight.

"Where were you last week? You missed band practice. I blew a few notes when Harmon wasn't looking." The side of his neck is purple, as if someone squeezed hard and wouldn't let go.

"On vacation." I gather my books. "What's with your neck?"

"Vacation? Where? The county jail?"

"You should consider taking your show on the road."

"No, really. Where were you?"

"A small trip my mother likes to take. Nowhere you'd go."

Tim nods his head, pulls a sandwich out of his bag, and eats it. I ask him about the sandwich, the details, because these are the things that I need to know: the composition of a meal down to the condiments on the bread. I'm relieved when Tim tells me that he's got turkey and cheese on white bread with just a little bit of mayonnaise because his mother still makes homemade mayonnaise while everyone else in town gets theirs out of a jar. Tim doesn't like mayonnaise, but he loves his mother. He offers me a bite: "Why not see for yourself?" I take the sandwich and pause, nervous, and Tim says, "This isn't an engagement, Ellie. It's just some cold cuts on bread." As I devour the rest of Tim's lunch, I wish he could know it's more than that. I wish he could know.

"You heard about Delilah Martin?"

Everything in me seizes. I bite my lip so hard it nearly bleeds. Is it possible to feel your blood vessels constrict? I try to keep my voice even. "What about her?"

"She's disappeared. Her sister came home from the market and no Delilah. Strangest thing. No one broke into the house. No bags were packed. No one saw her, and you know everyone would have noticed Delilah leaving the house. It was as if she just up and vanished."

Why did I immediately think of my mother? "When?"

"Last Sunday. The whole neighborhood is in a panic. It's been in the paper, and there's even talk about national coverage on account of Delilah's condition. Her sister sleeps at the church now because—would you believe this?—when she walked through her door last Sunday she could just 'feel the hand of Satan all around me,'" Tim says, mimicking Joan Martin's slow drawl. "'Rising up through the floorboards.'"

"My God," I say. My hands quake.

That corpse you planted last year in the garden, has it begun to sprout? Will it bloom this year? Or has the sudden frost disturbed its bed?

"You wouldn't believe the headlines: Satan Snatches Local Girl," Tim says. "Strange you didn't hear about it."

"We were on vacation," I stutter, thinking that I will likely faint. It's possible to fall right back into your history.

When I get home, my grandfather refills his pipe and tells me, by way of a hello, that he'll be living with us from now on. My mother strides into the living room with a tray of tea sandwiches and now I know I'll faint. "And if your mother has any objections to my being here, *Ellie*, she can move out of the house that I bought her. Isn't that right, Norah? It must be nice to eat off my plates and sleep in my bed." My grandfather holds out an empty mug and rattles it.

My mother refills his coffee. "Why would I ever object?" she purrs.

"Tell Ellie what we're having for dinner," he says.

"Roasted lamb, new potatoes, and peas. I didn't realize how many kinds of potatoes there were at the market. I didn't know which ones to get so I bought the most expensive, naturally. I've been all day in the kitchen; I'm practically living in it."

"Roasted lamb, new potatoes, and peas, *Ellie*," he warns.

"Roasted lamb, new potatoes, and peas." My mother sets down the carafe and cups my face with her hands when she says, "Ellie."

"Your mother likes it when I clean up after her. She's always making a mess—in the kitchen and out of it."

"I don't understand," I say.

"Father," my mother urges. Her face is a dam breaking, and this is her drowning.

When my mother leaves, I turn to my grandfather and ask, "What happened to Delilah Martin?"

"You mean the woman they found by the Pavilion with the Bible in her mouth?"

"The other Martin."

"You mean that troubled girl in the window?" We pass a few moments in excruciating quiet. Grandfather lays his pipe down on the table and taps his chin. This isn't the kind of silence where a story needs to be quickly crafted or a conversation requires diverting, rather this is a deliberate quiet. The kind of quiet where one anticipates the impact of the words that follow, how one should pay strict attention to them. These words are the air we're determined to breathe.

Time passes. Grandfather says, "I'm not sure you'd like the answer to that particular question. No, I don't think you'd like it at all. So let's leave it at this: Sometimes a man needs to do whatever it takes to protect his name. Especially when his daughter is hell-bent on ruining it."

My mother swans about the house and talks about dinner: How it's ready. How we need to eat before it gets cold. We use forks and knives because we're safe now. There's no more Ingrid. "We've closed that chapter," Grandfather says.

What we have almost resembles a family. We have the taste of it (the tender lamb, the hot butter pooling in the potatoes), the smell of it (my mother's hyacinths and my grandfather's aftershave), the feel of it (my face all sore from my grandfather's shadow, and the skin that nearly comes off when he kisses me). Finally, we have the sound of it: my mother's hands clapping.

"I brought you a sandwich," Tim offers after band class, months later. Ham and cheese with a smear of his mother's homemade mayo.

"Why don't you just quit band? Everyone knows you can't play," I say. "Everyone knows you're no good at it."

Shrugging his shoulders, Tim says, "Because it makes my mother happy. If she's going to spend all this time making homemade mayo for my lunch, I owe her a night away from punching tickets at the Pavilion. You don't know what it's like working two shifts and having to come home and make your family sandwiches. She deserves a night where she can get dressed up and watch me perform. Music is music; it doesn't matter if I'm not the one actually playing it."

"But you don't even like mayonnaise," I say, confused. His words are a riddle I don't understand.

Darkness stretches across Tim's face, and he regards me with the same look Grandfather did all those months ago when I asked about Delilah Martin. "I would think you of all people would understand the kind of people we come from and who we are as a result," he says, snatching the sandwich away.

There is no Delilah. There is no girl in the window, only the memory of it. While my grandfather remains in our house, we have normal feeding times. We open the curtains to let the light in, and wave to our neighbors when they pass by. We have something that resembles a family, a house that takes on the appearance of a home. Except in this house the basement is locked and only Grandfather has the key.

Sometimes, when they think I can't hear or see them, they grieve. Sometimes, I walk on tiptoe to opposite sides of the house to hear my mother's cries and my grandfather thrashing in his sleep.

FOLLOW ME INTO THE DARK
1958–1968

CAN I TOUCH you? Can I trace the archipelago of bruises on your face? Can I lay my hand on your heart and feel it beat? I want to put my mouth on yours and exhale so you can breathe. You're purple and blue and there's blood on your face from the men down the river who like to pick on boys who play instruments. My grandfather padlocked my mother's door just in case she gets the urge to play warden and executioner. Night after night she cooks rare meat but doesn't eat it.

I want to be normal. *What's normal?* What we see on television is normal: dinners at six, ankle socks, cheering from the field and stomping in the bleachers, gossip on Mr. O'Hara, who can't stop talking about the Cold War and the bomb that never dropped, *Can you please pass the potatoes?* I want this normal; I want to be afraid of the men on the radio, not what's behind my front door. As long as my grandfather is alive, I'm safe. In five years' time my mother will grow weak and her hands will involuntarily shake, and in ten years she will no longer remember her own name. I will find myself crawling my way back to her, and later I will become her. I'll drag my daughter Kate underwater in hopes that the mermaids will sing her a song.

Not yet, not yet.

In two days, Tim, *your* mother will lose both of her legs in an accident at the Pavilion. Weeks later, in a moment of weakness she'll make her mayonnaise, pack you a week's worth of lunches, and after she sees you to bed she'll pay a man to pour a bottle of pills down her throat so she can sleep full-time. You will both fall asleep at the same hour but she'll never wake. You will run down a half-deserted street shouting her name until the police pin you down and toss a sheet over your mother's cooled body. The police will tell their wives—*Can you please pass the salt?*—how you stretched out on the floor beside her, how you wept and prayed to the same God who couldn't save Delilah Martin—*What's Jesus ever done for me?* You will feel guilty for the accident and for her legs sawed off at the knees, for all of it. Your aunt will tell her friends that you sleep with the sandwiches wrapped in plastic under your pillow, as if this act of contrition will bring her back. *I am Lazarus, come from the dead / Come back to tell you all, I shall tell you all.* But we don't know any of this yet.

ELLIE LEFT A garden and walked into a cathedral, sat in the pew, tore a page from the Bible, and ate it. Outside, a man aimed his camera at the sky and photographed white. When they left, Norah shielded her daughter's body as they approached the crosswalk. Norah waved at the photographer, who couldn't see her because of all the light in his eyes. Temporarily blinded, the photographer walked into the street and got hit by a car. Ellie clutched the side of her mother's skirt. Norah screamed. The camera shattered the car window and struck the driver. The photographer was dead. The photographer was Ellie's father.

TIM WAKES WITH a start. Something's wrong. Something's not right. It's too quiet in the house in which they sleep. His mother never rests; she's always poised with one foot off the bed, ready to run. She takes naps standing up, but never does she allow herself to settle, to drift calmly to sleep. Rather his mother is a metronome, a body that oscillates from one part of the house to another. Now that body is missing a quarter of its total, confined to a wheelchair. Now that body needs a bottle of pills to keep it straight. Tim slips downstairs and sees a week's worth of sandwiches arranged in one long row on the counter. They're individually wrapped but he can still see the oil stain of the mayonnaise through the plastic. He smiles because although his mother takes pleasure in laying a wire hanger or a wrench on the small of his back on occasion, he knows she loves him in her own way. He opens the back door to see the sky painted black, pricked with stars. A man runs down the block. Even surrounded by all this beauty and quiet, something gnaws at him. Calling his mother's name, his voice is soft at first, and then it crescendos to a shout. His feet take inventory of the handful of rooms, until he runs into the bedroom and finds her there. He closes her eyes with the pads of his fingertips.

Tim kisses his mother good morning and goodnight before he calls the police. When they come he's in the kitchen, standing over the row of sandwiches.

There's a platoon of officers on Tim's street. He sits on his porch with a blanket draped over his shoulders while a woman leans in, talking, but he's not listening. Instead he stares out into the street, at me, as I sit on my bike and wave. What happened? Why all the gruesome blue? From then on I will forever hate the color blue. A policeman tells me to go on home, there's nothing to see. Tim pulls up his blanket and covers his head with it. Cradles his head between his knees. Ever set fire to an anthill and watch as the colony scatter and cover the ground only to inch their way back once the smoke clears, once the flames have gone out? All I can hear is a buzz, a whisper of *that poor boy, that poor woman.* I overhear something about legs all tangled up in a machine, and then I see an insurance adjustor and his notebook. He's just here to get the preliminaries, take some pictures, and file a report because there's always a claim, always an estimate and adjustment. I ride on home and later someone will tell me that the distance between Tim's mother's stumps and the ground were like a whole other country. I saw her in a wheelchair only once.

Ellie and Norah wore all black. Ellie didn't understand death, she only knew her father had taken a long trip from which he'd never return. Would he send postcards? she wondered, feeling blue. Would he write? Ellie clapped all the way to the funeral: *Miss Mary Mack, Mack, Mack. All dressed in black, black, black. With silver buttons, buttons, buttons. All down her back, back, back . . .* Norah remembered a holiday she and her husband had taken, before their child, before the glass that splintered his face, where they'd stood behind giant rocks in front of the ocean. Norah couldn't swim and he could, and he'd pulled her into the water, and she'd said, *No, I'm scared. Of what?* he'd asked. *Of everything.* So that day he carried her into the water, kneeled down, and held her as she dug her heels into the wet sand. *I will always carry you*, he'd said. It broke her now, as she rode in a black car, that she couldn't carry him home. That's men's work, carrying a coffin on your shoulders while the women sat in chairs with linen napkins and quietly grieved. But she didn't want to fucking grieve; she wanted the weight of her husband on her back. She wanted her daughter to shut the fuck up.

"You are not what I wanted," Norah said.

A WEEK AFTER Tim's mother's death, I call him. Winding a telephone cord around my finger I say, "You don't have to talk. We can just sit here, breathing. But if you want to talk, we can do that, too."

"Why are you calling me?" Tim says.

"I don't know. I wanted to," I say. "I guess I'm sorry."

"For what? Did you push her under that machine or shovel pills down her throat?"

"I guess I'm sorry you lost her. I'm sorry for your loss."

Tim laughs, so loud I have to pull the receiver away from my ear. "*Lost* her," he says. "You make it sound like she's a mitten. I didn't lose my mother, Ellie. She was here, in my house, in her room. I didn't lose her; she didn't run away. She killed herself. So there's no way you can be sorry about that unless you were standing over her bed handing her pill after pill."

"I know your mother's not a mitten," I say. My mother stands in the doorway and tells me we're having beef stroganoff for dinner. Mashed potatoes, peas—the whole lot.

"Maybe what you can be sorry for is the way your family won't take responsibility for my mother's accident.

Your grandfather sent a man out here with his forms and big words, talking to me as if I couldn't read, but I can read, and the words on the claim form said *free of culpability*, which is just a fancy way of saying *we get away with murder*. Think about that when you're eating your beef stroganoff with mashed potatoes and peas."

Before Tim hangs up, I hear the sound of paper ripping.

At dinner, my mother inquires as to why I haven't touched the food on my plate.

"Is it true?" I ask my grandfather. "We won't pay Tim's family what we owe them."

"What is it that you think we owe them, Ellie?" Grandfather says, wiping sauce off his chin.

"His mother is *dead*," I say.

"Have you ever seen the inside of a hospital? Have you ever had to pay a bill? The Pavilion—"

"Our family," I interrupt.

"The Pavilion paid for all of her medical bills and aftercare. We hired a nurse and made sure she received a monthly allowance so that she could survive. Considering that woman did more drinking on the job than actual work, I'd say that we were more than generous. So if she's going to get it in her head that she wants to swallow a bottle of painkillers because the going got a little tough . . . well, I don't see how we can be responsible for that."

I feel like Tim now. I feel like laughing. "She lost her legs and we gave her nothing."

"No," my grandfather interrupts. "You're just not satisfied with what we gave."

"I think we can do with a little pie," my mother says. For a moment I wonder how badly she wants to lock me in the basement again. How deeply she longs for the return of Ingrid.

"*We* gave?"

"I don't know why you insist on asking questions you already know the answers to. It seems to me that I've given you a lot," my grandfather says.

"I think apple," my mother says, laying a plate before me.

WILDFLOWERS GREW IN the field where the husband was buried. Norah picked them and pulled a ribbon out of her daughter's hair. She bound the flowers together before laying them down on the grave. Norah couldn't bury him alongside those other people and their crumbling headstones, arranged lilies, and relatives with their perfunctory grief. No, the husband belonged here, in front of the water; he belonged where her eye could see. There was a moment in the space between her inhales and exhales when Norah considered following the husband into the dark, but then Ellie sang and she was reminded that this child was what her husband had wanted. Sometimes she thought it was all he had wanted, and he would never forgive Norah if she abandoned her child. This made Norah resentful of a daughter who trampled gardenias and sang nursery rhymes, and every day that Norah was separated from the husband, every day she couldn't smell his sour breath or feel the worms that stuck like pearls on his withering skin, she would remind her child of the dark. The depth of it, the ache of it, the pain of it.

A place of origin doesn't exist. It's just beyond our sacrifice.

TIM BLOWS INTO his saxophone as if it's the first time he's played it. His chest is flooded with air, and he heaves like he wants to storm everyone in his wake. Mr. Harmon sits down on his conductor's chair and places his wand on the music stand. There's so much anger in this room—it hovers over us as we play sonatas and fidget in our seats. But there's also sadness, and we feel that too. Words exist that can pull Tim out of the darkness and into the light; we know they exist, we're sure of it, only we don't know the arrangement. We only know the music. So we do what we know how to do: we play off-key until the bell rings. Clutching his instrument to his chest, Tim doesn't move. Even as the guys lay hands on Tim's shoulder as they file out, even as the girls smile and carefully tiptoe over his feet. There are no words, only the silences in the beats between them.

"I'm sorry I'm related to greedy assholes," I say.

Tim shrugs. "At least they're still alive."

Outside the window a girl in a cream sweater conceals her face with her hands while five other girls dressed in matching cobalt blue form a human pyramid. Tim and I watch the smallest one flip off two shoulders—back arched, chest to the sky—to the ground. A group of boys sporting letter jackets toss around a football even though they're not really good at it—our team hasn't won all year—but they don't care. They cackle and snort over every fumble and talk about the big plans they have for the summer. This will be the summer they score. I think of Delilah and her belief that the whole world was her private television.

"I think my mother had something to do with Delilah's disappearance. I came home from school one day, sick from what I don't remember, and I heard them in my bedroom. In my fucking *bedroom*—how weird is that? Delilah and my mother were sitting on my bed, and I watched my mother take Delilah's hair in her hands, saying, 'This could be yours if you want it. Do you want it?' And Delilah said, 'Yes, but what do I have to do to get it?' I hid in the closet and then my grandfather came in and I still get the chills when I remember how he howled, 'Get the fuck out of my house!' My mother had to have known it wasn't possible, right? She had to have known that you just don't bring strangers into our house. But maybe she hoped that she could, and that was enough to make her stand up to her father, who cared only about our name and preserving it. And now Delilah's gone. The only question is, who got what they wanted? So when you tell me that my family's still alive, I have to disagree. I have to tell you they're not. I live among the remains of people."

"I miss the sandwiches," he says, laying his instrument beside him. He stares out the window, stares through it. "I can't bring myself to eat the ones she's made, but I can't throw them away. It just feels wrong, you know?"

"You're playing," I say, pointing to the saxophone.

"Everyone knew about your father and Farah Martin. About the affair. But no one knows about your mother."

"She performs on cue." We sit for a time and the sky folds into dusk. "I heard you're moving."

"California. My aunt's moving here until the end of term and then I'm gone."

"I'm sorry."

"For what?"

"That I didn't try to know you more."

Who are you again? I'm Lazarus. I've come back to see you.

SOMEONE TOLD NORAH that she needed to consider the possibility that she would never be reunited with her husband. This time, this earth, are all we may ever have, so why not use it to watch the daughter grow, everyone told her. As if Ellie were a geranium that required tending to (watering, repotting, small words of whispered encouragement). After a respectable mourning period, perhaps Norah should consider remarriage? Norah considered killing all of her friends, but decided against it because her husband would be furious that she would abandon their daughter as a result. Years ago the husband had built all of the furniture in the house with his hands, and Norah remembered the smell of pine and how she'd laid her naked body on the kitchen table to feel the raw, unfinished wood against her skin. She'd endured the splinters because that meant a piece of him would always remain in her. If she stood still, she could almost feel him again, swimming. Then Ellie, fucking Ellie, ran in with her arms extended, begging to be held, asking to be loved.

It was late one night or morning, Norah couldn't remember which, when a friend knocked on her door and said, "I don't know if your husband's accident was an accident. There's been talk." "What talk?" Norah hissed, her hair coming undone at her shoulders. "He knew things, horrible things, and he was going to tell."

Ellie was at the foot of the stairs, for the knocking had woken her too.

"Your father loved you. I endure you," Norah said.

TIM'S AUNT, MINNIE, is a baker of pies and tarts, and will torch you if you make any reference to "that Disney character." Minnie will say, most emphatically, that she is a woman not a mouse. However, she will acknowledge the character of Minnie Castevet from *Rosemary's Baby*, because Ruth Gordon is "one sharp dame," and who wouldn't relate to a childless woman who drinks root beer in bed, and only wanted to take that guileless Rosemary under her wing?

"So they tricked her into giving birth to the Antichrist. Think of the upside. Living in Beverly Hills, taking the sun. What wouldn't I give to be with a man in tails, drinking out of a champagne glass, instead of living in this fleabag of a town? What is that? Is that a mosquito?"

"A wasp," I say. "They come this time of year."

"Like a plague, no doubt," Minnie says. We are at the Pavilion because Minnie wants to see the beginning of the end, although she confides her younger sister's end was a long time coming. "That woman's been yearning for the grave as soon as she came out of the womb. It's like she took one look at this place and decided, 'No, not for me. None of it.'"

"Tell us what you really think, Aunt Minnie," Tim says.

"If I had half a mind to tell you what I really thought, you'd be on some headshrinker's couch with a blanket, crying crocodile tears. I know you don't see it now, kid, but my sister, God rest her soul, did you a favor."

"This used to be a resort in the twenties," I say, and with a mixture of pride and shame I recount the history of the place that indirectly killed Tim's mother. As we walk, I describe the main building, which used to be two stories high. The colonnades were made of stone, and when you stared up at the ceiling from the inside, you believed that paradise was possible. Regardless of where you stood you were bathed in light, so how do you explain the warmth that felt like an embrace, a lingering kiss on a cheek, otherwise?

Those headed farther west in search of luck paused to bathe in the man-made pools and make love in the rooms concealed only by flimsy gossamer curtains; the Pavilion used to be a stomping ground for fathers who waltzed with their daughters under the glare of the afternoon sun and, glass of gin in hand, foxtrotted with their wives and mistresses in the evening. Many a bastard child was conceived here, and sometimes, young brides were abandoned on their honeymoons when their husbands fled for the desert. This used to be a place where the sun gallantly rose and fell.

"People came here to be found, even if they didn't think or know they were lost," I say with a wistfulness that was borderline embarrassing.

"Then the thirties happened and everyone lost their money and their hope, and soon everyone stopped jumping into the pool and started hurling out of windows," Minnie says. "Back then, that was the more gallant option."

"Something like that," I say.

"I'm much more interested in the other stories: the one about the starlet who drowned her mother in the pool. Or what about the stockbroker, all tangled up in his greed, hanging himself with those pretty curtains you spoke of. Tell me about the avaricious. Tell me *those* stories. I imagine they make for more indecent conversation, but who cares, because, quite honestly, who gives a flying fuck about the entablatures and Roman-inspired architecture that influenced this dump."

"I want to go home," Tim says, as we approach the ride that excised his mother's legs. Children bury their faces in tufts of white cotton candy while girls adjust their skirts; they fold them above their knees in Tim's presence. He doesn't notice, but Minnie does. It seems as if Minnie notices everything. Eyebrow cocked, she says, "Maybe we should stick around, kid. Perhaps this town is more interesting than I thought. I'm always looking for a good show."

"We're leaving," Tim says. The certainty in his voice is a clock ticking, a reminder that every moment with him is a moment not with him. Why is it that death casts a light on all the things you never notice? When Delilah Martin's mother died, I suffered from horrible migraines because suddenly everything was so loud. Rustling leaves were landmines. Hushed voices were bombs. After Tim's mother died, something shifted. I felt the texture of things. Colors appeared violent in their willful saturation, and I could *see*.

All I could see was Tim.

"So, kid," Minnie turns to me. "Tell me a story."

"I'll tell you a story about a man and a woman that you won't read in any of the guidebooks. It's 1919, and a husband discovers his wife has been having an affair with his father. The husband takes her on a trip to the bathhouse and says he has a surprise for her. The wife doesn't want to go for obvious reasons, but she suspects that the husband knows something—maybe it was the tone in his voice when he issued the invitation, or his insistence—because he never cared about spending time alone with her before. So she goes, and when they arrive and settle into their room, he tells her that he's been taking magic classes and tonight he'll debut some tricks. The wife is confused, naturally, because her husband is a stockbroker, and she's practically speechless when he asks her to be his assistant for the evening."

"Now this is what I want to hear," Minnie says.

I continue. "Later on that night, he puts her in a wooden box and says he's going to saw her in half. He wears a cape and tails. He looks the part of a man who knows tricks, and suddenly the wife feels unsettled. Something's not right but she can't move, and there are a hundred people beyond the lights cheering her husband on. But he never took a magic class and the trick is on the wife as he works a saw down the box and proceeds to cut his wife in two. The room thunders with applause, which muffles the wife's screams, and everyone talks about how real it all looked. They talked about the terror they felt. Yet no one ever mentioned, until later, until a body was found buried ten miles down the road and the husband was found with his face blown off from the barrel of a gun, that maybe it looked *too* real." I finish, triumphant in my eerie tale and Minnie's smile.

"Now you'll find this place pretty tame. My family rebuilt it from the ground up five years ago, and nothing really happens in this town except for teenagers on heavy dates and kids sneaking rides on the Ferris wheel." As I say this, I watch lacquered mares go around, and I can't help but think that, in one way or another, children are forever held hostage.

"Except for the Bible-thumper drowned by the lake, and the suicide in a bed," Minnie says.

"That *suicide* was my fucking mother, for chrissake. You may not have loved her, you may have even hated her, but I love her," Tim says. He kicks dirt all around him and the earth rises up, converges, and falls. "She's not one week in the ground and already you've got your one-liners cued up."

I hold my breath and suddenly become aware of the

chill. It's as if I've interrupted an unfinished conversation between Tim and his aunt, the words jutting out are entirely too painful to bear. When I think what it would be like to lose my mother, the only feeling that registers is relief. I would be relieved. My mother would not be mourned or argued about in amusement parks, and I wonder if she knows this. I wonder if she understands that anger and sorrow, not relief, are what happens to your loved ones when you pass to the other side. I wonder if she realizes that no one in our family loves anyone. But maybe she does and that knowledge is what keeps her going.

"Your life is your life, and you only know it while you have it," Minnie says. "There's a difference between hate and anger over a woman who wasted her life, who didn't know what she had when it was right in front of her. So she lost her fucking legs? I don't hate my sister, Tim, but she was cruel, impetuous, and selfish, and there's no denying that. She didn't beat death; she opened up her front door and let it in. Threw it a goddamn parade."

Tim's voice was hoarse. "You don't know that. You don't know anything about my mother."

"I know she did nothing about the bruises on your back. I know about her drinking, how she liked her anesthesia."

I think about my mother and how her father provided the dressing for the daily wounds he inflicted. We have meat every night and our pain is private, but we're the same as Tim's family in all the ways you couldn't see.

Do I just walk away and give them their privacy?

"I've got an idea," Minnie winks at me. "I picked up a steak at the butcher's today. Why don't you be a good egg and invite your family over for dinner? As you can imagine, I'm not good at taking no for an answer."

"Leave these people alone," Tim says.

"Calm down. I'm asking for a meal, not the Antichrist."

I start rummaging for excuses but Minnie is fast. "My mother and grandfather don't really go out all that much. We tend to have dinner at home."

"I find that hard to believe," Minnie says, pointedly.

"Jesus, Minnie," Tim says. "I want to go home."

"You tell your grandfather that either your family sits at my table or I'll sit at theirs."

I open my mouth to speak, but Tim pulls Minnie toward the car. I follow.

Before they drive away Minnie rolls down the window and says, "Did anyone ever tell you just how good you look in blue? It suits you."

"THERE'S NOTHING HERE for me," Norah had told her husband once, before they were man and wife. "Just give me a moment of peace," she'd implored, "to be still amidst all this sadness." Her husband took her hands in his. "Squeeze," he'd said, "so I can feel how much you hurt." And she did, so hard she thought his fingers would break, but he didn't let go. This small gesture awakened a great love. Had she been asleep this whole time to suddenly wake up? Had the sun shone her entire life? If so, how was it that this was the first time she'd seen it? Norah felt sick, fell to her knees because love was not supposed to become her. Then her husband kneeled down too, and in his eyes she saw church. Let me run my hands along the pew, she'd thought. Let me breathe in the mahogany. Let me stare through the glass window and see the sun and feel the ache of you. Let me feel this heart that suddenly stops.

"There's nothing here for me," Norah said, as the coffin closed over her husband's face. "Let me feel this heart that suddenly stops," as the coffin was lifted up and gently lowered underground. "Just give me a moment of peace," she snapped at Ellie, "to be still amidst this sadness."

"Why did you show me the possibility of love only to take it away?" Norah cried over an open grave.

"IT'S A SHAME about Delilah Martin. Did they ever find that retarded child?" Minnie says, sawing through tough beef. Dressed in fuchsia, she's an assault to our dining room with its gray walls and dark furniture, and I suspect she knows this.

"Delilah Martin isn't retarded," my mother says coldly, and I regard her tireless defense of Delilah with suspicion. None of us really understood her condition, much less had it diagnosed. The doctors observed that Delilah Martin was many things, but not one thing in its entirety.

"Past tense, dear," Minnie says. "Unless you know something the papers don't. I'm always game for a good gossip."

"My granddaughter tells me you're a baker," Grandfather says, refilling his pipe.

"I put things in and out of ovens, yes, that's true."

"I never could get my head around the chemistry of it," my mother says. For the whole of the evening, she circles the table, picking up things and putting them down.

"You could say chemistry agrees with me while biology always eluded me. I lived here with my sister for a time, and, as I said before, I do love a good gossip. We lived in that house up on Cavanaugh Street."

"I know the place," my mother says.

"Odd," Minnie says. "I've been here for a total of thirty-four minutes and I've yet to hear one condolence, a word of sympathy, not even a pithy 'I'm so sorry for your loss.' Even the butcher, a man I don't know, got teary-eyed at the counter. Told me he was sorry, and I said, 'You better save your apologies, unless you plan on gypping me on that cut of beef.'"

My grandfather takes a puff of his pipe and clouds the air with his smoke. "We're so sorry for your loss."

"How is Tim?" my mother asks, following suit. "He must be devastated."

Minnie snaps her fingers. "You're fast with the platitudes. How is Tim? Well, his mother's current address is a box six feet below. And while that woman, my sister, was a horrible human being and a terrible drunk, she was his mother and she's dead, leaving this boy with the fantasy that he could have done something about it. Prevented it, somehow. In two months' time, he's going to have to uproot his life, change his school, leave his friends—your daughter, the silent one over there, being one of them—to come live with me, a woman he doesn't know, much less like. 'Devastated' is one way of putting it. I'd say 'fucked up beyond words' is better. For people like us, the hand Tim got dealt, the hand I have to play out, is the only kind we're likely to get."

Do I detect a smile? Is my grandfather smiling? It seems Minnie amuses him.

"I'm sure we can arrange to have the funds that were allocated to your sister after the accident transferred to Tim."

Minnie regards my grandfather with mild interest. "I'm sure he'll be grateful. We'll never be without toilet paper and a leaner cut of meat."

My mother finally sits down and tucks into the steak. Her hands quake. "I remember you. You used to make the cakes for the church banquets. It's all coming back now."

"Most of the ladies pass off that Betty Crocker shit as homemade, but I make my own, from scratch. Why, a cake's just some butter, sugar, and flour. Once you got the basics, there's a whole wide world of possibility. Before this business with my sister, I nearly signed a lease on a small place back east. I had the idea of calling it Minnie Cakes and Pies, and I'd sell miniature cakes of every variety. Picture rows of cakes behind glass—chocolate, lemon meringue, banana cream, and coconut—stretched as far as the eye could see. Imagine a mini Baked Alaska? Just the talk of it will give me business for months. But I've said too much. I can do that sometimes. Not know my limits."

"Do you have a fellow?" my mother asks.

"I tell you about my dream and you ask me about a man."

It seems as if Minnie is pushing for a fight but nothing sticks. My grandfather looks amused and bored while my mother regards Minnie with confusion and terror. But something stirs, bubbles right below the surface.

"I like the name," I say to Minnie. "I like it a lot."

"She speaks! Kid, did you finally get hold of some of the life rafts I've been begging for?" Minnie's eyes glint, and I relax in her presence. It takes everything in me not to plead her to take me with her. I'll be as quiet as a mouse.

"You do say what's on your mind," my grandfather says. "That's rather bold for a woman."

"Well, Simon, if I said what was on my mind, I'd tell you that the first time Tim introduced me to your daughter, I felt as if I'd met her before, which is impossible, of course. Yet, every time I look at Ellie's face I'm reminded of someone."

"Small town," my mother says.

"Too small for my own taste," my grandfather says.

"And in this, we agree." Turning to me, Minnie says, "You remind me of your dead father. How long has it been since he died in that accident? Ten, twelve years? How many years, Norah?"

"It was a car accident." My mother seethes. "A camera smashed his face."

"Did the car kill him or the camera? No, I don't think it was an accident," Minnie says. To my grandfather she says, "But you would know more about that than I would, Simon."

"For a low-grade piece of trash, I have to admire your verve. Coming into my house, eating my food, taking advantage of the fact that your sister was an incompetent drunk. For what? Petty threats? Blackmail. What is it that you think you know, Miss Mouse?" my grandfather says.

"You're insulting me if you think this is about money. Or perhaps that's the only hand you know how to play. Stuff wads of bills into people's mouths until they choke—that sound about right?"

"What is she talking about?" I ask. You don't just raise

your voice at Grandfather, you whisper. You speak when spoken to, and you certainly don't come into his home and antagonize him. Something about Minnie frightens me; perhaps it's the way she's unafraid of my grandfather when everyone else perpetually tiptoes around him.

"Take your dinner upstairs," my mother says to me.

Minnie rises and drops her napkin on my grandfather's lap. "Your dead father, rest his soul, was a good man. But he was also a man who knew things about this family. Secrets I'm sure your grandfather didn't want other people to know."

"I think it's time you leave now," my grandfather says.

"Do you remember your father, Ellie?"

The only response I'm able to give is a whiplash of the neck, a shake of the head, no.

"GET OUT OF MY HOUSE." The storm assails.

To me she says, "These two could start a knitting circle with all the lies they weave. Your father didn't die in a car accident, as these two would have you believe. In fact, there wasn't anything natural about his death at all."

"Remove the woman."

"Oh, the woman doesn't need removing, Simon. The woman is leaving on her own accord."

I try to run after her, but I can't. My legs buckle and I fall to the floor.

Outside Minnie shouts, "You come see me, Ellie. I'll tell you stories."

HAVE YOU SAID *your farewell to your father, as you sent him where he is now? He said you didn't. He said you just killed him,* said Ophelia, said Norah, to Ellie who wasn't listening. Norah choked from the stench of the white lilies that crowded every vase in the house her husband built. *Everyone seems so slow, so immobile, that I sometimes wonder if I'm living amongst statues,* said Ophelia, said Norah, while Ellie chased fireflies and insects in the grass. They lived in a home plagued with shadows, old music, and everything they could want but never needed. Norah was often lonely. It had been two weeks since she was laid to unrest, and during this time she realized their home was not dissimilar to the box in which her husband was buried. There were windows, yes, but her view was the undertow; she looked out to see the waves pulling her further under. *You will forgive me in time,* she said aloud to her dead husband. And just as Norah set out to join her husband, her father burst in with Ellie and said, "Every day I look at the child I'm reminded that she is not the image of you. In fact, she's the image of me. I gave you my seed and you gave me what? A girl? If only she were a boy. If only she'd grow into something useful."

"Stop talking," the mother said.

"I wonder," her father said, "are you sad because he died, or because you had something to do with it? Does it break your heart to know that when given the choice between you and someone else, you will always, invariably, choose you? What would have happened to you, to our family, had people found out about our indiscretion? Do you feel proud that you seduced your father and bore his child? That dirty little secret you fought so hard to hide, finally let loose upon the world because that God-fearing man you let crawl into your bed planned to go to the police? Things had to be done. In the end, we do what we have to. We do what we must."

Ellie played hopscotch over the flowers inside the house. "Don't play inside the house, *Ellie*," she snapped. She even hated the sound of her daughter's name. Ellie. Ellie. Ellie.

Norah's father picked up the bottle of pills, laughed, and said, "Don't play inside the house, Norah."

FLAMMABLE WOMEN

1968–1974

A WEEK LATER I see Tim through glass. He's on a bus, waving, and it takes everything in me not to shout, "Take me with you." Before he boards he presses a folded piece of paper into my hand and says, "This isn't goodbye. This is I'll see you soon." He's leaving for California to live with his crazy aunt Minnie, who registers him in a school that allows him to play the saxophone as loud as he wants to. If you ask me to remember the evening Minnie came for dinner and the aftermath, what remains is my mother whispering in my ear that grief will undo you. It will make you drive to someone's house and unload lies, as if the unburdening will relieve them of their grief. That night my grandfather found comfort in a bottle of scotch and my mother invited me to pray for Minnie, even though we were a family who lied about our devotion. We were Christians on paper, and I remember a few Sundays praying for a woman who lost her sister at the Pavilion.

IT'S BEEN SIX years since then, and now I wonder if there was a grain of truth to what Minnie said. Mother and Grandfather, a knitting circle of two—did they conspire and plan my father's death, too?

"Hey. Where did you go?" Tim asks, interrupting my memory.

We're in bed and my body caves from the weight of his. We're making love, although *love* isn't quite the word I'd attribute to my fiancé. We're making *escape*, making *safe*, but he doesn't know this. I want so much to love him but I don't have it in me; it's as if I'm not physically built to endure it—love, and the magnitude of its inevitable loss. Everyone I've loved I've lost, so I have a hard time distinguishing the difference between the two.

People were initially suspicious about the match: the son of a woman who died working for our family. Was this our penance, a plea for forgiveness given too late, or was this his retribution, revenge served cold? However, the talk died down when everyone learned of the minor wealth Tim accumulated in Sacramento—real-estate speculation—and my mother, already panicked over my advancing age, settled for a man, any man, who was able to place a respectable ring on my finger. My mother rules over our small town by default. She's like the china you hide in glass cabinets. Over a series of endless show-off-the-ring lunches—where I suspected I might only survive by burning my eyes out with a blowtorch—my mother regaled everyone with stories about Tim's self-made position as if I were marrying it instead of the man. She spoke of the small house in Carmel that Tim purchased for the two of us. A shabby cottage with a porch, a garden the size of our house, and some chickens—all attached to a small shop where Tim plans to sell the organic food we'll grow. When he showed me photographs of our new life—the life that will begin after we return from our honeymoon in Fiji—as much as I want it, need it, part of me knows I'll never leave this house.

"I'm right here," I joke now, in bed. "Can't you see me? We're not even married and already I have to manage the side effects of your old age."

"You're here but you're not. You know what I mean," Tim says, pressing his nose against my cheek. "You're nervous about tomorrow. That's it, isn't it?"

"About you, us, the vows and white dress? No. About everybody else? Yes."

"Forget it, then. We'll get our clothes and sneak out of the house. Get in the car and go."

"If only it were that easy."

"It *is* that easy, Ellie," he says, and he believes it. To Tim, you can leave and take the love with you. His certainty is palpable. "Do you want to go? We can go."

There is so much goodness in his face, it makes me want to cut myself open and let him in, all the way, but

I don't. It would be like dumping Alice in the Inferno instead of Wonderland. Letting Tim in would be akin to sitting a child in front of a horror movie and telling her, *Don't blink.* "No," I say. "I'm right where I need to be, with you."

"Cassidy will be there."

"The last wedding she went to she set the bride's dress on fire. I don't think Harper ever recovered."

"It was an accident. Completely unintentional. Cass wouldn't harm a fly."

"I found her asleep, wrapped up in the dress, holding a cigarette, Tim." We laugh. "Remind me to keep her away from anything flammable."

"I'll carry a fire extinguisher down the aisle if I have to."

"Now that's the man I love." We resume our love/escape-making, and then fall asleep in one another's arms like children. In the dark, the band of my engagement ring glints. This is the light, I think. This is it.

Come morning I watch Tim stir in his sleep and think, I want so much to love you. I want us as we were: two teenagers in band class watching kids play in the grass. If I close my eyes, right now, I can see that spring before Delilah disappeared and his mother died. Light breaks through the trees and children get lost in the street and find their way back again. A girl shouts, "You're IT!" Watch the children run as fast as their miniature hearts can beat, as swiftly as their legs will carry them. Before the blue hour, before the sun settles along the horizon, I sneak into my mother's car and play the radio as loud as I can. My bare feet sway on the dashboard of my mother's car and I pretend we're driving, counting headlights on the highway. I pretend my mother is a woman she never was—a woman who sings bad songs off-key, who colors outside of the lines; I want her to get in a car and drive. I pretend to hear her laughter and I feel it in my heart. I want someone's childhood again, scraped knees and ice cream melting on the lips. Children create these magical worlds that adults find ways to ruin. I want the before-the-ruin, to feel the heart as a colossus, to bury myself in the forest that was my mother's hair. I want all of it before I realize that love is impossible, before I learn that black and white will never burst and bleed into color, that life is what we smother until there is nothing left. Until I become what I am now—a weaker version of Norah—a woman whose heart breaks, is broken, only to discover that there's nothing left in her to break.

Downstairs I hear Norah banging things—her signal that we should wake. My mother always hated being the first one up in the house, alone in the cool quiet of morning. None of Grandfather's nurses to admonish, no one with whom to gossip—solitude frightened Norah because it reminded her of her death. Death is the great equalizer, the supreme silencer of small talk, and what would Norah be without her finger sandwiches, daily intrigues, and money? The day I told her about my engagement, she said, "He's not what I wanted for you, but at least you won't die alone." I responded, "Look on the bright side; at least you can curl up with your father's money and an almanac." My mother smacked me across the face and said, "What a mouth on you, Ingrid."

Sometimes my mother forgets. Sometimes she remembers.

Norah bangs a plate on the table. Throws flatware in the sink.

One day I too will be strong enough to wreck things.

We're in a fast car and Cassidy drives with one hand on the wheel while the other adjusts the mirrors, opens and closes the glove compartment, rolls the window down and up—it's impossible for her to keep still. I watch the road shimmer, unveiling itself in degrees. This morning I read an article in the paper about a teenager in California who stabbed thirteen of her classmates with a kitchen knife because, she explained, "I don't like Mondays."

"It'll be another hour," Cassidy says. "You sleep while I drive."

"She told me not to scream. Save it for the bedroom," I say.

"You know you have this habit of starting a conversation from the middle. Let's rewind back to the beginning. Who told you not to scream?"

"My mother. This morning. And then she got me a scrip for Valium."

"How fifties of Norah."

"Say something nice, Cass. I need to hear something nice."

"Something nice." Cassidy laughs. "What's wrong with you? You're marrying into the Garden of Eden. This is the against-all-odds story. This is the nice boy who played the sax. Why are you acting like this is some long walk to the gas chamber? Should I break out the harmonica and play sad songs?"

"Nothing's wrong with me. I'm happy, perfectly content."

"It's the sex, right? I told you to ball him before the wedding night. No one needs the stress of bloody sheets and faked orgasms."

"We're not discussing this," I say. I have this habit of pulling at my hair. It's not a yanking, more like a desperate tug, and pulling out a clump thrills me. Tim swatted away my hand the moment he saw a tug, and for a while I stopped the tugging. When Tim first met me all those years ago in band class, he called me "impenetrable," but he was persistent and fell in love with me anyway. Even after he moved away. Even after we found one another at

Berkeley. We swore we would never go back to Nevada; rather we'd start new lives in California. We'd make our own history.

"There's a lake just over there, behind the trees. We could go for a dip. Have a little smoke." Cassidy holds up a joint, an invitation.

"I've got five hours. They let me out. Time served on account of good behavior."

Cassidy cuts the engine, lights a joint, and we pass it between us, taking long, measured inhales. "Let's roll," she says, bits of her long hair tangled in her mouth. She smells like meatballs, always, even though she's a vegetarian. *That's not the kind of meat I need in my mouth*, she often jokes at formal dinner parties, creating the kind of silences that make me love her more.

"You smell like meatballs," I say.

"I fucked that guy last night. The one from school."

"But you dropped out."

"Good thing I did, because you know what he gave me at the end of it, right as I'm pulling on my pants? A five-by-seven of his cock. All color, blown up to scale— the real deal. Wild, right?"

"You threw it away," I say.

"Are you kidding? It's in the glove compartment. I don't need to trip; I'm already having flashbacks. Ellie, it was like a wall of flesh coming at me." Cassidy's eyes are wide and bright, a deep green under the curtain that is her hair. I envy her this—hair that is unkempt, cut with her own hands. A month ago Cassidy, drunk, shouted outside my window, "I got bangs!" "What that woman needs is some self-control. Restraints," my mother said. "Women need to know their limits."

Intrigued, I pull out the photo, study it, and say, "That's not a penis, that's a Mack truck. Why would you keep this?"

"Hope," Cassidy says, and we explode into laughter.

"Tonight won't be the first time," I say. "We've slept together before. Satisfied?"

"Innocent Ellie, not so innocent. I like," she says. "I like this a lot."

"It's happened," I say to myself. "I've made him my own."

"Home?" Cassidy says over the engine. "What about home?"

We run through the trees down to the water like we're fifteen again, when Cassidy nicked red lipstick from her mother's vanity and we spent an afternoon puckering our small mouths. When I came home, my mother smacked me, hard, and rubbed off the lipstick with the back of her hand. Back then everyone called Cassidy *spirited*, she was a rich girl who lived in a big, empty house replete with paintings of dour spinsters and rugs from the Orient. The house is still empty and Cassidy hocked a rug to a buy a car, some smokes, and a trip farther west, which she refuses to talk about, except to say that things "got pretty fucked up, really fast." Everyone calls Cassidy an undertow, but I don't mind this. I wouldn't mind sliding in and under.

I live in Nevada; I'm trained to breathe underwater and survive in the desert.

The sky is cloudless. The waters recede. Nothing would dare interrupt two women on the verge.

"Go on in," I say, holding up a book, rattling it. "I'll watch our stuff."

"You like to watch?" Cassidy teases, lowering her bikini to a point where it's dangerous.

"Funny girl." Only now do I notice Cassidy's T-shirt, which reads, "In Cock We Trust."

"So if you're getting balled, what's with the sad face? Is Tim putting your feet to sleep? I always thought the nice ones were craftier."

"You had to take it there, Cass."

"The extreme makes an impression. Maybe it'll make you realize that you need to run, Ell. I've been mopping up your sadness since day one. Tim's a sweet guy but he's not your way out. You'll live in that house and end up a repeat of Norah."

I thought about Delilah Martin: *I'm scared that she's going to make you crazy.* I repeat to Cassidy what I said to Delilah: "Already there, baby."

"I'm giving you a way out."

"How? How is getting in a car and driving who knows where with no money, out? *Out* is not in my plan. It's not even on the fucking map." I rake my hair with my hands, depleted. Finished, last call, boxed in, no way out.

"That's Norah talking. You make your own plans. Think about what I'm saying."

"This coming from a woman who carries a picture of a man's cock in her car," I laugh, wipe tears.

"Hope, sister. Hope."

Before Cassidy leaves and breaks into the water, she teases me. "Imagine if I don't make it back."

Today of all days this threat frightens me, holds a weight it normally wouldn't, but then I realize that Cass would never settle for a meager curtain call. Hers is a plane hurtling into the ocean, a great machine crackling and hissing with black fire. Wings floating and somber men narrating the six o'clock news while we clink our forks on dinner plates and refill tumblers with gin, neat, to the brim. Cassidy would never go quietly.

"You'll make it back; you always do," I say.

"I guess that's my trip."

Cassidy treads water, waves at boys on a boat. I watch my friend swim toward the boys, her body inching closer, and they lift her up and onto their boat. It's a small dinghy, a scrap of wood and a prayer, but Cassidy doesn't seem to mind. For an hour Cassidy drinks and smokes with the boys, and they inch closer, start rubbing her back, and suddenly I'm furious that my last day of freedom is being spent watching my best friend spring free.

"I'm pregnant," I say to myself, out loud. Once spoken, the words feel permanent, regardless of whether anyone has heard them. Looking down at my stomach I can't help but think that I am choosing to build my own prison; I am the warden of this body, my small but growing penitentiary. This body will never be in that water with those men; it'll be beneath Tim, always, smiling for the camera. The body will be a repeat of Norah. The body will never move to California.

I'm fine, really.

Clothes hurled overboard. Liquor poured on Cassidy's back. I crawl down the green to see skin. How one boy grabs her hair while the other cups his hand under her chin. My mother is right—men are forever lunging for things.

Suddenly I'm ravenous, starving, and I gather my things, run up the hill and through the trees to the car. Click the key, fire the engine, and take it down the road. Drive the car to the only place I know—home.

Another key, another door, up the stairs and through another door into the room where all I can see is white for days. Tulle and silk, oceans of it, cover the floor.

"You're back early," my mother says.

I turn to my mother, take her by the neck, pull her in,

and kiss her on the mouth, hard. My mother shrieks at first, recoils, but then her body falls slack, allows the kiss, the violence of it, to settle.

My mother stands, shaken, while I finger my dress and pull clips out of my hair. I hum a song Cassidy and I used to sing. Cassidy's car is in the driveway, engine cooling.

"Don't worry," I say. "I'll be a good girl; I won't scream."

I'm fine, really.

"Where will your children sleep? I know your mother well and I can't imagine she'll let you leave this house. She'll find some way to ruin this day, keep you here." Cassidy is nowhere to be found, but Minnie is here. She snuck into the house and speaks to me from behind a shower curtain. She's in my bathroom, in my house, and I nearly scream.

"You need to leave now," I say, opening the door. "If Tim sees you here, he'll freak."

"Oh, honey. These aren't the movies. I'm not going to come at you with a wig and a butcher knife. This is the only way I could see you without your mother interrupting things. Your mother's a handful, but I guess you already knew that. And Tim, he's always been stubborn. He takes after his mother that way."

"What do you want?"

"You make a pretty bride. I wish my Tim could see you as I do, all dolled up, all knocked up—yes, I know."

"Why are you here?"

"I baked you a cake."

A knock at the door. A distant cousin tells me that the car is outside. We're ready to go to the church.

"I'll be there in a minute," I say, locking the bathroom door.

Minnie pulls the curtain to one side and hoists herself up. "My back is killing me. All this money and you'd think you'd have a more comfortable tub, something that pulls away from the wall. Anyway, I knew your father back when he was delivering papers and cutting lawns. He was a good man, decent, but not a match for your mother. He didn't come from much, and you can imagine your grandfather was none too happy to have his only remaining daughter—the prized calf—marrying a man who would simply be another mouth to feed. But no one else would take her. She was a strange type, but I guess you already know that too, and many felt the money wasn't worth the trouble. But your father loved her, and she loved him, and it was all going to be a fairy tale tied up with a bow, but it ended up being a noose."

"You're not telling me anything I don't already know."

"Is that right? Ever ask yourself why your aunts just up and disappeared? How your grandmother died in this house only a few months after? They *knew*," Minnie says.

Aunts, what aunts?

"They knew what?"

"What was going on in this house between your

grandfather and your mother. They knew each other in a way that a father should never know his daughter, and if the grief and rage didn't kill your grandmother, I'm sure someone in that house did. And when your mother got it into her head to disobey her father's orders, practically threatened to run away, well, money and the man had their way. Imagine what your father must have thought when he heard all of this—his wife, lying in her father's bed."

"I don't believe you."

"No? Ask anyone in this town on your family's payroll. The people who clean your house, launder your linens, and take out your trash, the invisibles, hear things. Ask Tim. Everyone knew, including his mother. What your family was doing in this house wasn't right. When your father said he'd bring this whole charade down, tell anyone who would listen—God rest his soul, he was too naive for his own good—your grandfather told him things."

"Told him what?" I say, impatient, uneasy.

"Your grandfather told him that the child Norah was carrying wasn't your father's. It was his. At first your father stayed quiet because how could he ruin the woman he loved, but knowing something like that changes things. Your mother couldn't handle the way he looked at her. And then one day he died in a car accident. Or maybe a camera hit him? Who's to say? It was convenient that you were both there, to watch."

I shook my head.

"You don't believe me? Ask Tim. His mother told him everything. He felt sorry for you. You were rich, but broken like the rest of us. Why did you think he was marrying you? Everyone loves a happy ending. He's got it in that head of his that your child is going to make it right. Don't you understand, Ellie? You're the do-over."

It's only now that I realize I'm naked, covered in hives. Red patches that burn and itch. My wedding dress is on the floor, little clumps of my hair are on the floor, and Minnie takes this all in and keeps talking. I interrupt. "Why are you telling me this? Now. Right before I'm about to get into a fucking car . . ."

"Because that's exactly why, Ellie. I'm telling you this because I want you to run as fast as your legs will take you. I have never liked your family, they're horrible people, and I hate to see another generation ruined by what they own." Minnie hands me a towel, not for my body, she says, but for the tears. "If I found out what I've just told you, I'd cry buckets."

"You'd like to see my family miserable."

"Are my motivations really relevant when you know the truth?"

The man I only remember from photographs, the man covered in wood and dirt, is not mine. My grandfather, my father. I clutch my stomach, my prison, and I collapse.

We sit like this for a few moments until my cousin knocks again. "Are you okay?" she asks.

"I'm okay," I say. "A few more minutes."

The cousin lingers. I hear her feet shift. "You can go."

"I'd think twice about having that child. Listen to your friend. Make your own plans."

"Get out of my house," I hiss.

After the wedding, before I fall asleep in Tim's arms, I palm my belly and whisper, "Kate. I think I'll call you Kate."

In the morning I tell Tim that we're staying in Nevada. He says nothing and sits in my grandfather's chair.

Later I slip into the basement. I cut the lights. I turn up the heat. I'm Ingrid again. Dangerous.

IN CASE OF AN EARTHQUAKE,
REMAIN CALM
1977

"TELL ME THE story about the autistic girl lured into
the men's room in a gas station in Reno by a man with
candy folded in his hand. When the men cover the girl's
body with a stained sheet, a reporter breaks down at the
scene: her face is a tissue forever crumbling. The man,
who cut the girl in two, wired flowers in her hair. 'She
smells like blood and old blankets,' someone mutters. Or
tell me that one about the couple who got crushed in an
avalanche because they thought it romantic to picnic in a
Sierra snowstorm. Open the door (slowly, slowly) to the
bathroom to see a woman lying on the floor, her jaw broken in three places. Watch her husband crawl in and bite
her toes in apology. The wife barely feels the peonies he
hails over her swollen face. Show me the veil belonging
to the girl pushed down the aisle to marry the man who
stole her childhood from her. 'Go,' says the mother, who
refuses to wince, even when the man puckers his fleshy
lips, rubs his calloused hands. If I hold the lace between

my fingers long enough, perhaps it will erase the shame we collectively carry. Perhaps it will undo the first and every hurt," I say. I'm in the kitchen in the middle of the night, rearranging food in cabinets because this house. This fucking house. "I'm right here. Tell me all about it, Tim. Speak slowly. Convince me a love exists that isn't a wound that never closes."

"Ellie, you're tired. Come back to bed," says Tim.

"I've got a confession to make: sometimes I lie awake and imagine men burning. When I was small, I used to watch fires in the country. Back then we thought it smart to burn rather than rebuild."

In the morning I shriek, "Why do you insist on hiding the matches from me?" I'm Ingrid in the basement again, and I've been robbed of light.

Later, a friend squeezes Tim's arm and says, "Don't you think it's time you put her in some *place*?"

The women in white hats buckle me in and I yell, "Traitor." "Snug like a bug in a rug, Ellie," they pantomime. Everyone tells me that the shocks are fast, that I won't feel a thing. I laugh because I've been down this long road to the middle before, and I feel everything. My affection for metal becomes a hunger that the men with their clipboards and pens aren't able to understand, much less diagnose. When I'm free to roam the halls, which I do as often as I can, I lick the undersides of tables. I bite down hard on metal carts and gnaw on lunch trays. As a result, I've been banned from silverware. Spoons are a delicacy and also my ruin. My world has been reduced to paper plates and plastic cutlery—*for my protection*, they say.

MORNING INVENTORY CHECKS:

— 22 identical rooms in square footage and decor.
— 44 blue sheets and white pillowcases with blue trim.
— 88 towels, 2 for each of the wards, often restocked due to hangings, tears, and stains that can't be bleached out.
— 44 women, mostly girls, mostly brown-haired, wide-eyed, and moneyed. The girls are nervous, paranoid, angry, ambivalent, and fragile creatures. There are a few who refuse food or eliminate it. We only know of one—a winsome girl, barely out of her teens—who eliminated two children before they were born.
— 44 men are to blame: fathers, sons, husbands, uncles, and brothers, who have signed us over. One Saturday a month they'll bring us lilies (death flowers) and books we'll never read. As if we need more propaganda.

Sometimes we trail the nurses as they make their counts. Some of us will shout out numbers to mess with them, but the nurses are unfazed by us and go on with their clipboards, pens, and endless boxes that require ticking. At night, they peer into our rooms with flashlights to make sure that we're alive, that we're still here. It's funny, if you think about it. No one entertains the notion of escape because where would we go? We would be the nuisances on our families' doorsteps, a nudge in the passenger seat, an elbow gripped and gently ushered back into our rooms where the sheets have barely cooled. The men are good at this, we realize, escorting women from one cold home to another.

Tim tells me that I'm here to rest. My family and friends repeat the word *cure* as if incanting a prayer, and I ask, "What's my disease?" Shaking their heads, they don't want to talk about a disease, per se; they just want me to *rest*. As if I'm a piece of china that could shatter and break.

"Well, then. Give me my fucking spoon and let me go to bed."

The next day, a doctor says, "Let's talk about your daughter. Kate."

I haven't told them about the incident with the bleach, but I suspect they already know. "Is this about the bleach? I assure you the burn was minor. Nothing more than a mild irritation."

The doctor inquires whether I think it's normal to

bathe a child in bleach. "Get your story straight; I didn't douse her in fucking Clorox. What do you think I am, crazy? What mother would bathe her child in bleach? Where I come from, they put you in the chair for hurting a child. Even in here, we despise women who *eliminate*."

"Your husband found you cleaning your child in a sink, with the windows closed and the room smelling of bleach, Eleanor."

"It's Ellie, and my husband is dead in the head. Maybe I'll send you an invitation to the exhuming." I pause and consider my words. "It's perfectly normal for a mother to clean her child. Perhaps we differ in our methods, but don't judge the intent."

"Do you consider yourself a good mother?"

"What does that even mean? A *good* mother," I say. My laugh is a series of hiccups and snorts. "Does wiring me up like a car that won't start make you a good doctor? Have you ever considered that the car doesn't want to start? That all it wants is to be covered up and rolled into a garage?"

"Cars aren't capable of emotion, Eleanor."

I light a cigarette. I'm in custody. "Jesus Christ, how many times do I have to tell you? It's Ellie. My name is Ellie. Ellie. Ellie."

A nurse shakes me. It's time for shocks again. My body is ravaged with sweat; everything clings in all the wrong places. My sheets are soiled, and next thing I know they lift me up (*easy, easy, you got her too high*). They strap me in, adjust the dials and read meters, and they tell me to bite down hard.

"Why should I bother telling you that my body and my name are mine, when you refuse to listen? When you laugh and say that I will always come from, and be delivered to, a man; my name is part of a male lineage, and my body a receipt of the transaction. My hair done up in the shape of a bow." I say this to the nurses who chat among themselves, the women in white who ignore me so completely. I'm the mother who bathed her child in bleach. I am an inbred, daughter of a mother and her father. I've been put in this place—*Isn't it time you put her in some place?*—by my husband, for my betterment, so that the doctors can scrub away the bleach and the inbreeding.

Tell me, do you think they've been successful? Am I clean?

What I hear, in the dark, after the shocks: *The dreams I had. I dreamed someone was raping me. I think it was someone inhuman.*

In the morning, I tell the doctors that they've got it all wrong; I don't hate my daughter. There will come a day when I will have to hand her over, when she will emigrate from my husband's house to her husband's house, and her name will change and her body will breed, and on it goes. The incident with the bleach was my attempt to scrub the man out of her. Wipe the slate clean.

"Don't you see?" I say. "The thing with the bleach. What I'm trying to tell you. What you need to know is this: I'm trying to get my daughter back to zero, but I ended up burning her. No one gets it; no one wants to."

"You clean a child with soap and water."

"Water," I say. "Water. I'll keep that in mind."

How could I know that years later my daughter would cling to water and play with fire?

Months later, the doctors tell me I have a visitor. When I tell them that no, I don't want to see my husband, and no, I will stab someone with a fork if they put me in a room with my mother (*You know you're no longer allowed access to utensils, Ellie*, they remind me in a childish, singsong voice I've grown to hate), they interrupt my long list of refusals to tell me that my visitor isn't a member of my family.

It's Minnie.

"Jesus, kid. This is straight out of *Cuckoo's Nest*. What the hell did you do to yourself? Why are you in this place?"

"I'm taking a rest," I say, smoking a cigarette.

"People got beds in their homes for that. No one just checks into an asylum."

"It was suggested that I needed some time apart from my family so that I could rest." I'm starting to notice that my wrist twitches every so often. It's replaced the way I used to pull at my hair.

"I remember your wedding."

"Ah, yes. The day you ruined my life."

"Your mother had a flair for the melodrama. You chose to stay in that house."

"Why can't you leave me alone?" I say. A bitterness edges into the spaces between the words.

"Because you won't leave my family alone. Know that I am patient. I will wait. And know that no one in your family will be spared."

Minnie watches me take my medicine. I smile and wave at her body gliding out of the door as I fall quickly to sleep.

This means goodbye.

MY PREGNANCY WAS nine months of torment. When Kate wasn't practicing her in-utero karate, I could be found on the bathroom floor, sore and raw because my body had grown accustomed to expelling everything that entered it save the one thing that mattered, the one thing that needed to make the journey out. She was smart, this one, hurting from the inside.

I marked the time between breaths using a diamond watch that my husband wound around my wrist. "A little something," Tim said, blushing, "for becoming a mother." Confused, I wondered if the watch was a down payment for a life-long vocation of braiding hair, ironing dresses, packing lunches, and sitting through games, recitals, and minor victories that bored me to tears. Was I wrong for not wanting this? Was I cruel for desiring to hoard the one thing over which I had dominion: my time? I wasn't ready to let it all go. Part of me wanted to hold on to my daughter for as long as I could, for I knew that her inevitable gushing out would also be my drowning.

Branded like cattle, I thought. They're all waiting for me to push out the prized calf.

After Kate was born, Cassidy visited only once. Since high school Cassidy had been forever chasing smoke and dodging rabbits. Rolling a cigarette and licking it, she asked, "What's it like?"

"What's *what* like?"

"Being a wife, a mother. You've got all this love. Where does it come from?"

"How do you mean?"

Cassidy laid down her cigarette, let it ash all over the Formica. I noticed her hands, how small they were, how her nails had been gnawed to the quick. How they lunged for the cigarette and how her fingers curled and withdrew. I don't smoke, never saw the glamour in it, only the rot, but I was fond of watching my best friend tangled up in her addiction. I didn't tell her this.

"I always thought you got a finite set of feelings, you know? Like we have two hands and ten toes, maybe we just have the capacity to love, *really* love—over, under, and between the sheets, and under the skin—only a set number of people. It's not the same for each person. It couldn't be. Like my mother only having room enough in her heart to fill it with my father and herself. So by the time I came along, she was all tapped out. Drained, no refills, and I realized that was the kind of life I was likely to get. But it seems to me that you hit the lotto, Ellie. All these people and you somehow love them. Aren't you ever terrified that you'll hit your limit? That maybe the next kid you push out will have to fend for itself?"

Cassidy would live her whole life not knowing about me and my mother, about my time in the cellar, and her lying down, willingly, on her father's bed.

Something within me rattled. In the other room, my newborn daughter was swaddled, sound asleep. If I strained, if I listened hard enough, I could hear her breathing—the steady calm of her inhales and exhales that reminded me of a metronome. A clock reminding me of the time she gains and the moments I lose, an exchange of possessive pronouns: mine, yours, mine, and *yours*. At night I lean over her crib and watch her sleep. And while I love this innocent, beautiful thing, I can't help but look at her and think of her only as my subtraction. Me: a firmament no longer part of the sky. She: the eclipse.

"How do you know I haven't already gone beyond my limit?" I said.

Cassidy's eyes widened. She leaned toward the cigarette but paused. "Now you're in the game."

"I ALWAYS KNEW you liked to be tied down," Cassidy says now, during visiting hours. Leaning in, she examines my face, all of it. "You quiet types are kinky that way."

"They say it's for my safety." It's been two years since I saw Cassidy. Her hair is shorn to the ears, *like Mia Farrow*, she says proudly. The bruises are long gone, replaced by a body freckled and brown from the sun. More than anything I want to hide my arms under the sheets and drape a curtain over my face—all to hide a body that's been kept in a preserve. "It's been a while."

"I never told you what happened out West," she says. "You should know what happened. You need to know," she says, grabbing at my restraints, fingering the metal of the buckle that I'm desperate to lick. "How to get out."

Cassidy tells me about a man playing the guitar with gold in his hair, like the summer of love. He strums Paul Simon and Bob Dylan because he's going to be a star, and tells her that she is his *sweet girl*. They live on an old movie set out in the desert called Eden (*sound the alarm*, she says), where they've a handful of cattle, chickens, and cats that take care of the mice. Thirty of them live on the land, sing songs, read poetry, and talk about a world where everyone lets the shackles fall from their ankles. During the day, the women cook and sew and clean, and the men smoke joints and fuck the new girls. *Baptism*, they call it. *Bringing the pigs home*, they say. At night, they eat out of clean bowls and move from one body to the next like a game of musical chairs. Soon Cassidy becomes the *mare*, when she just wants to be the *sweet girl* who hums out of tune. She empties her pockets for the leader—whom they all call Father—all for semantics, for the desire to be small and pure and clean. But the only thing that changes is her name—they've given her a new one—and she can't keep the old and new nicknames straight. When Cassidy stops pressing money into the Father's hands, he has new chores for her to do: men to bring into the family and houses in the country ripe for thievery. One particular robbery gone wrong made Cassidy flee.

"How could we possibly know that the fucker would be home?" Cassidy says, lighting a Camel, smoking it. She tells me about a baseball bat, blood (*so much, you wouldn't believe*), and their footprints all over the mud-room. "Not the kind of shit you want to leave behind. So I bolted. I ran through the trees to the road. I had to blow some trucker from Barstow to give me a ride across the state line."

"My God, Cass. Why didn't you tell me this? I could have done something."

"What would you have done? Driven down with that husband of yours who would've given me a lecture all the way back to town? And remember that day you ran off with my car?" she says. "Left me with men who did the things they felt entitled to do. And then you left me again when you had that child. How could I trust you; you always leave."

I close my eyes. The waves recede. "You seemed . . . free."

"Oh, honey. I'm a fuckup with a bank account. Getting balled by men isn't free, sweetie; I know the game, and it's one where we'll celebrate our minor victories, but we'll never win. Not really. Freedom is having cash to bandage the wounds and run. Freedom is saying we're getting the fuck out of here *today*, Ellie. I read your chart and they say you're crazy, bonkers, off your rocker, but I don't buy it."

"That's not possible," I say. "I see now what I've done to Kate. I understand why I need the pills." Suddenly my face is a river. I've outlived my best-by date. I accept that I will never scramble eggs. I will always burn or break toast. My skin will itch and blister after a man touches it. There will always be marks and stained sheets. I will never understand the nuances of dinner parties, where conversations require constant costume changes. I will never gnaw down to the bone. I will be cautious of birds. I will live in a series of homes and never see the deed. I will pin butterflies to the walls of my room to replace the mirrors that have been removed. The days will continue to leave their scars. I will never take my own life because I can't bear the thought of writing the note. Instead, I'll let others leave their marks. I'll open the Bible and read the book without understanding the story. It doesn't matter. In the end, the men will save. This is what I was told. What I needed to know was this: my role was to own the books and believe. Men would do the work.

I think of my house and I see my daughter reaching for me as I fade and fall out of the frame. All I've got is a mouth that has a taste for metal and a desire to leave my three-year-old daughter and go.

"They tell me I'm getting better," I say.

"I don't think you were ever sick to begin with. So you realized you didn't want to be a wife and a mother—believe me, you wouldn't be the first."

"But Kate . . . the bleach."

"Momentary lapse of reason. I nearly beat a man to death for what? Pocket change? Because a man told me to? I'd say, under the right conditions, otherwise normal people are capable of doing just about anything. And what's normal, really?" Cassidy says, her face only inches away from mine. I can feel her breath on me; I can smell the meat.

The unbuckling of leather—guards, not belts—the crinkle of cotton pulled on and draped over, the fastening of buttons, the buzz of a door, the cool hallway and diverted eyes, the doors that unlock, the light that threatens to blind.

"Let's go," Cassidy says, folds my hand in hers. "Let's run."

We run.

LEAVING NEVADA
1977

WE DRIVE THROUGH Nevada. It takes a day to travel to a town so hot that corpses crawl up out of their graves because even the six feet of shade isn't cool enough. We joke about eating cactus and rattlesnake, picking scales and spines out of our teeth with nails we've grown too long, although we secretly know we're the kind who will settle for a ham sandwich. At least I would. We pass a smoke between us and talk intellectually about tumbleweed as if it were the one thing on this trip we're meant to see. I roll down the window, lapping up the dry heat with my tongue. At a pay phone on the outskirts of Tonopah, I call Tim and tell him I'll be gone for a while. I call my mother and tell her to go fuck herself.

Cassidy laughs and rattles dimes in her pocket. "Feels good, doesn't it?"

I feel the elastic band on the underside of my shorts and say, "Yes, it does." But as soon as it does, it doesn't. I think about Kate, in parts, but not the whole of her. I see her eyes, sometimes blue, often gray, but I can't make out the shape of her face or the body of a child leaning toward its mother, grasping for what's warm and familiar. I can't fit her in the frame, so as we drive I think about her hands, the smooth, webbed skin between her toes, the deep curve of her bottom lip. This part, the missing, doesn't feel so good, but I don't tell Cassidy this. Instead, I unfurl a map and tell her to head farther west. I want California.

"I've seen California," she says, "You don't want that."

I'm coming back, Kate. You have to know that I'm trying to get better so they don't take me away again. I'm trying to swallow all this sadness so they don't suspect me again, but there's so much of it. A woman is a dam, breaking. California is all for you, Kate.

In Tonopah, you can still get a hamburger for fifty-five cents, and for a dime you can play all the Perry Como songs your heart desires on the jukebox in the local luncheonette. One of two local radio stations plays gospel songs, although at midday everyone seems drunk on hooch passed around in old Coca Cola bottles.

"Fuck me," Cassidy says. "We're not in Kansas, Dorothy. We're in 1950."

"Good thing we're white," I say. "Good thing we blend in."

For a moment, a blankness falls over Cassidy's face, like a dark curtain that no one can see through. She's a ghost town, an uninhabitable country. I've seen that look before. When I was seventeen, we were both at a sleepover at Kit Ryan's house. I woke in the middle of the night and stole boxes of cookies and cake mix out of Kit Ryan's kitchen. My home was one free of sweets, and I desperately wanted an Oreo cookie. Prone to night terrors, Cassidy rarely slept, and she found me with my bounty. Same blank stare like the one she's giving me now when she called me the *Nabisco thief.* When Kit woke the next morning, she and her mother whispered in the kitchen, and all I could remember hearing is Kit, annoyed, saying *we probably ate them all* because who would just break into a house and steal all the biscuits? When I got home that night, I arranged all the loot in my closet and ate every last morsel. Every chip, every crumb.

In a small voice Cassidy says, "Good thing."

At the front desk of the Motel Tonopah, a sign reads, Voted Worst Motel in the World. Annie, the proprietor, greets us in a sweeping floral muumuu and a bushel of red hair. Pointing to the sign, she says with pride, "You read right. This ain't the Shangri La, ladies. We got none of that fancy-smelling bar soap and *amenities*. You get five channels on the television, and you're lucky to even be getting a television on account of me experiencing some downsizing. You keep your rooms clean because I ain't your damn maid or mother; I already got four rotten kids sucking on my teat. And I don't want to find anything funny on those sheets, if you know what I mean. They get washed once a week, on laundry day, so consider today your lucky day."

"You got a boy my age in that rotten bunch?" Cassidy asks.

Annie scowls. "That'll be ten dollars a night, paid in advance."

I wince from the heat, or perhaps it's the lone fan blowing dirt in my face.

After Cassidy pays the bill, I say, "I don't think this is a good idea."

Cassidy rolls her eyes, "What do you want, Ellie? The Four Seasons and malts?"

"I didn't realize clean sheets were a luxury."

The room! The room is a comedy of errors, straight out of an Albee play, all theater of the absurd. On the television screen, a taped sign reads, Do Not Adjust Television Antennae. On the toilet seat, someone has scrawled, Flush after Every Other Elimination. Water Don't Grow on Trees. Taped to the bathroom mirror, a sign reads, Do Not Use Towels or Wash Clothes to Clean Cars, Windshields, or Vaginas during the Time. Beneath the sign is a large arrow that points to a cardboard box on the floor filled with oily rags. Taped onto that box is another sign: Use Me.

"You think they got cameras in here?" I say.

"This is back-ass Nevada. They've probably got holes drilled in the walls. They're probably watching us right now. They'll use the good towels to clean up the evidence."

"I've read about hotels like this."

"I've *lived* in hotels like this," Cassidy says, flushing the toilet twice and shoving one of the clean rags between her legs. When I gawk, Cassidy shrugs and says, "Evidence."

The blood is a torrent, drowning everything in its wake. Through the red foam that sweeps across the hospital bed and spills over the tray tables, I see my husband collapse against a wall, and then a head. A swatch of pale blond hair and eyelids shuttered white. Then a fist burying itself in me as if it wanted to crawl back to where it had come from. Then come the gurgle and scream, and then Kate, white hair darkening in the sea, rolling deeper and deeper underwater.

Cassidy snaps her fingers in front of my face. "Earth to Ellie. Did I lose you to the little green men from up there?"

Be normal, I think. "More like the green shit growing on the walls." Next to the black-and-white television set, mold spores spider up the wallpaper, and the corner of the room teems with miniature mushrooms. "Don't take off your shoes," I warn.

"I wonder if old Annie's got a sign for that," Cassidy laughs and sprawls out on the bed while I wonder whether Clorox could make this room habitable, bleach it to the bone. I want it to be winter. I want to feel what it's like to drive through snow. But I remember the sun and the fact that my license was taken from me.

Cassidy says, "I thought we'd go out. Let's get wrecked."

"No cactus or rattlesnake? You're not even in the least bit hungry? Because I'm starving." I cover the lower half of my bed in Saran Wrap. I'm starting to see inkblots on the wallpaper. I blink them away. Focus on the task at hand.

"I'm working up to it. Once I get a little drink and boy in me, I'll be ripping the heads off live snakes and picking needles out of my hair. That's my kind of night. I hope you're not wearing that shirt. No one will fuck you in that shirt."

"I met my husband in this shirt."

"My point," Cassidy says. "Wait, is that plastic wrap? Are you wrapping your bed in plastic wrap?"

"There could be lice on this bed; I'm not taking any chances."

"You think you're taking this germaphobe thing a little far? Maybe I shouldn't have broken you out of the loony bin," Cassidy teases.

"That's not funny," I say. After a while, "I hate gross things."

We move like fog in the night. The road ahead of us is dark and we make a game out of kicking beer cans and rifling through our empty cigarette packs. Tonopah is the sort of town where everyone draws their curtains to one side and gathers around a couch to watch the black-and-white television. Cassidy talks about group sex and cult blow jobs. There are no street signs.

"There's a difference between wanting it and having it taken from you," Cassidy says. "From being on top to waking up with a knee pressed on your back. When I came home, nobody even noticed I'd left. But they all talked about you. How your husband put you in the nut-house."

"He was right to do that," I say.

"We're not crazy is what I'm trying to tell you," Cassidy says. She grabs my hand and squeezes it two times. "We're not."

I see a coral snake wrapped around Kate's mouth. Her eyes are lidless, white, and wide. The snake hatches an egg in my daughter's mouth and she chokes. "Of course not," I say, knowing that the pills have made their exit and the shadows will become voices will become people will become shocks will become Kate. *I will return.*

"I'm not so sure," I say.

Cassidy looks around and asks, "Where are we?"

"Back-ass Nevada."

It's ladies' night at the Motel Tonopah, but men try to buy us drinks anyway. Everyone asks us where we're from and Cassidy says, "Sun, moon, and stars, baby."

She drinks whiskey neat and licks her lips so much they get dry. Her hair is longer now; it covers the scars on the back of her neck. But every now and then I see her touch them, like habit, and I think about our day at the lake and all the hope.

A fat man named Fred sits next to me and he smells of raw onion and tobacco. I turn my back to him so he's left talking to my hair. After a few moments he grunts, "Queer as fuck," and moves down the bar. A woman walks in with a fox skin draped around her neck, and Fred pulls out a chair and buys her a drink. Boys play quarters on a table filled with chipped glasses. Fireflies dart in and out of the windows while two men haul out a broken jukebox to hock but no one pays them any mind, and the bartender drinks gin straight from the bottle. Somebody orders food but nobody eats it. A man yells, "I used to be in shipping. I used to move things."

I remember the bleach, the sting of it. I remember brushing Kate's hair out of her eyes. I remember the smallness of her hands. She's so small; she won't always be this small. One day she won't be the thing that fills my hands. Her body will spill over.

Eyeing the jukebox men holding court across the room, Cassidy jumps out of her chair. She's a woman who loves things in twos, who forever desires to be in French films she's never seen and travel to places her parents abandoned her for. I want to shake her. I want to tell her that people always leave.

"Nothing deep," Cassidy says, unbuttoning a button. Strands of her hair cling to her neck, all slicked with gloss and sweat. "What do you think of those guys? The ones with the box?"

"You've never had a more receptive audience."

Cassidy comes closer, leans into me, and bites my cheek. "That day when I first met you at the carnival, I had you pegged; I had you made. You only have eyes for me." She sticks out her tongue and I watch her run to the men.

Outside, thin snakes dangle from a tree like livewire. Stars paint the sky silver. The first month I couldn't feel Kate, I only knew that cells were thick in the business of multiplication, and as a result a person would take shape. A person I wasn't ready for, but it didn't matter. Women are born to serve and breed, and when we fail at this, what else is there? What is it that we can do that men can't? We bring their screaming mouths into this world only to be told by those mouths, now grown, that we're lesser than. Only good for being on our knees, backs, and perched over stoves. We're told, *You're smart for a woman, you're mouthy for a woman, you're brazen for a woman.* They tell us we're dangerous and emotional, prone to hysterics like landmines, and I wonder, if this is true, why aren't they afraid?

Why was it that I was the only one afraid of this person occupying my body?

During the months that followed I prayed for a fall,

a kick, or the will to plunge a hanger all the way in, but I was afraid that losing my daughter would hurt me in some unimaginable way, so I stayed home, locked in my room. Removed all the hangers from the closets. Took the cords out of the phones. Every night my husband would come home and return the hangers to the closets and plug the phones back into the walls. Every morning I'd wake to the same nightmare all over again. I prayed for amnesia.

Now, I close my eyes and feel the night, the stillness of it. A few blocks from the bar is a diner. I eat eggs off a white paper plate and leave a ten-dollar tip. When I leave, I see a man's arms covered in scales. On the way back to the Motel Tonopah, I see snakes, so many of them, but I know it's my head playing tricks and I crouch down on the curb of a street and make myself lose all the eggs. I press down on my stomach as if it's a part of my body that doesn't belong; I'd give anything for a pair of scissors or a steak knife. The eggs are still there and I need them gutted out. I require a scalpel and a knife; I need things to be removed. *We all go a little mad sometimes.* A couple passes and the woman says, "Look at that, will you? Woman can't even hold her drink."

Woman can't hold anything, it seems. But I did hold Kate, until I couldn't, and two years later my husband pried the bleach out of my hands. They didn't understand how I needed to undo all of her history. Take back the years. I tried to kill my daughter; I tried to save my daughter. I don't know what to think. For some reason I can't get the smell of bleach out of my skin. Is this my haunting? Forever made to wear the perfume that imprisoned me, the smell I now associate with shocks? They tell you that you won't feel a thing, only a jolt and the taste of metal in your mouth, like you're sucking on coins, but they're lying.

When I open my eyes I see Annie, proprietor of the Motel Tonopah, wearer of muumuus, and she says, "You ignored the signs." She sits on the curb alongside me eating fried onions out of a paper bag.

"What?"

"The room," she says. "I heard the flushing. It was like Niagara Falls in there."

"That wasn't me," I say.

"I figured as much. Your friend's got sass to her."

"That's one way of putting it."

"Where you from?"

"There are a lot of snakes in this town." The eggs are still in me, multiplying.

"By the looks of it," Annie says, raising her eyebrows, "your friend is about to get acquainted with two of them firsthand. They even got her pushing that old jukebox." She points to Cassidy trailing the two men from the bar. From the sidewalk I can hear her grunting as she drags a dolly holding the jukebox along the concrete. The men pass a bottle between them, walking ahead, and I open my mouth, ready to shout Cassidy's name, but I don't. I watch my friend, who is a little drunk and a lot lost, getting her hands dirty.

"I'm from my father's house, my husband's house, and sometimes a hospital, which is to say I don't really know where I'm from. It's still Nevada but far from this town." After a time I ask, "Why do you have all those signs in the rooms?"

Annie laughs. "It started as a joke in '69, but now it's something that passes the time. It seems to me that all we have is time—that's the one thing that can't be taken from us."

"Speak for yourself. I lost nearly a year of my life in a hospital."

"You sick or something?"

"Some might say so. But I don't know. All I know is that there was a time when I had a lot of pain and I didn't know where to put it. I was supposed to have a version of a life, and then I started seeing things that weren't there but *were* there, and one day I stood over my daughter in a sink with a bottle of bleach and I don't know, even now, even after all this time, how I got there. I don't remember the bottle or putting her in the sink. It was as if I'd been sleeping and I woke up and there she was, cold and crying. There was a window of time when I thought I was happy . . ."

Annie's eyes are red and wide. "Some women aren't built for children."

"What else is there? Should I take up dictation? Or should I be like Cass, feeding off the remains of her father's money? There is no life that isn't in service of a man. There is no time my grandfather or husband hasn't accounted for. There is only what you can endure, what you can bear, and sometimes it feels good to lose time, to not be here for any of it."

"One morning, years ago, my daughter packed a bag with her shirts and shorts and a few sandwiches and got as far as the highway. It was the cars that scared her—the fear that one would hit her—that drove her back. We didn't even notice she'd been gone until she came back, face full of dust, and said she'd run away. She was five. You don't see the boys running. It's always the girls." A kind of clarity registers on Annie's face as if I am a puzzle she's suddenly pieced together. It's the opposite of Cassidy and her confusion, but it's still exhausting. It occurs to me that I don't know why I'm here, only that my head hurts. I should be home with my child. The pain colors everything white. I can make out the shape of things: trees, car parts on the sidewalk, and Annie—the lump of her, the mess of her hair. Why is she here? What is she telling me?

"I don't understand."

"Sounds like you've had a rough time. Like somebody took you by the hair and rubbed your face into the world until you got the taste and feel of how things are. Why else would you be out here, alone, puking your guts out onto the street, and not over there with your friend?"

"What are you doing here?" I ask. The words, as they leave me, are sharper than I intended.

Annie points to the house across the street and says, "I live over there. Twenty-seven years in that house with two dead husbands, a father seeing his life at the end of a dribble cup, and four kids who know this town is as good as it'll ever get. All I've got left are boxes in the attic, a life spread out across pages of a photo album, and a run-down, shit-bag motel where I get to practice my sadness and watch it play out like an old movie. Maybe you need to ask yourself, What movie I got playing in my head?"

"But this is real."

"No, it ain't. Let me give you a piece of advice, speaking from personal experience. Don't betray your kin. Now I'm not talking about your husband—fuck your husband because they all run around on you or lie about it. I'm talking about your kids. Don't do wrong by them, because it has a way of coming back to you."

I heave on the sidewalk.

Annie shakes her head and sighs, "Go on home, girl. It's about time we all go on home."

Back in the room, Cassidy's alone and she slurs, "Where the fuck have you been?"

"Out," I say. "With Annie."

"Who's Annie?"

I point to the television that's airing nothing but snow and say, "Front desk lady."

Cassidy sits up; hair clings to her face. "I'll tell you how my night went. Two men and me load a jukebox onto a truck. We drive to another bar outside of town. One of them buys me a drink, and they keep buying drinks until I black out, and then I wake up here in this room. They carry me in. They wrap my stomach with your Saran Wrap and they fuck me until my smoke burns down to the filter. They put on their pants, one pisses in the toilet, and then they go back to where it is that they've come from. And I'll tell you about tomorrow. I'll wake up and vomit into the toilet he didn't flush while you play the rebellious Stepford wife who tries to forget that she almost bleached her kid. One of us will have a breakdown and then we'll go home. Want to place a bet on which one of us will crack first?"

"You don't know me," I say.

"That's the rub, Ellie. I know your kind. I know *you*."

The next morning, Cassidy vomits and we pack without speaking. I return the keys to the office while Cassidy packs the car. When I reach for her she says, "Don't."

Behind the desk is a man that's not Annie, not even close. "Where's Annie?"

"Room number," he grunts, and I realize it's fat Fred from the bar.

"Where's Annie?"

"Annie's dead. Shot up her four kids last night and then turned the gun on herself."

"That's impossible," I say. My hands start shaking. "I saw her last night, in the street, in front of her house. I talked to her."

"Then you might want to talk to the police, lady. Room number?"

"Wait. What are you even doing here?" I shout. *Shhh, sweet Kate. This won't hurt one bit.*

Fred laughs. "What am I doing here? What am I doing here? Well, little lady, this is a bit awkward, you see, on account of Annie being my wife."

"Your wife?"

"I think you better go now," Fred says.

I stand in front of the car. Cassidy's inside. The engine runs. She leans over to the passenger side and says, "Get in."

"Annie's dead."

For a moment Cassidy's quiet. Then she gives me the blank stare, again. "What did you do?"

CONSTANT LAND MOVEMENT
1977

"STOP THE CAR," I say. I gather my things from the back seat and lay them on top of my lap. I am not crazy. I didn't kill Annie, proprietor of the Motel Tonopah. I'm just a sad woman who never wanted to be a wife, shouldn't have been a mother, but now I have this child and Kate is what I will inevitably go home to. There's one more trip I have to take before I make my reparations, before I take my pills and sleep through my waking life. This is the end of the line for Cassidy and me. "I'm leaving."

"Quit the drama, Ellie. I'll take you where you need to go," she says, gripping the steering wheel.

"If you don't stop the car I'll jump out," I say.

"And do what? Walk? It's over 110 degrees out there. You'll get burned." Cassidy pulls onto the side of the road and cuts the engine. "This is about those guys last night, right? Why don't we just get your judgment all out in the open so we can keep going like nothing happened."

"You don't like me very much, do you?"

"I never gave the matter much thought."

"Why did you come for me? On my wedding day, at the hospital."

"Because you're the kind of woman who needs saving."

"And you're the one to do it." I open the door and get my suitcase out of the trunk. The heat bears down on my back and I can feel my skin grow hot. I stand there, sleepless, with dust on my shoes. I'm ready to walk away. For a moment I think of Charlie Manson and his family. Is this where they went? Crawled back to a ranch in the desert, living among rusted railway cars, blackbirds, diamondback snakes, and prostitutes named Candy? Was it Cassidy singing off-key next to a beautiful ex-con, whose calloused fingers strummed Beach Boy songs on an old guitar? His eyes were the world she orphaned herself to. After bleaching her hair, did Cassidy tell him she was the sun? If I stand still long enough I can feel Cassidy trembling in the car.

Cassidy rolls down the window. "So that's it? We have one argument and you take off? Where are you gonna go? Back to Tim, back to playing wet nurse? I'm all you have. I'm hope, Ellie."

"You know, the day of my wedding I had a visitor, Minnie."

"That crazy cake baker?"

"Oh, I think you know her better than that. She told me that I should listen to you. That I should make my plans."

"What are you talking about?"

"So I'm making my plans." I slam the passenger door hard, wheel my luggage to the gas station, and hitch a ride to the bus station, leaving Cassidy standing in front of her car, one hand shielding her eyes from the sun. Who knew this would be the last time we'd see one another? Who knew that in a few years' time cancer would breed in Cassidy's body, annihilating everything in its wake? Tim will tell me that she weighed seventy pounds when she died; she'd become a bag of rattled bones. All that beauty, unrecognizable, and all that *hope* stolen by cancer. I lie. I will see her one last time when my daughter is older and I lay wildflowers on Cassidy's grave. The bunch is messy, prickly, and riddled with weeds—exactly what she would have wanted. I will see Minnie standing at a distance.

When I am old and gray with eyes drowning of sleep, I will finally feel the weight of Annie's words hurtling back to me. I will lie in a bed and see my daughter standing over me. I will see her pry the bottle of pills from my hands. She will smell of butter and burned bread. I will see her hold a pillow over my face. I will hear her say, *I've always loved watching you sleep.*

Not yet.

It takes nearly three hundred and fifty miles to get to Bakersfield, and I'm awake the whole way. The bus rolls along Route 6, through the desert, past pickup trucks and men who chew tobacco in ten-gallon hats, and all I can see is the stretch of road ahead. Truckers honk as they race by, and the woman beside me occupies herself by knitting pink wool booties.

"It's a bit warm for socks," I say, by way of conversation, and the woman looks at me, looks at her socks, and resumes the needle clink.

"I have a daughter," I say.

The woman glares at me and says, "What do you want, a medal? Can I get back to my business now?" Startled, I press my face against the glass for the remainder of the ride. When we leave Barstow, I see a hand-painted sign that reads, Everyone Who Passes through Here Gets Pulled Under. Cassidy used to tell me about her nightmares, how she dreamed of Indians in the desert.

We arrive in Bakersfield in the evening when the air has cooled down to hot. It's quiet save for the sound of cicadas and the row of old men at the bus station spitting into tin cans. Inside, I ask the man who takes the tickets where I can find the nearest motel. Without looking up from his magazine, he points to a building across the road. "That's the Bakersfield Inn," he says. "Rooms are eight fifty a night. You go there and ask for Marla, and she'll fix you up." When I thank him he says, "You're a long way from home." And in this, we agree.

There are two lamps in the hotel room, and I turn them both on before I call Tim. Sobbing, he says he can't do this on his own. He's not built for it. A child needs its mother, not a grandmother who's out to lunch and not taking any calls. "Your mother calls her Ingrid," my husband says. "Who the hell is Ingrid?"

"Someone we used to know." Delilah Martin: *I'm scared that she's going to make you crazy.*

"When your mother's not acting like Greta Garbo, she plays it like she's got a bad case of amnesia. I swear, Kate and I will be in the room with Norah and she'll act as if we're goddamn strangers. Twice I had to call the doctor to sedate her. And this morning, she up and disappeared. Do I call the police? What the fuck do I do? I can't take another day of this. Not another second. You have to come home," Tim says, in a way that's less of an order and more of a plea. He doesn't mention the hospital and my jailhouse break, fearing, perhaps, that I'd never come home. I know what awaits me, what I'll have to return to eventually—imprisonment: my daughter, that hospital, my *life*. But not yet.

"Call my grandfather. He'll take care of it." We are so far from that home Tim had made for us in Carmel. I need California; I need to see this through.

My husband sighs and speaks slowly, the way he used to right before the hospital. "Your grandfather has been dead for six months. I held your hand at the funeral. I don't know what ideas Cassidy's put in your head . . ."

"She's gone," I interrupt, but he's not listening.

"But you have an obligation. You took a vow."

"You know what they did. The things they put in my mouth. I can't go back there."

"Okay, no more hospitals," Tim says. He's crying. I can hear his halting breath over the telephone line. "Just come home, Ellie."

"I've just got to do this one thing and I'll be back tomorrow night."

"Tell me where you are. I'll get you on a plane."

"I'll call you when I'm done," I say, and put down the phone. It's only then that I realize I haven't once asked about my daughter. The thing with the bleach, well, maybe it's not as horrible as I thought.

After I've covered the bathtub with cling film, I step in, lie down, turn on the shower, and feel the waterfall cool on my back. I fall asleep to the sound of water. That night I dream about a man standing in front of a refrigerator; the light illuminates his body blue. He removes his belt and coils it in his hands. Outside there are horses. We are in Ireland, on a farm where the sheep and lambs are painted red. A fat woman punches her daughter in the stomach, yanks out her hair in clumps. The daughter whistles in my ear. I wake to the sound of my mother's voice: *We used to have another girl, but she died. We didn't want to upset you.*

I wake to a man shaking my shoulders. The room is a river. "What the hell is wrong with you, letting the water run like that? You could've died. You could've drowned."

When I wake, I feel restless. I am the wound my mother keeps dressing.

HOW TO GRIEVE THE TERMINALLY ILL
2013

I ONCE PLUCKED out the eyes of all the dolls I owned because I couldn't bear to have them as witnesses. I might have been ten, twenty-five, or thirty-two—at this point, does it really matter? I couldn't allow the dolls to see me being driven away from my home when I was ten. They can't see the years I spent baking cakes in my home because I found it difficult to make friends. And the dolls could never bear witness to my mother's steady, heartbreaking decline: the thirty pounds skinned from Ellie's already slender frame because cancer booked passage into her body and proceeded to breed.

Sometimes one needs to remove things.

I watch an interview with Charles Manson where he calls Ted Bundy a mama's boy, not fit to roll with his tribe, because Manson can only stand people who can stand to be with themselves. Manson shouts: *Who do you think I am, girl? If you can pick all the words of the vocabulary that your mother told you, who do you think I am? This is only a couple of hours. Can you imagine a couple of days with me?* Manson pleads for more time.

Experts think Ted Bundy hated his mother. Reports say his mother was a prim, modest department-store clerk who bore Bundy out of wedlock. He grew up in a home where he'd sometimes see women tossed down flights of stairs if they overslept. As a child he was horrified. As an adult who had been betrayed by his mother and first love, robbed of his identity and manhood, he understood hate. Women needed to be taken, possessed. Women required instruction.

While Ellie lies dying, I occupy my time observing the habits of strange men and reading grief manuals online. I learn how to bind myself to my mother's pain and how to cope with loss.

I spend hours watching Bundy pay homage to the heads of his victims. He recounts how he posed and cleaned them, watched the skin turn gray then purple then blue. Inevitably, the skin would blister and crack, removing itself from the skull. Chrysalises aroused Ted, and in these moments of reliving the murders and the careful care of the remains, his voice is deep, melodic. I bake cakes. I pipe roses. I learn the term *anticipatory grief.* Ted was handsome, arresting. Sometimes I change the color of my hair. Other times I comb frosting through it.

I don't want to talk about that. No, no I do not.

STAGE 1: CRISIS

Your family's equilibrium will be disrupted. Anxiety is the most common initial reaction, but with estrangement, you may feel guilty, resentful, or angry.

Drinking softens the edges. The day Ellie is diagnosed with advanced lung cancer, she buys a pack of cigarettes and takes up smoking again because why not? What does it matter that she quit ten years ago when she won't be alive to see another ball drop? She pours glass after glass of Sancerre because she likes the taste of it. She shreds the prescriptions and tosses the paper in the air like confetti. She hasn't considered death until she's had to reckon with it. There was a time, years ago, when she wanted to die. When she was in a hotel in Bakersfield and turned the faucets on, full blast, to see if she could drown in a room. When she was on a street in Tonopah and didn't know if she had the strength to go on, to be a dutiful wife and mother. Maybe if she took all the pills, she could rub all of it away. Why didn't the cancer come for her then?

"So this is what I get," Ellie says, "for the woman I've been."

"We should get a second opinion," says James.

"Why?"

"People get misdiagnosed all the time. We can't take this lying down. We have to fight this."

"You sound like a fucking Lifetime movie," Ellie says. "I'm not going to another doctor. What I am going to do is finish this bottle of wine and start on a new one. And then I'll smoke through this pack until I need to send you out to buy me a new one."

"I think James is right," I say, timidly.

"When this is all over, I want to be burned."

"No one's getting burned," says James. "We have time."

"*You* have time," Ellie says. "Both of you."

No one mentioned that all the anger and resentment in the room would belong to Ellie. No one feels guilt.

This will go on for hours until Ellie is passed out and James locks himself in the bedroom with Nic Cage movies. I remove the lit cigarette from my mother's hand. I rub it out. I drape a blanket over her sleeping body and tuck in the edges. I'm careful with the hair, the feet.

"What's one less person on the face of the earth anyway?" Ted Bundy says during an interview.

My mother is dying. She's fucking dying. I bite down on my wrist, hard, until I can see teeth marks.

STAGE 2: UNITY

The needs of the dying become paramount. Not only does each family member have to define their role with respect

*to the terminally ill, but existing grudges or ill will must be
resolved. But being a team player admittedly is challenging.*

We don't seek out a second opinion and live with the fact
that Ellie's on a clock. Her coughing causes her pain and
the tissues surrounding her bed are covered in blood and
phlegm. The cancer is spreading. I watch movies about
death and I'm confused. Why does everyone appear to be
encased in white light when we know there's only black?
We have to consider the possibility that nothing exists beyond our final breath except for a pine box or gray ashes
flecked with bone.

In the yard I yank weeds from beds and James talks to
me about putting some distance between us. The chemo
was working, now it isn't, and we don't know what to do.
The cancer has metastasized. It's in the house.

"I know you're angry," he says.

"You have no idea." I yank.

"I'm human, Kate, and this is me trying to do the
right thing. But you got to take some responsibility in all
of this."

"You fuck another woman and it's my fault? I was a
witness. I saw what you did, I saw—"

"Kate, you were there."

"Don't." I stand, wipe the dirt from my hands on my
pants. A tiny worm winds its way around my finger. "And

while you're trying to do the right thing, I'm going to give my dying mother her medication and arrange for hospice. Is that enough distance for you, James?"

"We need to be on the same team," says James.

"And whose team would that be?" I say, walking into the house.

Ellie tells me about a friend named Cassidy. "I was sick and she took me for a ride. We planned on driving all the way west, through California down to Mexico, but we only got as far as a small town in Nevada. And we got into a fight, over what I don't remember, and the last time I saw her was in a car speeding away."

"Do you know where she lives? I could find her for you," I say.

Ellie closes her eyes. "She died. Cancer. Funny how time sorts things, delivers retribution when you least expect it. At least she went quickly. My sickness is fucking with me, baiting hope only to snatch it away. It sits in a rocking chair with its needlework and sips lemonade. But I deserve this."

"Is there anything I can get you? What can I do?"

"You can close the door behind you and let me sleep. Let me pretend that I could go back. That I could've stayed in the car with Cassidy. Could've heard the engine run." She speaks so softly that I suspect she doesn't think I can hear her say, "I could've been the one who ran."

"I love you." I edge closer to her on the bed.

Ellie's eyes are still closed when she says, "I know you think you do."

I leave her alone because the websites tell me that I need to put the dying's wants and needs before my own. Grief is slippery—once you think you've grasped it, it changes its form. You know there's pain in the room—it rises up all around you—but you can't identify whose it is. Ellie will die. She'll die even if I manage to resuscitate the hyacinths in the garden. She'll die even if James and I come to a kind of reconciliation. I don't see the sense in studying the grief guides, but I do it anyway because this is what you do when someone you love is dying. I'm Kate, playing the daughter of a woman dying from metastatic lung cancer, a cancer that has crept into her liver. These are the feelings you're told to feel, the calls and arrangements you have to make. You're given a timetable and you take solace in the fact that you can follow an outline. Right now we're all in stage two and I do everything my mother tells me. I play daughter. I play nice.

Yet I feel nothing. I think about my dolls' eyes, my mother's cancer—how they have the ability to *see*. I feel nothing if not the by-product of their harvest.

Later that night I read a collection of Ted Bundy quotes while James soft-knuckles my door, begging for forgiveness. *I haven't blocked out the past. I wouldn't trade the person I am, or what I've done, or the people I've known, for anything. So I do think about it. And at times it's a rather mellow trip to lay back and remember.*

In this, Teddy and I agree.

STAGE 3: UPHEAVAL

Your anticipatory grief is running out because the ill family member still breathes even though their life is falling apart. Rage and resentment become constant states. Everyone needs to communicate in this stage, but who really wants to?

People must think, when will it be over? While they'll never admit it, everyone craves closure. There's no joy in watching pain played out on an extended tour. There's a moment when something in you shifts. You've done the work. You've made the arrangements, interviewed the hospice nurses. You are told in the end she will require oxygen, and part of you wonders, why bother? Why bother torturing her with air when she'll invariably lose it?

At one point, you and James sit in a room that is not in your house and you both wonder aloud, when will this be over? When will she die? When will her illness cease making demands on your time?

You need "you" in this stage because resorting to the first-person "I" is unimaginable. Sometimes you need to move through different voices, varying points of view. This makes life tolerable.

You need distance.

You need to play daughter, play nice; your part is the grief-stricken daughter and there is no dress rehearsal. This is the show. Curtain rises. Hit your mark.

You hold James in your arms while he weeps.

You don't cry, you only sleep.

A young Jim Jones once threw his Bible to the floor and shouted to his associates, "Too many people are looking at this instead of looking at me."

When will you die?

One day near the end, Ellie studies you. Says with a sincerity you don't recognize, "I worry about you. What will become of you when I'm gone? How will you live your life then, now that the war is over?"

You tuck her in, crush pills, and press them onto her scabbed tongue. Lately she's complained that it hurts to swallow. Even water has become an assault.

"I'll manage."

STAGE 4: RESOLUTION
The terminal family member's health rapidly deteriorates, yet these moments are punctuated with false hope. Stabilization occurs, corners are turned, and everyone considers the word "hope." But in the end everyone knows what's coming, and this is the stage where grudges and old jealousies

are settled and everyone boards the memory train. Everyone pantomimes: remember when? Everyone dusts off the family albums they were all once too excited to keep hidden.

Ellie drifts in and out of consciousness. But today, she's stronger in a way that makes all of us think she's turned a corner. Maybe we should've gotten a second opinion. Maybe we didn't need the stages, a manual for grief. She's laughing. She's talking to Cassidy again, and she says the words *photo* and *cock*.

"Hope, sister. Hope."

Ellie climbs out of bed, says she has an urge for toast.

"You know you can't eat that," I say.

"I'll eat whatever the fuck I want," says Ellie.

The phone rings.

"Tim?" says Ellie.

Life's unfair, really. You're given hope only to have cancer snatch it away.

"THERE ARE NO pictures of her before she was ten," I say. I hold a photo album in my hands. I cup a photo of Ellie and me in my hand.

"You know why."

"I wasn't asking a question."

STAGE 5: RENEWAL

The terminal terminates. The final stage of grief begins with the funeral and the celebration of the now-departed family member's life. The marker of loss is weighted with the celebration of life. Everyone's looking forward.

I leave her room for the yard. There are seeds to plant. I watch Ellie and James in a room. I scan photographs of urns on my phone. I think about my mother. I think it's time for rest.

THE DAY ELLIE DIED
2013

"I SAW A television show about a woman who loses her husband in an accident. He was on that damn phone of his, and at the moment he starts laughing at some video of a man pretending to be a cat, a real man, a really drunk one, smashes into his car. The husband dies instantly. But the woman lives in an age somewhat like our own, but more advanced. A technology exists, available only by invitation, where you can communicate with the dead if you're lucky enough to have most of your life online. There are no guarantees. The woman's lucky because the husband was attached to his phone, captured and shared every moment of his life with it, so when they finally speak, she hears his voice, which is generated from all the videos he shot of himself: husband in front of the Grand Canyon, racking up roaming fees, then threatening to jump (he was kidding); husband recording the woman while she slept, whispering, *I love you, I love you* . . ."

There are tears in Ellie's eyes.

Outside, Kate yanks at things.

"What's this all about, Ellie?" James says. "What are you getting at?"

"How about staying the course for a change. With you, with her, I'm never able to finish a story."

"You've always been the story."

Ignoring James, Ellie continues. "So the woman goes crazy with grief, orders a physical version of him. He arrives on her doorstep and she activates him, the love of her life, with chemicals and bath water. When he gets out of the tub, he's naked, born again, and she looks at him and says, 'You look like him on a good day,' and he says . . ." Ellie can barely contain herself. She kneels down to the floor and sits there. "He says, 'Why did we only keep our most physically flattering photos? Those were the times we were most unhappy?' Over the course of the night they make love, he cracks jokes—all from the memory track in his phone, and at one point the woman says that he's not enough. This version of her husband is good enough on a good day, but never enough. He doesn't come close to the man she loved."

"Let me take you to bed." James kneels down gently, moves toward her, and she recedes. Inches back along the carpet to the wall.

"Don't come any closer. Don't you fucking come near me. I know you. I know what you've done. What you're doing and how long you've been doing it. We had a fucking deal and you blew it because she wagged her pussy in your face. You couldn't wait a few months, until they threw dirt on my face and talked about how beautiful I once was. *She was taken too soon, oh the humanity*, or some such shit—you know how everyone we know talks." Ellie looks at him as if for the first time. "You couldn't wait for my death and the money that comes with it. Tell me, James. Was I ever completely enough, or just enough on a good day?"

"Oh, I get it. Suddenly I'm the villain because I spent the better part of my life lying next to a woman who didn't want me and I got sick of it? I'm the bad guy because I woke up one day and realized that I'm hired help and maybe the payday wasn't worth it? That I'm no better than Tim and those other men you left behind. For over twenty-five years I brought your coffee, asked about your day, and fucked you when and how you wanted me to—I gave you the best parts of me while you gave me leftovers. What else do you want?"

"I want nothing," Ellie says. She remembers a time when James was a paragraph in a personal ad, when he was four lines of hope and possibility. He could take her away from all her familial history, but when she'd pulled up to his home with her daughter, he'd lost his sheen. *If the wings of the butterfly are to keep their sheen, you mustn't touch them.* James was a man like any other man, and the only difference was he won because of his geography. He would never move to Nevada; he would never live in the house in which Ellie grew up, the place she'd once called home. He was a trip to California she couldn't complete on her own because all those years ago, she was the girl in Annie's story. She was the girl who saw the speeding cars on the highway and turned back. Headed home. She was the girl who became a woman who went home to a man. The road home was long and dark and scattered with the breadcrumbs she left in her wake. Ellie kept a house, raised a daughter, and swallowed pills. How do you explain that you didn't have leftovers to give because nothing existed to begin with? Ellie thinks about Tim. We don't choose who we love; we only choose to live with the parts that come with that love, and only now does she realize that she has devoted the whole of her wasted, brief life to bearing the penuries of that devotion.

Ellie loved the fact that James was a fixed point on a map, immovable. Who would've known that after all these years she would be the one who wanted to move back to that dark country, to any country really, if only it would allow her to love, to *feel* all of it again and again? Now her heart is breaking more than she thought it could, and when she finally wants everyone to care, no one does.

"I tried, Ellie. God knows I tried. But you never let me in, all the way in."

Ellie wonders if under his skin lies a beating heart. Or has it gone cold, like the rest of him? Ellie remembers how her heart was a door that opened once. *Be careful, his bow tie is really a camera,* Tim sang Simon and Garfunkel loud and off-key. They were children faking snow angels on spring grass. Their arms moved so fast it was as if they were preparing for flight. *If we could stay here, just like this,* Ellie said. *What would happen?* Tim asked. Ellie turned to him, smiled, her heart and eyes as wide as the ocean when she said, *We'd be happy.* But as swiftly as that door crept open it slammed shut when Tim's mother died and Ellie was left to marry a man, Tim, with whom she'd pass her life but never live it. Tim and James tried, with their skeleton keys and crowbars, but they never managed to push their way in. Ellie's deepest regret is the fact that she never thought she could go with Tim.

James and Ellie sit across from one another. He picks lint off his sleeve and she traces the edge of a mug filled with coffee that has gone cold. Ellie will die in five hours, but now, right now, all she feels is the enormity of everything she's lost.

"How could you fuck her in my house? *My house.*" Ellie's voice splinters.

Kate walks into the kitchen and takes a loaf out of the cupboard. Ellie reaches for two slices because the only thing she can bear right now is toast. Ellie looks at her daughter, regards her as paper—a body that could easily crumble, a heart that steadfastly cuts.

"I have to go," James says. He takes one of the hairclips that Ellie left on the counter and puts it in his pocket.

"I wonder," Ellie says. "Where does everyone go when they say they have to go?"

Kate grips the counter with her hands. James slams the door shut. The toaster oven breaks the silence. The kitchen smells of things burning.

WE PASS IN PARTS
1985

"DO YOU KNOW sometimes, at night, my mother burns her hair in the bathroom? She pulls it out of her hairbrush and creates little balls, like tumbleweed, and sets it on fire? She says she likes the way it smells, but it makes me sick and I have to breathe into my shirt or this blanket I carry around. She hides matches all around the house, places where she thinks no one will look, but I always find them. The matches. It's like hide and seek, only Mom doesn't know I'm playing."

I am ten and doctors ask the strangest questions.

"Why don't you tell me about the pool, Kate? Can we talk about the water?" one of them asks. I know they're doctors because my mother tells me this, but they're not wearing white coats or metal tubes around their necks, the instruments they use to listen to my heartbeat. They wear pants and shirts and write in their notebooks with blue pens. They ask so many questions.

"What's there to say? Water's cold and it kills you. I can't eat lobsters, you know. Can't stand the sight of them. Once, Mom brought a bag of them home, and I screamed—wouldn't you after seeing giant red bugs moving real slow? And then she threw them in a pot of hot water and I waited for them to scream. Do lobsters scream? I know I would if my skin was being burned off. Now I can't look at red things, like the sky before it gets dark or Stop signs." I chew the end of my braid because I like to get my hair wet, not like the water in the pool, but my wet. Hot water kills you too, I guess.

I am ten.

I look around my room for my clock, a windup that sounds like a ringing telephone when the alarm goes off, but it's been moved. Somebody moved it. It used to be over there, next to the chair with no legs. "How long do we have to keep doing this?" I ask the men.

"For as long as it takes, Kate."

"Why do you keep saying my name like that, like I don't know it?"

"If it makes you uncomfortable we don't have to say your name at all."

It makes me uncomfortable.

I hear my mother's voice coming out of a tape recorder: "I can't take those pills anymore; they mess with my head. Make me see things that aren't there. These pills are picking at a wound until there's nothing left but the ache of a life that used to be there. What I did in that pool was merciful. Because who wants this for their child? To crawl into the same hole her mother can't bandage up?" The men press the Stop button and her voice is gone.

"Do you always touch things that aren't yours?" They put the tape player in a bag and zip it shut. No one trusts me with their things.

"Yes." I tap my fingers on each of their thighs, high up, and say, "Mine." Their mouths make an *O* and they write things in their notebooks. I ask them if they're writing a story, and they say, "Yes, a kind of story. A story about you and your mother, and we need help filling in the blanks. Can you do that for us? Why don't we start with the pool? Can you swim?"

"Fish tank," I correct. "Four feet of water, and I dog paddled and kicked my legs, fast, like a fish. I wore the blue bathing suit my father gave me. It felt so soft that I kept rubbing my hand across my tummy, until the heel of my hand got real hot and I wanted to crawl into the pool to cool off. I brought my marbles with me, the clear kind, the ones you can see through. I put them in the pocket of my shorts and held them in my hands. Safe."

The men look at each other, and then they look at me. "Where was your mother? Was she already in the pool?"

"Of course she was," I say, rolling my eyes. "She's always everywhere first. She was in the pool wearing her nightgown. Told me her name was Ingrid."

"A nightgown? Ingrid?"

"Yes, *yes*. Can't you hear me right? For doctors, you

guys don't seem all that smart. Anyway, people got used to her wearing funny stuff in the pool. Sometimes Mom would swim in my dad's suit, other times her wedding dress, or in a sheet she'd wrap around her body. She'd wave her hands in the air and yell, 'Just call me Mummy!'"

"Let's get back to the nightgown, to yesterday. Did you notice whether your mother was acting any different than usual? Headaches? Saying strange things, anything out of the ordinary?"

Why are these doctors asking stupid questions? I thought doctors were supposed to be smart. I'm smart because my mother tells me so. Mom told me to forget about the pool and it's forgotten, so why are these people, these men she let into our house, making me remember? I chew on my braid again. The men walk around the room and I hate that they're touching things. Did they take my clock? They pick up some of the books my mother reads to me: *The Awakening* and *Laughter in the Dark,* by some Russian writer whose name I can never pronounce. They pause in front of a videocassette of *The Shining.* The men ask me where all the children's books have gone off to.

"They're for simple people," I say. "My mother says I'm not that kind."

"What kind are you?"

"The kind of girl who doesn't want to read stupid books about seeing a dog run, or stories about stupid Ramona helping her dad quit the smokes when everyone knows that you can't beat an addiction." The doctors write in their little books. "Did I tell you about a boy I saw today, a boy who pulled the wings off flies? He just sat there in the middle of the sidewalk, just him and his jar of flies." I hold my breath for a minute, trying to get brave, and then I ask, "Did you take my clock?"

"No," they say.

"Someone did."

"You watched this movie?" they ask, pointing to *The Shining*. I nod, proud, and say that I saw it when I was five. Back then it was confusing and loud, but now it comforts me like a record played again and again. "How does this comfort you?" They hold up the box cover with a picture of Jack Torrance. I roll my eyes because again with the stupid questions. "It's nice to know there are others like Mom, except she doesn't run around with an axe like some crazy person shouting about three little pigs. Ha. Ha."

"It didn't scare you?"

"No. It's a movie. Make-believe. Also, my mother would never wear the same outfit two days in a row like Jack. I've seen her change her clothes, sometimes, three or four times in one day. Watching the movie is like being with Mom even when she's asleep. See?"

"I see," they say, nodding slowly.

I know they have my clock. I can hear it ticking.

With my books I create a circle around me so the men

can't get in. Safe. "My mom always has headaches, says strange things. But that's the way it's always been. That's just Mom. All work and no play," I singsong. "Burning hair in the bathroom. Swimming in panties and a hairnet. Mom told me that adults have to lie to children until they're found out, until the lies pile up so high like snow and they can't see past them."

"I wouldn't call it lying. There are some things too complicated for a child to understand."

"Tell that to the Easter bunny, the tooth fairy, and the fat man and his reindeer that can't fit down a chimney."

"You're very perceptive for a ten-year-old."

"My clock's gone."

"Do you have any friends? Play with kids your own age?"

"Mom says a girl's best friend is her mother."

"Do you know why one of your neighbors would call the police on your mother? Do you know why we're here?"

"I thought doctors were supposed to know the answers instead of asking all the questions. Why don't you come out with it? You want to know if my mom tried to kill me, right? Because some lady in the pool screamed and told the cops that Mom held my head underwater for a long time. It *was* a long time and I *was* scared, but I'm here now. Mom told me all she wanted was for me to see light because it was so dark and she couldn't see. She didn't want me to catch the sads, and I believe her. I believe her!"

While I'm telling the doctors this, I start crying and the tears won't stop. All this water could kill you if you're not smart about it. "You don't understand us."

"We have an idea."

Downstairs my mother is smoking a cigarette because she has an addiction. My father, Tim (I have to say Tim instead of father because those are Mom's rules), puts a bowl of noodles in front of her and she gives him that mean look (sometimes she growls but not today, not in front of the doctors), and says, "Why would I want this?"

I love Mom but sometimes she can be a little mean.

She holds her gold lighter, the one she bought at a yard sale, the one the seller said used to belong to Lionel Barrymore. When I asked, *Who's Lionel Barrymore?* my mother shoved me away and said, *An actor from old movies.* I hid under the bed and kept saying *Lionel Barrymore*, imagining an old man with cotton-candy hair living in a castle. Like a king. Not like Santa Claus, or God, who's Santa Claus dressed in white—no, not like those make-believe men. A king in a kingdom is real, and I could be queen.

Lionel and me. King and queen.

The doctors don't notice I've followed them downstairs. When they ask if I could sit in the other room, my mother says, "Kate stays here. Kate stays with me." The men grow quiet and when they speak it's so slow and soft you can hardly hear them. They don't sit on the chairs; they stand behind them. Why won't they sit down?

"You want to speed this up," my mother says. "I'm not five, or a moron, so don't speak to me like one." She holds her cigarette but doesn't smoke it.

"You're not smoking your cigarette," I say. "You're holding it, but you're not smoking it. You're a smoking addict, Mom, so smoke your cigarette."

"Oh honey, you'd be surprised just how much restraint I can exercise. Even now, as these fine doctors don't deign to sit in my chairs, but they'll drink my coffee and rifle through my things." One of the doctors begins to speak, but the other shakes his head, and they just watch my mother playing with her lighter, watch my father watching her.

Tim doesn't speak. You see, this is Mom's kingdom.

"Or maybe we can talk about that drunk who called the cops, the drunk who probably thought the water in the pool was an extended happy hour, a well from which she could drink, because wouldn't you get sauced if you came home to find your husband fucking some illiterate Fabco Shoes cashier on the bed you just made? And if the whore cashier was wearing your shoes, the expensive ones with the sequins, while she was fucking your husband? If it were me, and that sure as hell would never be me, I'd probably pour a bottle of vodka over my eyes. Then

I'd start seeing things that weren't there. So tell me more about your star witness and the tape recording you made of me before you read me my rights?"

"Why don't we talk about the books you've got in your daughter's room? Do you think they're appropriate reading material for a child?" one of them asks. He's the angrier of the two, and when he talks to my mother he spits through yellow teeth.

Mom notices the teeth and points at them, says, "You should do something about that. What kind of doctor are you if you can't fix your own teeth? And don't go blaming it on nicotine because I've smoked a pack a day since I was fifteen and I'm all white."

"Mom, my alarm clock is gone. The windup."

"I have it," she says, annoyed. "You don't need a clock when you have me. I keep good time."

I could cry! I could scream! Like lobsters in hot pots. Instead, I ball up my fists and count to one hundred.

"We saw the books. And the fact that you've completely isolated her from children her own age concerns us greatly. We are concerned with Kate's development."

Why are they talking about me as if I'm not here? What is my *development*?

"Maybe I should pour sugar down her throat or grow strawberry patches in her room and clip unicorns in her hair. Tell me, Mr. Hoffman, would filling Kate's world with delusion and fantasy be more appropriate?"

The other one sighs and says, "Your daughter owns a

movie about an alcoholic who tried to murder his family with an axe."

"There's more horror in one episode of *Sesame Street* than in *The Shining*."

"We're going to recommend that the child be removed from this environment while you seek professional help."

The child. This environment. Help. Those are the only words I hear.

"Should I lie down on the bed and have you fuck me? Or do you prefer the floor? I know you love it when my back burns," I hear my mother shout through the wall later that night. I crawl out of bed and sit outside their room. The door is open a little, and I see Tim wearing a white mask and a blue jumpsuit; he holds a big knife in his lap. Mom turns the lamp on and off, and all I hear is a constant click, and all I see is Tim moving the knife from knee to knee. I shake.

"Look at me having to do everything. Making you dress up like a murderer just so I can find you remotely interesting. So here's your script for the evening, Michael Myers. You meet a blond riding a blue bus and you take her home and kill her. Let's give her a name. Let's call her Ellie. But first you tell her how much you want to die. You tell her about the canaries your mother bought you, and how one day you opened the cage and the birds went wild, scattered, and flew out the window. You thought you did a good thing, right? But here's the rub—birds don't really come home or escape; they fly as high as they can and then they fall right out of the sky."

I see my mother's feet at the edge of the bed and Tim kneeling down and kissing them. I am ten.

"What if I told you that girl was already dead?"

"I don't even know what any of this means," Tim says. "This mask is making my face itch."

In the dark I feel a hand shaking under my sheets. "We've got to go. We've got to go," my mother whispers. I'm cold and confused. "What?"

"They came in my house and smashed all the windows," she says.

"Windows? What windows?" I ask, rubbing sleep out of my eyes. "The windows aren't broken." Mom is starting to act like Jack again, before the axe.

"It's like Humpty Dumpty, but I can't put it back together again. I collected all the shells but they only ended up cutting me. Stop eating your hair," Mom hisses. "You're always eating your hair. You got a lunchbox hidden in there?"

"I don't know what you're saying. Who's Humpty Dumpty?"

Mom turns on my night-light and I see her face, all wet with water. Again I ask about Humpty Dumpty— "Is he a real person or make-believe?"—and she mumbles out of the side of her mouth that this Humpty is no one I need to know. In her hand she holds a lamb mask. She pulls the mask over her face, covering it, and I'm scared. Not like water scared, but for real scared. Mom tells me we need to go. Put your clothes in this garbage bag.

I reach for the blue swimsuit I've hidden under my pillow. "What about Dad? Is he coming too?"

Mom shakes her head. "No, he's not. I left him with my parents' remains and I'm never looking back." With the lamb face on she sounds different. Funny.

What is she talking about? Remains. My body shakes. "Where are we going, Mom? Why are you wearing that face? Take it off. Take it off."

Oh the places we will go. We have brains in our head (she pulls a hat over my head). *We have feet in our shoes* (she puts on my shoes, left, then right). *We can steer ourselves in any direction we choose* (she shakes the car keys). *We're on our own, little lamb. And we know what we know* (Why does she have my bathing suit?). *And I am the one who will decide where we go.* Mom grabs my hand; she grabs the trash bag and says, "Run!"

I am ten.

Mom drives fast. The lamb face is gone, replaced by a cigarette, and she looks over at me when she says, "We'll need new names."

"I don't want to change my name," I say. "I like Kate just fine."

"It doesn't matter what you want; this is about what we need. Pick a name, any name. Think of it as a game. When I was your age, my mother gave me another name every other year, whenever she was bored or forgetful. Every new name meant I had to become a new person until my mother decided I would be someone else. Those were the rules. When I was Vanessa, I was a mean cheerleader who didn't wear underwear and played card games for smokes. When I was Amy, I played the flute and wore fake prescription glasses from the drugstore. One time I was Chuck, and I stuffed socks down my pants and didn't shave my legs."

"What did your teachers say?"

"They didn't know. It was a secret. And I only wore the sock in my pants when I was home."

"Weren't your friends confused?"

In a small voice Mom says, "I didn't have many friends. I wasn't really a cheerleader; I stole a uniform and practiced in the basement where no one could see me, until someone did and all the kids laughed at me. And I was a shitty flute player on account of I didn't know how to breathe, so I gathered up all the flutes and threw them in the pool. Back then I wasn't what you'd call subtle."

"I'm tired, Mom."

"The glasses used to give me headaches, and the principal called my mother when he found me banging my head on a locker because I wanted the pain to stop. But it never stops. No one tells you that, but it's true, Kate. The pain is with me, right here, right now, in this car. Even as I drive."

She's running red lights again. It's quiet outside except for a few dogs barking and a can being kicked into the street. I roll down the window to feel the air on my face, and part of all this feels good, like the night only belongs to Mom and me. But the more she drives the more I get tired, and soon all I want to do is go to sleep and wake up as Kate, in my bed, in my house, with my books around my feet. But there's Mom asking me to "try on Meg for size," as if I'm a shoe.

I am not a shoe!

"When are we going home?" I ask.

"We're not," she says. "They want to take you away from me, sweet Kate, and I can't have that. Besides, you don't even love your father, and we can always get new books."

"That's not true. That's not true at all. I love Tim."

"See! You can't even call him Dad."

"But those were your rules!" I sputtered.

"You always have a choice, Kate."

What choice?

"And besides, that man can't open a jar without saying, 'Mother, may I?' You want to grow up to be that weak?"

"I love him," I whimper. I look up at Mom and see shadows of trees on her face.

My mother stops the car, leans so far into my face our lips touch, and she says, "You love *me*."

In the morning the sun is hot and I can't see. A man leans into the car, kisses my mother on the lips, and says, "She awake yet?"

"You awake yet?"

"Where are we?"

"Morning, Gillian," my mother says, "It's time."

The man leans in further and shakes my hand. His name is James.

"Come closer," Mom says. "He won't bite."

James laughs and makes a joke about nibbling, a joke that's not ha-ha funny. "Your mother told me all about your father. It was brave what you did. Escape. After two days on the road, you must want to see your new room, right?" James opens the door and takes my hand. "You've got the biggest room in the house, Gillian. All the books you can read. All the dolls you can play with. No one's going to hurt you anymore."

Two days? Who said anything about hurt? I look down and my clothes are different.

We go inside the house.

My mother smiles like that day in the pool. "Don't worry," she says. "At home, we'll call you Kate. Our secret."

A boy sits on the couch and stares at a blank television screen. He looks at me and he laughs. My mother is here. I will soon learn that the woman who used to live in this house abandoned her son and husband for another man.

"Gillian, this is my son. Jonah."

COLD COMES THE NIGHT
2013

"CAN I TELL you about the first time I saw you? You looked sleepy and sad because Ellie had dragged you to come live with us in California, having made up some story about your father beating her and fucking you. They tell you kids never make up stories—that's for adults to do—so part of me wondered if Ellie's story was actually true, even if parts of it didn't belong to her. Who knows, you know? In the end, I remember sitting on the couch, meeting a girl called Kate. Do I keep telling you stories? Do you finally remember?" Jonah says.

"There's this thing with Minnie," I say. I've left the window open and I notice how the rain comes down in sheets. Tiny pools of water eddy under the sill. It's been a while since I've heard thunder and my body shudders from the thrash of it.

"There's always a thing with Minnie, with the cakes, with Ellie and that woman—there's always something that is never about you," Jonah says.

"Those girls on the news . . ."

"I don't think you're ready for that just yet."

I can only nod. That's all my body will permit me to do. Instead of closing the window I lean out of it, feel the cold on my face and the rain snake down my back. My instinct is always to close and recede, but I want to open. I want to run.

I ask Jonah how he knows all of this—my mother's history, my grandmother falling from the air like some weary star, Delilah Martin, the water and the bleach, Nevada.

"Ellie loved me," Jonah says, plainly. "Stories were the only thing she owned, the one thing that was exclusively hers. You were hers, but you weren't. I can't explain it."

"You're telling me I'm your sister, that *woman*."

Jonah takes my hand and guides me into the one room that has a mirror. He stands beside me and takes my hair in his hands and I imagine it feels like gristle to him. Charred edges already bluntly cut. A neck (now shivering, now slick) dressing that requires constant changing like laundered sheets on an old mattress. Skin removed because of a lifelong betrayal—*Fuck. You have to know I didn't mean it*, said Gillian, repeats me—and reborn because of a chrysalis, because of a stepbrother who followed me and dragged my screaming body (and I was a kicker, I was) out of that dark hotel room I paid for with my stepfather's credit card. I remember Ellie telling me about Nevada. In life, would I ever make that kind of journey, if a journey were indeed the one thing that needed to be made? Will you forgive me, Mother, for being a silent observer as you ended your single, sad life? Here is my shorn, dead skin in my hands; I mix my skin with your ashes and wonder if that is the very definition of forgiveness. Will my burning in a cheap hotel room ever be enough punishment? When does one broken life cancel out a deliberate death?

Jonah said then what he repeats now, all baritone and tenor sax: "I will not lose you to the dark."

"What if I deserve it? What if the thing I broke can't be repaired?" I remember a car ride into the black night and my mother humming: *All the king's horses and all the king's men, couldn't put Humpty together again.*

"Everyone needs to be broken in some way," Jonah says.

"Gillian," I say. "I'm that woman." I'm a woman carved in two, a delicate caretaker of masks. I went into this thing with James as Kate and remained as Gillian. Jonah is here and I am here and you know how it is. Gillian wanders in and out of the frame. And Lionel, I suspect he's making the rounds, too. The storm, you wouldn't believe. I think: I'm lonely. Does it hurt? Yes. Does it stain? Yes.

All of the children have come home to play house.

"Kate," Jonah says.

"Kate," he repeats.

"I am so sad," I say.

"And tired, I imagine," Jonah says.

That night we sleep like children, curled up under the

kitchen table. Clutching our clothes for warmth, we're soothed by the lullaby of each other's breaths. I dream of Alice's mother, Lulu, a woman I once knew only slightly. A mother who carried wind chimes in the shape of airplanes in her purse. Through a face full of tears, I remember telling Lulu this: "But we *are* children."

SHE HAD HAIR the color of animal pelts, a mix of mink and sable. Jonah told himself, this is the last time, final straw, last call, no refunds or exchanges. He lay down on the bed, simply to feel the imprint his sister's body made. This was Kate's room, sacred territory, and he felt sick for having violated it. Jonah contemplated the burden of murder and the stains humans leave behind. There was a woman in the bathroom and her hair was on fire, homage to his stepsister's desperate attempt at punishing herself for sleeping with her dying mother's husband. What was important here was the hair and how the perfume of it hung heavy in the air, even after this woman Ikaria's death. Had that been her name? Lionel was right about him botching the basics . . . As if the completion of this act absolved Kate of all that she had done to herself. As if he could erase his sister's pain and replace it with a fresh wound, a new hurt. For a moment Jonah believed his own fiction until the rain came down and the fire alarms blared. This time he didn't wrap up his gift; the shower curtain remained intact and the body, the wreck of it, limbs akimbo and eyes supplicating and wide, remained untouched from the time when he'd urged her last breath out. There were prints everywhere. What he did take was her wallet. Her name was Ilaria and she had a small child. He shoved the wallet in his mouth as far as it could go.

Later, in his car, Jonah curled up in a ball and sobbed. He'd taken all the mothers he could take, but the ground continued to give way and his fall continued to be bottomless. There was only his stepsister lying in a hospital bed from burns whose origin doctors couldn't understand, and she woke as Gillian even though he pleaded, he fucking begged, for Kate. The small girl rubbing sleep out of her eyes with balled-up fists, the teenager who was content to live within the confines of her head, and the woman who ran through the trees—in the mess that was Gillian, somewhere was Kate. And Kate gave him hope when Gillian was so intent on taking it away.

"SHE KNEW, DIDN'T she?" I say.

Jonah is in the kitchen scrambling eggs. "You mean about you and James?"

"Yeah."

"Not at first, but in the end she knew. You weren't exactly discrete."

"I was lonely, and he was just . . . there."

Jonah turns to profile and smirks. I remember this. He comes back like a torrent, and we're teenagers again, waging our minor wars. Too stubborn to wave the white flags we never owned. Those eyes, so impossibly blue. "You fucked my father out of proximity? I'm not judging here—I mean, who am I to judge—but you can't honestly tell me you took up with James while our mother lay dying because he was in arm's distance. Pick up a man in a bar, take him home, and fuck him rough and raw—that's convenience. This thing with James was about love, hate, and revenge."

"*My* mother," I snap.

Jonah places a plate of eggs and charred bits of bacon in front of me and smiles in a way that implies victory. "You keep holding on to that."

THIS ONE WAS older. She had the face of a bird: pinched mouth, sallow cheeks, and squinting eyes. She couldn't be more than thirty, but there was something different about this one. Just below the surface of her skin, Jonah could detect a ravaging, as if the layers beneath had become impatient, as if her body wanted to get on with the business of decay. This one wanted death, opened her doors to it. Before he could pull the blade out of his pocket, she laughed, and in that laugh Jonah felt something inside him shift. He felt with the pickup of this doll—What was her name? He always knew their names—that he was on the precipice of a new horror. He didn't know that this would be the last time he sat beside a woman with a knife edging out of his pocket. It had been a month since his sister came home from the hospital and she didn't even remember being there. She was Kate, baker of cakes, and Jonah continued his night work.

"I know who you are. Why do you think I picked you up?" The woman paused. "I want to get the job done, but I'm too much of a pussy to do it."

"Now what job would that be?"

"I'm looking for a fast exit, and I think you're the one who's going to get me where I need to go. I just ask that you close my eyes and be quick and clean about it. I'm kind of a perfectionist."

"You think this is a joke? Some sort of game?" There was no begging, only a willful surrender. Why else would a woman take the back roads in the middle of the night, if not to drive directly into the dark, into a predetermined ruin? It struck Jonah that this had been the thing he'd once loved about Lucia—her desire to tumble below the surface, to become less than zero—until he realized, albeit too late, that she didn't want the dark; what Lucia desired were twinkling indoor lights, a carton of slick noodles, and a marathon of romantic movies. All the things that Jonah wasn't equipped to give. What Lucia wanted was to flee her wounds. In the end, it was Jonah who was the scab-picker, pain-burrower, fucking *pain tourist*. But this woman—*What was her goddamn name?*—with her hand steady on the wheel, was already measuring her own grave.

"Am I laughing? I put an ad on Craigslist, but everyone I met thought I was into S&M. It's like, I'm the only one looking for a killer and I get suburban men in dog collars."

Jonah thought: I should kill her. I should take off this belt and wrap it around her neck. Tie a fucking bow. In the distance he could feel Lionel, practically see the fucker tapping his feet, as if he were announcing his retirement. Jonah remembered his father and a story about a dog with mange he'd made up. Why was Jonah thinking of a shivering dog biting at its skin until there was no more skin? Remember the tweezers in your hand? Who do you think put them there?

"You're going to leave this to me, aren't you?" Jonah said, without realizing he'd said this out loud. He thought, Not you, but her smile, in profile, was an affirmative, Yes, me.

"I've got a gun in the glove compartment," she said. "I'm thinking that might be quicker than that belt you're carrying. Unless you're a lousy shot—I didn't think of that. All those other girls were choked. Or maybe we should go with the knife, but aim for the big arteries. I don't want to be lying in the middle of the road for hours, bleeding."

There was no Lionel. There was only Jonah in a car with a headache. He considered jumping out, going for one of the regulars, a doll who pleaded, someone who had someone to go home to, but he was in the middle of nowhere. He'd have to walk all night to get to the nearest town and he didn't have the shoes for it.

"I'm dying," she said.

"We're all dying."

"Yeah, well some of us are on an accelerated timeline. I've got leukemia."

"Don't you get that when you're a child?"

"Are you seriously second-guessing my illness? Look in my bag. Read the labels on the pill bottles, smart-ass. While you're there, can you grab my smokes? I'm suddenly concerned that you're not going to go through with this, because who kills a woman dying of cancer? There's just no kick in stabbing a woman with one foot in the grave."

Jonah checked the bag. Read the multisyllabic labels: clofarabine and methotrexate. How would he know which medications someone who has leukemia takes? This woman was dying—the sack of pills and barbiturates confirmed *something* was wrong.

"During my third round of chemo, my husband left me for his yoga instructor. It would be funny if it weren't such a cliché. Can you hand me a smoke? Don't deprive a woman of her addiction."

Jonah lit a cigarette and pressed it into her open mouth.

"And then there were my friends, who walked the

breast-cancer walks even though I didn't have breast cancer and created a website for me, a fucking online memorial. I mean, were they searching for every unflattering photo of me to post on Facebook? Was this payback for blowing their boyfriends in high school?" The woman sighed. "It's amazing how all of the energy wears thin after round three of chemo. At this point, everyone wants a miracle or a casket."

"That's pretty cold, lady."

"That's cancer."

"What's your name? It occurs to me that we've been driving for an hour and I don't even know your name."

"Does knowing that help in what you do?"

"What is it that you think I do?" Jonah said. "Don't you think I'd be doing it already?"

"This could be your foreplay. It's not good unless you drag it out: make the girl feel like she has the possibility for survival, that maybe she's the one who will be spared. She'll run barefoot into the road with blood on her face and some trucker will flash his lights at her and pick her up. But listen here. I'm handing you a sure thing: the girl with her panties at her ankles and a rubber in her teeth."

"You watch a lot of bad movies."

"I know you," she said. "You want to know how I know you?"

It was as if Lionel were nailed down to a rocking chair, lighting a pipe, and taking in the scene. Wondering how it was all going to play out. "How do you know me?"

"You're the Doll Collector. I know this because my sister is the girl who got away. Mia. Left for dead, you know, before you got into the doll thing, and the cops got her in a safe house for the past year because every case needs a living witness."

"I don't know what you're talking about," Jonah said. Mia. Black bangs that curtained her eyes, and he only remembered her vividly because right before he plunged the knife in her stomach, she started to sing Leonard Cohen's "Hallelujah." He'd been messy that one time. Wouldn't you be if you learned that your sister had been fucking your father? Sorry, *stepsister*, but did that really matter in the scheme of things?

"Oh, I think you do. Before you get it into your head that this is some sort of vigilante thing, I should tell you that my sister is the yoga instructor my husband's fucking. It would be funny if it weren't such a cliché. The police have a sketch of you, but you're good. Always in disguise—sometimes you're dressed up like a woman with red or blond hair, right? You're hard to find."

"*You* found me."

"It took time."

"You're going to drive to the next town, and you're going to leave me there. And then you're going to keep on driving."

"So you're a cocktease? Is that what you're trying to tell me? Is it my sister? I can tell you where she is. I can write down the fucking address."

"God, no. You're not even listening. You hear how crazy you sound?"

"I'm not the one taking a needle and thread to a dead girl's mouth." The woman was hysterical. "All I hear is some little bitch who can't get it up. What? I'm not good enough for you? You stab my sister in the stomach but you can't even put a knife in my back. What is that shit? Act like a man."

In a small voice, Jonah said, "Pull over."

"Like hell I am. You're going to take that knife you got under the seat and stab me in the neck."

Jonah punched her harder than he meant to, and the car spun out of control and crashed into a tree. He's a child again, playing with Kate, with Gillian, with his father's blood on his hands. The woman's head smacked against the glass, shattering it, and when he leaned over and felt for her pulse, checked for signs of life, he couldn't help but laugh over the fact that she was dead.

Jonah carried her out of the car and laid her down gently onto the grass.

"Let me hold on to this," he said aloud.

THE DAY MY mother dies we make toast. We're watching an old film from the 1950s, *The House in the Middle*. My mother is often tense with the remote, never quite satisfied with the channel she's on because the possibility of something else, something better, exists just out of her reach. So she spends a few minutes flipping through the channels, everyone's voice a note in staccato, until she pauses at this film on the History Channel. She says, "You know, Kate. This reminds me of . . ."

We watch as a home that bears the earmarks of untidy housekeeping—cluttered papers and unkempt linens inside, and decayed wood and dead grass outside—is doomed to destruction. We await the bomb and the fireball, the fate of a house left to neglect. When the house in disrepair explodes, my mother says, "Can you believe this is the kind of bullshit we were raised to believe?"

In a few days, I will take a match to my hair and quietly watch the blaze from down below. My hair will smell like the sourness of sick children. Just in case I don't make it out, I'll tape a note into the palm of my left hand. (I'm left-handed, which will make the striking of the match tiresome for both of us.)

But right now the phone rings and my mother mutes the volume on the television set. Houses like mine detonate in silence while homes with whitewashed walls and hanging succulents remain standing; the clean and austere endure the devastation. I glance at my mother and then at the trembling wood and I can't tell which will blow first. My mother utters, "Tim? I can't. I just can't." When Ellie puts down the phone she repeats his name without speaking; her mouth moves but no sound comes out. When I ask her about Tim, the man who is not James, not a man who exists in the space between my stepfather and lover, she is shrapnel. She is bone.

"I bet you'd like to know who he was," my mother says.

"I don't know what you mean," I say.

"Tim will be dead so it doesn't even matter," she says, ripping the plastic off a loaf of bread.

Ellie makes a tower out of the slices, placing one on top of the other, brick by brick. This is her house within her house. I lose control of my mouth; I tremble. There's still time to explain. There's still time for her to understand that fucking James wasn't my doing; I wasn't flashing No Vacancy signs in a house teeming with leftovers of a family. She has to understand there are factors at play beyond my control. There is a father who requires constant surveillance. There is a woman whose body is a house that won't withstand the blast. When I was small my grandmother, Norah, waved to me from the roof of our house before she tumbled through the air and landed in the grass. All those ruined flowers, I thought. All that theater to show that she could fly. I raced over to her sleeping body and shook it. *Wake up*, I said. *Quit playing pretend.*

Come back and play. Why is it that no one likes to play? Why is it that I'm always left alone to invent the games?

"Men are always ready to trade in for younger versions of you. It's still you, but with lighter hair and a tighter face. A body that has not traveled like I have," Ellie says, slathering cold butter on toast, tearing it, but not noticing it.

I take my mother's hand in mine and pry the toast from under her clenched fist. She leaves the room as violently as she entered it. The ticking is the bomb. The house is on fire. No way out. The voices are here with me and they are shouting.

Pausing at the doorway she says, "You keep holding on to that."

THE VICTIM, IDENTIFIED *as thirty-five-year-old Julia Cassavetes, suffered severe face lacerations and contusions to the skull. The victim is at McGinley Hospital where she is in a medically induced coma. Family members are devastated, as Ms. Cassavetes has been fighting a five-year battle with leukemia. Police are on the hunt for a suspect after another blood sample was left at the scene. Investigators are hesitant to link this incident to the Doll Collector murders . . .*

Jonah regards the scar on his hand from where the knife burrowed its way in. Jonah also thinks this: the woman isn't dead.

"Want to talk about it?" I say.

"Not particularly."

"Was it you, Jonah? Did you hurt those women? Were you in the car with that woman?" I point to the television where a woman's face is splashed across the screen, along with a website and the name of an organization that is accepting donations for Julia's treatment. The photo of the woman isn't a particularly flattering one.

Jonah peels the skin off an orange and seems momentarily satisfied by it, as if this small act of savagery is a Band Aid for a monstrous, incurable ache. He peels all the oranges in the bowl but leaves the flesh intact. "Remember Alice? The roommate who had you sucking cock for blow?"

I flinch.

"See, I knew it. It's all coming back, isn't it? It was only a matter of time. I know the things she made you do when all you wanted was to come home. It was James's idea, you know, to ship you off to boarding school. All he needed to do was put a fucking whisk in your hand and all was forgiven. It's because of him you were forced to do what you did."

"I don't want to talk about this," I stutter. "I want to talk about you, about those girls." I see a girl on all fours in the snow. You can never get the bloodstains out.

"And you know, rich girls like Alice never want to do the dirty work."

"So you killed her," I spit out.

"I still have to hold your hand, sweet Kate? Even after all this time? Alice was your masterpiece. Alice was all you. That little carve-up inspired a lifetime of work," Jonah says. Then something shifts—a movement of a voice from the front of the lips to the side of the mouth, and blue eyes that burn.

"Don't worry. I cleaned up your slop then, just like I'm cleaning out his slop now. Correction, cleaned, because apparently Jonah's in semiretirement."

Lionel.

"Lady, this is getting old. You gotta start taking responsibility. Own up for what you've done. Before you got on the scene, Jonah here was your garden-variety bed wetter. Sure, he dismembered a stray cat here and there, but he probably would've grown up to be a real pussy. Probably would've found him locked up in some shithole bathroom with his wrists all cut up. Then you came along, the girl with two faces and a man, me, who was just itching to come out of your skin. You gave Jonah a vision, a partner in crime, as it were, and an alibi. Women always get in cars when they see other women. Makes them feel safe, and you knew that. Hell, you gave Jonah *me*. Remember the lighter, Kate? Does Lionel Barrymore ring a bell? Or do you still believe your grandmother threw herself off the roof, when really she was pushed because that was one of the games you liked to play. Poor kid;

what you wouldn't do to get Ellie to love you. Hell, you even hate your stepbrother because Ellie loved him more than you."

Jonah shakes my shoulders. "Don't you see," he says.

My lips stop moving. I look in the mirror. I see Gillian. I see Lionel. I see all the dead girls, photocopy after photocopy of me.

I see me.

"Do you see now, Kate?" Jonah says.

I turn away from the mirror and recede. I see Alice's hair all matted in my hands. I see the rusted metal of a shovel as I dig a shallow grave for Lucia. I see my hands on wet mouths and on knives searing through necks. It occurs to me that my mother didn't die on that day from all those pills slipping, *slippery*, down her neck. No, I watched her death, and it was slow, invisible, a disappearing into nothingness. It occurs to me that there's no difference between her hand holding thirty pills in one moment of quiet desperation versus months of her smelling her husband in my hand. I had to burn it down; I needed to eliminate, *excavate*.

"Tell me that you see," Jonah says. There are tears in his eyes. Why is he crying?

I see James.

Sweet Kate, said James, before the pills and the fire. Before all of it, I was eighteen and on the floor with my stepfather watching dough rise.

After his wife's and my mother's body went up in flames, James stood at my door and said, *She didn't want to die. I know it was you. I don't know how I know, but what I do know is this: She was frightened of being alone with you. She was always frightened of you. Maybe that's why she let this thing . . .* (You fucking me?) *slide,* he finished. I haven't seen him since.

"I don't want to see," I cry out, closing my eyes.

WHERE THE CHILDREN SLEEP
1989, 2003–2005

WHEN I WAS fourteen, I saw a body in the snow. It was a boy, no more than five; his mouth gaped wide. He had hair the color of linens. When his heart gave out, he had been bouncing a ball in the snow. Yes, a ball in the snow. The boy had been a little slow in the head, and when they found him his mother sighed and said, *Good riddance.* Before they found the boy and wrapped his small body in a trash bag, I kneeled down in front of him and saw a speck of blood on his lip. I kissed him three times and ran away. Sometimes, if I close my eyes tight, I can still taste him in my mouth. How is it that beauty and ugliness could be one and the same?

When I got home that day, Jonah said, "Everyone dies. Sorry to break the news to you."

"Spoilsport," I said. "When I die, make sure you bury me right. No cutting corners. No polyester in the casket. Okay?"

"Even corners. Silk all the way," he said.

I was frightened of death, but I couldn't tell Jonah that. There was no room for fear in our house.

We had our own world, Jonah and I, and in this world there were rules. I would be called Gillian until the heat wore off, because, "Do you want to end up in a home for girls?" my mother threatened. "Try on orphan for size and see how fast you come running back to me," she said when I pleaded for my books, my room, and Tim, my father, who made sloppy peanut butter (the smooth kind, obviously) and jelly (strawberry, clearly) sandwiches with the crusts torn off. James tried hard to pick up where my father left off, down to the sandwiches. But he used that expensive jelly, those preserves, when I would rather have had Welch's strawberry. James tried so hard—you could feel the enormity of his love. Serving my lunch on a clean plate, James would bow and say, *Your majesty.* We'd collapse into laughter as I pulled apart the bread with my fingers, which had already gotten sticky from the jam. This was our secret ritual, our small world, which was a welcome retreat from all the books about deformity and despair, and the darkness my mother wore like a veil, as if she were a bride wedded to depression. I tried to make sense of the complicated stories she told me and I memorized as many words as I could—so much so that I made it my practice to memorize fifty words a day from the dictionary—but the space between us grew wider with the passing of each day, and I could never, for the life of me, get closer to her. Ellie was slippery, always just beyond my reach. It was as if she wanted me *not* to love her.

"Do you want me to lock you in the basement like my mother did to me? Because I can and I will. Don't you see that I'm trying to protect you? Don't you understand that all of this is for you? Can't you keep this going for me?" The intensity of her tears frightened me, and I folded into myself, desperate to be shielded from the steady pulse of her breath. As soon as she left the room, Jonah would parrot back her threats in a shrill, which made me laugh. "At least in a home we wouldn't suffer her perfume," Jonah countered. "Do they call it Chanel No. 5 because one whiff of it would send you fleeing to the nearest toilet for five hours of dry heaving?" He had a way of opening up the sky and letting the light in. His eyes were an industrial blue, and through him I felt my heart beating. We had to be patient; he continued with the rules. We had to swallow our voices, bide our time, and play the parts of the dutiful children, until one day our revenge would be the loudest sound. I understood Jonah's anger toward my mother—a recalcitrant, chain-smoking runaway whose clothes occupied the closets in his bedroom—but I never got the rage against his father, James, a man who appeared docile and liked the heat. When I pressed him, Jonah said, "You'll see in time."

Be Gillian. Swallow voice. Wait the stretch. By the way, be Gillian.

"You being here makes me stronger," Jonah said, flicking my mother's lighter, which he'd stolen. "You should know that, Gillian."

"Kate," I whispered. I'm good at this, I thought. Playing him. Pretending to be a girl.

Jonah narrowed his eyes. "You know the rules."

"That's Lionel," I said.

"Who's Lionel?"

I pointed to the lighter, to the fire Jonah was making. "Lionel," I said.

"Lionel," Jonah repeated, smoothing my hair.

My mother might have manufactured the name, but Gillian was our invention. We made her from scratch using a notebook and two pens. Gillian loved blueberry muffins, Holocaust films, and the volume on the radio turned way up. She blasted Joy Division and old Depeche Mode (specifically, "Never Let Me Down Again"), because there was something about artificial sounds that felt right to her. From my mother's drawer we stole a tube of lipstick, Cherries in the Snow, and colored a sheet of white paper with it. Our girl was free, clumsy, and willful in all the ways we weren't. We made her tumble down the stairs and trip over her feet. Her laugh was a series of open-mouthed snorts. Hers was a world that was lived, while ours was one in which we endured.

We spent days contemplating her hair and went through boxes of markers in pursuit of the perfect hue. Was it possible to fall in love with a color? To be so consumed by a single shade that it haunted your waking hours? One Sunday, we shook a bottle of peroxide onto my hair until it was bone white. "You look like a piece of chalk," Jonah beamed. In the bathroom mirror I surveyed the shape of my clavicles and fingered my ribs as if they were individual parts of an instrument I hadn't yet learned to play. When my mother crept up behind me and placed her hands on my shoulders and chin on my head, something in me stirred. Ellie said, "God, you're beautiful," and I finally understood how, the more I disappeared, the more I became visible to my mother. I began to fade into the scenery as my mother's affection for me swelled.

Barely a newborn, a half-written story on the page, and we'd already foretold Gillian's death by drowning, because although the water fascinated her, she would never learn how to swim.

"But *I* can swim," I said, to which Jonah responded, "That's the discipline."

"When they finally pull her out of the water . . ."

"Boys will find her. Notice how boys always find the dead girls?" Jonah said.

"They'll find her covered in leeches."

Jonah closed his eyes. "Gillian," he sighed. "Ellie can't come with you."

When no one was listening, James called me Kate. "Our secret," he said. It was fun sometimes, returning to me. Four years had passed since we moved to California, and I was getting the taste of Gillian and liking it. Meanwhile, Ellie was getting the taste of every man in a ten-mile radius.

"I'm bleeding," I said, one morning.

"What? Where?" James shouted. He grabbed my face, my arms, and my scalp.

I lifted my skirt and pointed to the naked space between my legs. "There," I said.

"What the fuck are you doing?" he said, retreating.

"You ever watch that movie *Carrie*? The scene where she gets her period for the first time and she thinks she's dying. All the girls in the locker room think it's fucking hilarious, and all you want to do is slap her in the face and tell her to get a maxi pad because the blood will always, inevitably stop, just like it'll always, inevitably start again. You just don't bleed out. Remember? *Plug it up! Plug it up!*" That day I wore my mother's lipstick, Cherries in the Snow.

"What the fuck is wrong with you?" he said, eyes wide and unblinking.

"Don't worry. No one bleeds out."

"We're going to have a little talk about this—me, you, and your mother."

"I'm giving you what you want. I'm giving you Gillian. Don't be pissed because you don't like how the story turned out."

He slapped me so hard it stung. "Kate's gone, baby," I said.

Jonah came from behind the door where he'd been listening, and clapped. His applause was like thunder. "Good work, your majesty," he said, handing me a sandwich.

Sometimes I could see the pictures as if it were yesterday. Dozens of blurry Polaroids of a boy's head bashed in with a shovel. Amid the twigs, leaves, broken bones, and bloodied teeth, I recognized the boy as Johnny McIntyre, a senior. All the girls called him Johnny Panic because he had a habit of forcing girls to their knees—even the young ones coming out of grade school—and making them say yes even when they shouted no. You never knew if he was going to hold your hand or hold you down.

"It didn't start out that way," Jonah remarked when I threw the Polaroids on his bed.

"What is this?" I shrilled.

"Well, that *was* Johnny McIntyre."

"I know who this is, asshole. I'm asking you what you've done."

Jonah fixated on one of the photographs until I snatched it out of his hand. In the foreground was what was left of Johnny's face and Jonah at the edge of the frame, smiling, one hand waving. *Tweezers in a hand. One blue eye, bleeding.* Sometimes I wondered if I did that to him. Made him bleed. Told him afterward that no one ever bleeds out.

"What *we've* done," Jonah corrected. "Who do you think took the picture? Who do you think always takes the pictures?"

"I was *here*," I said, emphatic. A flash of white—was it my hair or the clouded sky? A lip torn off and two knees cracked with a hammer. A cry for forgiveness, which echoed a cry uttered in a car in the back of a gas station. *Stop. I don't want to do this.*

"That's right, you were. And so was I." Jonah waved the photo, now aflame, and said, "It's a shame. You know this is the only picture of me smiling?"

"My God," I said.

"Don't worry," Jonah said. "You cleaned James's hammer."

I pulled the sheet over my head and closed my eyes.

"By the way, I liked that thing you did with your voice back there. It's sexy."

"We killed someone," I said. "A person."

"You act as if Johnny was the first time. You know, you really need to stop talking about the dead granny in your sleep."

"I wanted her to play with me," I said. I don't like them seeing me do it, but I know they can feel me do it. It's important that you feel this pain, that we feel it together. It's important for you to know that love is about the delivering and receiving of pain. This is about love. You have to believe me.

"Tell me about your first time," I said. Jonah and I lay under my bed. Just us mice with all our snacks.

"No, you first."

How could I know that my grandmother wanted to fly like some sort of bird? There's no way to describe the flutter of arms and the smack of a body onto grass; you only see the blood that stains it.

"One day my grandmother woke up and she stopped being here. She was in some other place, and she was happy. Every time she'd blink there'd be another face to replace the one she'd just seen in the mirror. So many eyes, she'd lost count. And the voices, my God, they were loud and constant. But they were comforting because they each represented a different part of her father, who died this gruesome death. My grandmother told me her father was a man who plucked out her heart and squeezed it until there was nothing left, so it was a relief to see it in pieces, not complete. Complete was terrifying. Complete was Norah in the house with nail clippers and bloody sheets."

"I don't understand."

"My mother was feeding my grandmother drugs that made her normal again. So one day my grandmother climbed on our roof because her father was afraid of heights and the roof was safe. I followed her up the stairs and held her hair back when she cried, because her father had found her! He was here! But no one was there, only the two of us. *Can you help me, Ellie?* But I wasn't Ellie; I was never what anyone wanted. So I pushed her and ran down the stairs and saw her on the ground. For a second, I regretted what I'd done, but then I realized this is what she wanted, and I gave her a kind of peace."

"It's always peace," Jonah nodded.

"Then people came into our home and talked to my mother about grief, about the method in which one should mourn a woman who landed a few feet from where her child stood. They never suspected me; they were strangely frightened of me, of what I'd seen and what it would do to me."

"Remember that boy you found in the snow when we were kids?" Jonah said.

"Yeah."

"That was mine. Think of the life he would've had. Last one picked for teams; a full scholarship to a school where he'd learn to build bombs while his roommates date-raped all the girls who told him they *just want to be friends*; a mother who passed out under the tent during his valedictorian speech; a bomb built in a shed that exploded in a building that he'd visited seven times for eight interviews only to hear the words, *We regret to inform you.* I did that kid a favor. He was Ted Bundy in the making."

"So you're a savior now?"

"Better than pushing Granny off a roof. The problem with you, Kate, is that you lack vision."

I didn't have the heart to tell Jonah that he was a liar. The boy we once knew died because his heart suddenly stopped. When the boy collapsed to the ground, he smacked his mouth on a rock and all this blood gushed out from a body that was no longer living. I guess it was easy to claim the kid when you didn't have the stomach to do your own work. I felt bad for Jonah, never able to finish what he started. I gave him his ego and strength for no other reason than the fact that I loved him. I would allow him to be the man that I was, would always be. I gave him me, Lionel, everything, until there was nothing else left to give.

We passed a box of Little Debbie cakes between us.

"I've got a problem. Gillian won't leave."

Jonah smiled. "The heart wants what it wants."

"Can you not do this? Quote TV movies of the week?"

"When you get like this, sometimes I wish she'd stay. You know, when she's here, your eyes get different. You also do this thing with your hair."

"What thing with my hair?" I demanded.

"You get it all messy, cover your face with it."

"You love *me*, right? More than Gillian? You're mine, right?"

"Who else's would I be?"

We wanted it all back, a childhood edited for television. Thirty minutes of joy with all the heartbreak and sorrow cut out. We wanted to hold the remote and press all the buttons.

Two years later, the police found Alice in parts. They dug up her blistered feet bound in twine and discovered her manicured hands in a bodega freezer. For two weeks, the owners lit red candles and covered their hands in prayer beads because they believed that Alice's hands were the beginning of the rapture.

The local news fixated on the "grizzly nature" of the murder, as if we were bears or something. They completely ignored the hair. How it was singed at the ends. How chunks of it were yanked out of her scalp and scattered around her face, which was found under the boardwalk at Coney Island. How I braided a strand of it into my own hair. I didn't mean for things to get messy with Alice—I just wanted her to apologize for what she made me do. We argued, and all I could remember was her screaming that I was a *hysterical joke*, and I got so close to her that I could smell what she had for breakfast, and I hit her until I felt the bones in her face crack.

Then there was Jonah. "I thought we were just going to scare her."

"Did you really believe that?" I said. Sometimes it was hard to appease his simplemindedness.

Then there was Lionel, *me*, with Alice's bank card in our hand. "We got to get rid of her." Ninety-five pounds never felt so heavy. "We got to get her light; we got to get her clean." I giggled uncontrollably over the thought of hauling a bag of Alice's bones to the dry cleaner. Could skin be starched? Could bones be pressed? The image of Alice covered in plastic, dangling from a wire, her face obscured by an I Heart NY logo, sent me reeling. I fell to my knees, laughing so hard I cried, and then I vomited. *Is evil something you are? Or is it something you do?*

Jonah dumped a duffle bag of tools at my feet. I held Alice close, took a lighter to her hair. Said my goodbyes. Lionel shook our head. "Don't get sentimental about this."

A week after I returned home from boarding school, James shipped Jonah off to art school. "He wants you all to himself," Jonah said, shoving shirts into the duffle bag that had once stored Alice's torso.

"You take everything from me." I confronted Ellie in the bathroom because I knew this wasn't James's doing. Divisions and subtractions were the exclusive dominion of my mother.

Ellie applied eye shadow to the creases of her lids. "Nothing's been taken from you, Gillian. You don't own Jonah. In fact, I can't think of a single thing in this house that you own."

"I liked you better when you were off your meds."

Ellie stared at her reflection in the mirror when she said, "I never liked you at all. I should've left you to rot in that school, but no, James wanted you home. Didn't want people to think we weren't concerned parents due to the fact that a murderer was loose and all. As if you had anything to worry about. As if I didn't know that Jonah used my credit card to take a little trip on a plane back east. Tell me, Gillian, do you think I'm blind? Do you think I don't know?" Her words were a wound that would never close, and I wonder now if her honesty was the only act of decency she could muster.

"My name's Kate," I seethed, and closed the bathroom door behind me. I leaned into her, close. I was taller than Ellie, and I knew she could feel my breath in her hair.

"Open the door," she said.

I kissed the back of her head and pulled her close. "Say my name," I said. "Because how long was I good to you? How long did I sacrifice?"

Tears flooded her eyes. Her eyes darted left and right.

"Look ahead, look at me," I said behind her, forcing her hips against the sink.

"Kate," she said.

"See? That wasn't that hard. Now we're going to stick with Kate for a while because I'm starting to realize that she is so much fun."

That night I watched her sleep. I opened my mouth to scream but no sound came out because no sound ever comes out. That's what it was like to love my mother.

WHEN I WAS eighteen I packed two suitcases filled with books. I would board a plane that would take me back to Alice, or at least my memory of her. I felt fear and it felt good. Every hour James delivered the weather report through a locked door while Jonah bounced a ball against the wall and shouted for James to *please shut the fuck up*. Reports from back east warned of storms. Maybe I should stay home, James wondered aloud. Maybe I shouldn't fly into the blinding dark. To which Ellie responded, "She's getting on that plane tonight."

"Gillian's gone now, for good?" Jonah said.

"Whatever made you think that?" I held the lighter in my hand. I was hungry.

"What's the plan?"

"Hibernation," I said. Ellie stole my childhood from me and I planned to spend the next eighteen years taking it all back. I traveled the distance between love and hate and all the desire, grief, and sadness in between, but in the end I found that I'd only inched my way to the middle of the two, and I would be forever stuck in this place of hating myself for needing my mother's acceptance and love.

"What do you need?"

"I need you to stay here and play house. I'll call you and you move to New York and I'll come back here to do what I have to do. What I need is for us to be on opposite ends of the playing field."

"That's cryptic. What is all this?"

I smiled, leaned over on the bed, and kissed Jonah on the cheek. "Reconstruction."

"YOU GOT THE keys I left you?" I said over a telephone line, years later.

"I met a woman on the plane," Jonah said. "She's the cover girl from the underwear catalogs you used to get."

"I don't wear underwear. And I don't need you meeting girls on planes—I need you out of California. I need you to not be a source of strength. Did you get the keys? Is the apartment like I described?"

"Haven't I always been your playmate? Fucking Christ, Kate, sometimes I don't think you ever want me to be happy."

"Who the fuck is *Kate*?" I said. "Is the glue uncapped? You're off your meds again? Wake up, Jonah. It's Gillian, your *sister*."

"Right," he said, quietly. "You're back."

"What are you talking about? I never left. Did you get—?"

"I got the keys. I'm in the apartment. I won't come back until you call for me."

"Good. I need you settled while I set things up here."

"Where are you?" Jonah asked.

"Home," I said. "Playing house. Mother sends her love. Don't worry. You'll see me in time."

I always wanted to be all of someone else.

WE WENT WHERE no one could find us. A year before my mother died, James and I met where the barnacles sleep and the ocean washes away what others discard. The sky settled into the horizon, the sand was still warm, and we dug our feet under the grit to find the cool spots. I pressed a handful of shells against my face to take in the stink of salt and sea, and he sat behind me, tugging at my hair while we spoke.

"I don't know why I continue to come here with you," James said.

"Do you have a better option?"

There was a day when the wind blew in the afternoon rain and my mother woke from a deep sleep. I'd moved home the previous month and we barely spoke. I stood over her bed and she pulled the sheet over her head and said, *Go away.* I tried to talk about that morning when Norah fell off a roof and plunged to the ground. I could never get the blood—there was a flood of it—and her wide-set eyes out of my head. I kneeled down and tried to close her eyes, as I thought that was the sort of thing you should do for the dead—don't tease them with a light they'll never see again—and later a man in an ambulance told me that you had to be dead for a good four hours for the eyes to properly close. The body was still rattling; perhaps refusing to accept that it would fade into the forever dark. Over time it would be forgotten. The roof would be painted and new grass and trees would be planted to replace the soil that received Norah. I tried to tell Ellie this but she stared at me with a blankness that made me think that she permanently resided in a place between her and her mother. *Why did you have to come back?* she asked. *Why did you make your brother leave?* Shaking my head, I said, *I made him leave? Don't you know about the girl he's living with? She models underwear, or used to. Now I think she just models it for him. Cruel world we live in where beautiful women are simply thrown away after they've passed their prime.* Ellie pulled the sheet from her head and said, *Aren't you tired? You must be.*

"I want to make something clear," James said. "I still love her. I never stopped, just because we come here and do these things."

"You fuck me but you still love her?" I said. "I guess I can accept that."

"It never bothers you, what we do? Sometimes I lie awake at night thinking she knows, she *must*, and then part of me wonders if we're slowly killing her. We're taking away the one thing your mother never had—a family. I tried to give it to her, all of it, but I couldn't. Not in the end. And you can't either. I guess that's how we ended up where we are. This is how it always happens."

Later, we took a room in a cheap place and James lay in bed, glowing from a single lamp that I kept flicking on and off. The evening descended, piece by piece. I saw Ellie's hair hail down in the shower.

James placed his glasses on the nightstand next to an empty glass of water. "I'm thirsty," he said. He twisted his ring round and round on his finger and tossed it in the empty glass.

"Suddenly you have a conscience about fucking me? Where's this conscience when you're shoving my head into the sand or renting hotel rooms where you strap belts around my neck? Conscience is convenient; it lies dormant and rises when the guilt rushes in or when the condom comes off. Whatever comes first, right?"

I started to turn around when James held my neck in his hands. "It's better if you look straight ahead."

In a certain light, I'm the image of my mother's mother.

"You should take off your shoes," I said.

"We'll get there."

Back then I still made mixtapes, and I pressed play on *Tosca*. An aria separated us.

"You should take off your shoes," I repeated. A libretto.

"We'll get there."

"I know I'm not supposed to say this, but I love you," I said.

I thought of the smallness of a child's hands.

"You're beautiful in all the right places," James said.

What are the wrong places? I wondered.

I LEFT MESSAGES, dozens of them. Why didn't Jonah pick up? He was playing me hot and cold. It was always late when I called, and sometimes I'd pass the time with Lucia.

"He doesn't talk about you," she'd said once.

"He doesn't talk about you either," I said.

The last time we spoke I said, "Let me tell you a secret." In a day's time I'd board a plane to New York because my dear brother wasn't holding up his end of the bargain—he'd refused to come home, acted like my calls were something he could dodge, *excuse*. Didn't he know that I was not one to be ignored? But I didn't tell Lucia this. Instead I said, "I'm coming to visit. It'll be a surprise. By the way, did you get the check I sent?"

Lucia had a surprise of her own. "I'm leaving him," she said. "So it's good that you're coming. He'll need family."

"That wasn't part of our arrangement." Why did everyone think that they could shirk their obligations? I lived in a world where no one saw anything through.

"Make new arrangements. The guilt has been killing me. How is it not ruining you?" Lucia said.

Who are we without our family?

"Goodbye, goodnight," I said to Lucia. *I'll see you in the morning.*

THE BUSINESS OF LEAVING
2013

"I TRIED TO kill you once," Ellie said a week before she died. I'd already planned what I was going to do to my mother—the pills, the pillow—I just didn't know when. "Well, twice actually. The first time didn't count because my motives were altruistic. I wanted to scrub your history clean with a little bleach, a little water—our family's sicknesses—but I wasn't successful. The second time, you were ten and I saw you swimming in the deep edge of a pool, and I knew you would never be as beautiful and innocent as you were at the moment when you were hungry and tired. Yet your life's ambition was for me to see you swim from one side of the pool to the other, and that kept you moving through the water. I had my chance," Ellie said, her face awash in tears. Her heartbreak and hurt were palpable. "So I took it! I held you down as hard as I could, and you kicked and splashed and you filled the surface with your desperate need to breathe. Our instinct for survival is primal, and your need to live eclipsed my desire to love. Then someone grabbed me—of course it was a *man*—and you broke the water, shaking, crying, and gasping for air when all I wanted to do was rob you of it. You have to believe me when I say that I did this for you."

When you grow older you become accustomed to death; you become aware of your mortality simply for the fact that people around you die. Of course there are exceptions—that one friend you knew from college whose body was ravaged by illness from a needle she used one too many times. At the funeral, everyone lamented over a life snuffed out in the prime of youth. Everyone was vengeful of a God who neglected to fulfill his part of the agreement—give us our due time in this life, and we will humbly return to you in the afterlife. Some passed by the casket to see our friend for the final time—face all flush with false life and eyes brushed with blue shadows the color of certain skies—and stopped believing. Others, like me, waited until the end, until the casket was sealed and the body lowered six feet down. We walked away feeling nothing because we never believed in the first place.

In this life we are the property of someone else. We are claimed by our father's name and passed, at a certain age, to our husband's house. But what if your family disowns you? What if every man refuses to give you his name? What then? To whom do you belong? Who claims ownership over a body that is merely a deed ready for transfer, a piece of property? Who will stand over your still, sleeping body and feel what it's like to lose you?

"I don't know what you expect me to say." I roamed

the room, adjusted the curtains. I examined the few objects of my mother's affection—a silver comb, a book—and set them down. "Do you expect gratitude? A thank-you note?"

"What I expect is for my daughter not to crawl into my fucking bed."

"I don't understand what you're talking about. Crawling into your bed? What bed? *This* bed? I have my own bed."

"I *see* you." Ellie sat up, wrung her hands. "I also know about that underwear model you hired. Are you so intent on ruining your brother? Of breaking whatever's left of his heart?"

I went numb. "I don't have a brother."

"Is that the story you're telling yourself this month, Kate? Sometimes I think your lies, and that life you've created in your head, keep you alive."

"The life *you* created for me," I said. Remember the car ride, the lamb mask? I do. My life has always existed in between two homes in ruins. I'm Pompeii. I'm the second Vesuvius. They didn't see me coming.

"You're ungrateful and unworthy of my love," Ellie said.

Doctors will later tell me that after Lucia's death, after Jonah told me he wished he'd had the strength to kill me instead of her, I blotted him out. I made it such that it was as if he ceased to exist—a family of four reduced to three (subtraction). While I might have loved my mother once, my devotion to Jonah was a constant, and the morning I stood over Lucia, clutching a belt and rage in my two hands, I saw an unrecognizable look wash across his face: disgust. A common thief, I stole Lucia's last breath, held the bounty in my hands, and he hated me for it. Hated that I'd extinguished possibly the only woman he loved, a woman whom I paid to love him, but then she fell in love with him anyway because that was Jonah. You attached yourself to him.

No one needs to finish me off in a sink, in a pool, or in an apartment in Manhattan, because I've been gone this whole time. Yet, I breathe, and as you grow older you become accustomed to that too. Hurt wounds you, it alters the shape and swell of your heart, and his hate was one I couldn't bear.

"I think you need to rest," I said to Ellie.

"I've been where you are and I've seen what you've seen and worse, and let me tell you this: there is no light in the dark. There's no nobility in living in perpetual blackout. The last thing I need is *rest*. The clocks in this house remind me time is running out. The joke's on me, apparently, because I discovered that I could be happy and it's all too late. That's the one luxury you have, Kate. Time. And you don't even care."

The tragedy wasn't that she thought happiness existed beyond her reach; it was the fact that she believed it existed at all. Weren't we proof that we were generations of a family that had everything we needed but nothing we wanted? And my mother was wrong—I did care. I always cared.

"I followed you into the dark and you left me there," I said.

The day after Ellie died, I woke with scratches on my face and most of the furniture gone, and what was left of it had been rearranged. My dresses covered every inch of the floor, as if tangled together they'd formed a kind of carpet. I spent an hour unknotting sleeves, and removing clocks, combs, and shattered light bulbs and lamps from the confines of my dresser drawers. I couldn't take it anymore. Not one minute, not one day. There was a moment I thought about dying. Who was I kidding? I constantly thought of it. My days were a book where the space between words was infinite, and the words composed a single sentence typed over and over: *You were once here.* Once you'd been a small girl nearly drowned in a pool and stolen from her bed, and now you were a woman whose thighs didn't touch and you let parts of men crawl into the gap and rest there.

"You were Motel 6, flashing Vacancy in neon green. What kind of woman is that?" I said, as Kate. "I said, what kind of woman is that? I said—"

"I'm not deaf; I can fucking hear you. Hard not to," I said, as Gillian.

"I think you should leave."

"A little too late for that, don't you think? If you keep at this, Kate, it's going to be one long life."

"You're not real. You're an imaginary friend. A voice in my head," I said, as Kate.

"Really?" I laughed. "Tell that to Alice. Tell that to yourself. You're the story and you're tragic and simple and perhaps beautiful, but you'll never know this. You'll only realize it when someone else writes about it, and you read a story with a hint of nostalgia. This person sounds familiar, until you realize that person is you, and you're a character in a story rather than a real person who didn't have a beautiful life. This is your life. Not mine."

I thought about the pills under my bed. I could take them, two by two.

"Suicide again? Kate, you're starting to hurt my feelings."

"Shut up. Shut up. Shut up," said both of us.

"Do you honestly think, even for a moment, that Jonah would love you if it weren't for me? Your love is a return-to-sender, an address-not-found. A no-one-lives-here-anymore," I said.

"I don't know any Jonah," I cried.

"How convenient for you," I said.

I ached for the pills, the whole bottle. The pills, now in my hand. How did they get in my hand?

"Take them or shut up about it." To another, a distant voice in the background: "Do you really think our girl is the blood-in-the-bath type? Keep moving, nothing to see. You'll have your time. Isn't that right, Kate?" I said, as Gillian, as Lionel.

You were once here.

Now you're alone in the deep dark. You reach for James's credit card, rope, and matches. You call a motel and book a room. You know what to do.

ANIMAL KINGDOM
2013

WHEN I DREAM about Ellie, she's always asking me for things she doesn't need. She'll stomp into my room and ask for socks in the middle of a heat wave. She'll demand an avocado even though she's allergic. Once she asked for bobby pins with the plastic tips removed, and when I asked about this strange request, she said only, "I need to get into things." When I pressed her she said, "The only solace you offered me in life was pills and a pillow."

I dutifully comply with every request. I make small piles on my bed of pins, ripened fruit, and folded socks. Clusters of nail clippers and passages she loved torn out of library books, folded neatly in three. Her visits comfort me because I have something she might possibly need.

This is what I learn a few months after my mother dies:

1. I could have loved her shamelessly, recklessly, so much so that the enormity of my heart overwhelms her, breaks down her resolve until

she crawls into my bed and lies beside me, one hand over my quick-beating heart. She whispers, *Quiet, girl.*

2. That night she put me in a car and wore that lamb mask, I could have bolted back into the house. I could have burst into Tim's room and told him what my mother intended to do.

3. I could have said, *Go home to your wife, my mother, James*, when he buried his face in my hair.

4. Don't ask about love. Don't even risk it. "Did you love your daughter?" I asked Ellie once. It would take days to understand the shape her face made when she said, "Will *you* love your daughter?"

5. I could have spared Jonah's life when he came back right before the funeral, staking his claim on my mother's heart after I'd broken it. I could have shared her, but instead I viewed my mother's love as a territory I could occupy even after I'd scorched all the land and burned down the trees. I miss Jonah, but he had to go. Unlike my mother, he doesn't visit. Instead, he remains, mouse-quiet, in the basement. *Get to scraping*, I said one evening in his room; I pressed a knife against his face

and at the end of the evening I made cuts. All neat and tidy in that cooler. Instead, I speak for him, give him a part of my life, as reparations, so to speak. Admittedly, it's lonely in this house.

Love is a country you don't know exists until you reach it. When you're finally here, you plant your flag, but still you remain lost.

"HEY, KID. I'M on a pay phone. Can you believe they still make these things? It used to be a dime to make a phone call, now it's a buck fifty to get a dial tone."

"Minnie?"

"No, it's the repo man. Of course it's me. Who else would it be?"

"What happened to your phone?"

"It died. Although I don't understand how phones can actually die when they can be recharged. It's all very dramatic to me."

"Where are you?"

"Home. Things got crazy with the Colombians, and I finally realized I'm too old for this shit. I need beaches, not a banana republic. How are you holding up?"

"Oh, you know me." I wrap the phone cord around

my finger, and it occurs to me that I might be the only person in a ten-mile radius that has a landline. I still use the phone from my childhood—a powder-blue push-button, which never ceases to form a tangled web around my body. I remember thinking that I would pick up the phone and somehow Tim would answer, whispering the directions back to our house in code, and I would pack my backpack and escape when everyone was asleep. I would be Kate again. I would have my books, my blue dresses, and my blue bathing suit back. Gillian would be safely tucked away in my head, not unleashed onto the world like some kind of sickness.

Sometimes it's hard to keep track of all the stories in my head.

"I should've come home when I heard about Jonah. Who just up and abandons their family after a funeral? Even your rotten father had the decency to show up. Have you heard from him?"

"James?" How he kissed the soft patch of skin behind my knees and took my hair in his mouth and let it rest there . . . Why didn't anyone understand that memories are the things you don't want to see, a whole continent you need not revisit?

"God, no. Everyone in town knows James is at home baking pies and getting drunk. He never left, my dear. He never drove that car you spoke of farther west. The farthest he got was the liquor store. I meant Jonah."

"James is here? Of course he is. I imagine Jonah's on an island somewhere, finding new ways to spend what's left of my mother's money. He'll resurface; he always does."

"I'd like to see you, or what's left of you. Word is you don't leave your house much these days." The caution in her voice, the way she draws the words out, is palpable.

"My mother's ashes are in my bedroom, in a box. Should I be working the farmers' market? Making the town rounds so everyone can go home and tell their families that Kate's okay? That they did their duty in ensuring I won't crack up? That they need this small satisfaction to make their lives worth living? Tell me, what is that shit?"

"It must really be terrible having people in your life who care about you. Listen, kid. Your mother died, your father's a wreck, and your brother—who, in my opinion, is not playing with a full deck—went AWOL. You've lived in this shithole town your whole life and you're asking people, your neighbors, your *friends*, not to be concerned?" Minnie bellows. Her voice is the boldest it's ever been.

"I don't have any friends."

"And here I thought the idea of a cell phone dying was dramatic."

I fall into a fit of laughter.

"Now there's the girl I used to know," Minnie says. "Look alive, Kate. I'll be there in ten. You know how I take my coffee."

I REALLY LOVED Jonah. After two months of keeping him bound in the basement, I cried with him and held him all the way to his last breath, to home. His last word was *Lucia*. I'm trying to forgive him for that.

Jonah, will you forgive me for ending your life, for breaking the only trust that children have? Will you remember when I was kind? Is that true, really? Was I ever kind? Afterward, I was surprised how much it hurt to lose him, and how that hurt failed to recede with the passing of each day; in fact, it grew stronger, inverting how time has a way of removing color and sheen. In the weeks that followed, I scrubbed every inch of my home except for the rug where we last lay and the blankets he used to sleep on. Sometimes I sleep on the floor, cocooned in his scent because I'm frightened it'll fade. I grip counters with my hands. I keel over in dark bathrooms, and bite down on my lip so hard I don't notice I'm bleeding. I watch a television show where the voiceover tells me that *grief is like the ocean: it's deep and dark and bigger than all of us. And pain is like a thief in the night. Quiet. Persistent. Unfair. Diminished by time and faith and love.*

Sometimes I open my door and expect to see Jonah, a white star bolting from the other room. I ghost my home thinking that he'll somehow appear, from ether, from air, and it'll be a secret that he's come back, even for just a little while. Even if it's to lull me to sleep, even if it's to tell me that he understands that there was nothing else I could have done. I fill these rooms with the sound of his voice as I remember it, but still he remains mute in that cold box. Even Ellie comes flittering in with her requests or demands. She knows how it is, the defect of our lineage. I only have to assume that he's angry. Jonah, what else could I have done? The police were closing in. They'd find your collection of the dolls we'd stolen—playthings, really—from which I'd removed all traces of my existence, and they'd take you from me. I couldn't have them strap you to a chair and fill your head with shocks or your body with poison. You deserved to be taken home and buried here. Artists and their work are always revered in memoriam. Remember that awful *The Kingdom of Limbs* installation? *The real thing*, I said once, holding you close, *is always much more powerful than its representation.* "What did I tell you about getting sloppy? How many times did I have to tell you?" I say this aloud, in my house, and I am so alone.

In time Jonah will see why I had to do what I've done. He'll understand my sacrifice and he will thank me.

MINNIE GASPS. "HOW are you pregnant?" She does what women aren't supposed to do—she leans in and touches my stomach, uninvited.

"Jesus, Minnie, *thanks.*" I remove her hand and turn away.

"Well, at least we know *why* you've been shacked up all this time. The more pressing question is with *whom?*" Minnie says, coyly.

I divert my eyes. "No one you know."

"I thought you didn't want children."

"I didn't. It just sort of happened. And then my mother and Jonah . . . left. By the time I got around to doing something about it, it was too late."

"I'm pleased as pie, but are you ready for this? After all that's happened. Where's your boy? Is he here, in the house?" Minnie takes a sip of coffee, and I notice the mug shake. Minnie's afraid. The more she laughs and rearranges her hands on her lap, brings the mug to her lips and sets it down, it occurs to me that she's not actually drinking the coffee. She looks occupied, staring at me as if she's trying to sort something out.

"What's wrong?"

"What's wrong?"

"That's what I said."

"I just got back from spending two months in Cartagena with coked-up Colombians who had enough guns to supply a small army. I found fucking *bullet casings* between the sofa cushions. So let's just say that my retirement wasn't what I expected. Then I come home to discover you're pregnant because your pants are too damn tight. You could've told me on the phone, you know."

"I never thought I'd keep it," I say, and in a softer voice I tell Minnie the boy is no longer here. The boy is gone. What I don't tell her is that the boy is actually a man who used to occupy half of my mother's bed. *Never give away the coordinates*, Lionel whispers. The headache dulls at the back of my neck and slowly begins to spread like sickness. I feel something stir in my body and I know that what I need is silence because I can't go on like this. I need all of me here for my daughter. She can't know about the others, the *infestation*. How do I know it's a girl? Of course it's a girl. We are always girls.

"You know I knew your mother since she was a child," Minnie says.

"Jonah told me," I say.

"Oh he did, did he? That kid is the kind who picks up a book, reads the page, and assumes he knows the whole story."

"Minnie, don't. He was trying to help me make sense of things, of her. How she was."

"How would Jonah know how Ellie was? He wasn't even there. I was there, and I wish you would have known her then. Before her mother and her grandfather's money ruined her. You needed a compass to find that old man's heart. I spat on his grave when he died, I did."

"Why do you hate him so much?" I could feel her kicking.

"Your great-grandfather? That man came out of the womb with coins in his mouth. He had a taste for all kinds of metals."

"I mean Jonah."

"I woke one night, late, and I could hear him on the lawn. I could hear the bat come down hard on my pup's flank and all his bones crack. And there's your little angel with blood on him, smiling. Said something about mange. He dropped the bat and left, like it was nothing. There was a dead animal on my front lawn and that fucker whistled home. I called your father, said some things—back then I had a kind of influence on people—and next thing you know Jonah walks by my house, real slow, with bruises on his neck. I'm just sitting there, drinking lemonade, and you know what he says to me? *I won't forget you.* It was his way of keeping me away because he knew things. He knew I'd followed your mother after she left your father; your *real* father—long story, not much of a payoff—and he liked you. No way was I going to ruin that. No way was I going to take you from him. He wouldn't permit you to stay in Nevada."

My body goes cold. It was never James who kept me from my father. It was Jonah?

As if reading my mind, Minnie says, "James knew everything. Not at first, but in time. Your mother was difficult, a colt that had been kept in a barn now allowed to run in the field, and James made his entreaties. That man put on a good show, but he was fucking weak. But she didn't want to leave, and Jonah, well, Jonah was like your great-grandfather—it shocks me that he doesn't have the blood in him—always getting his way."

"It was never James," I say.

"I know what they did to you," Minnie says. "I know about Gillian."

Miniature feet knead, curl, and press. My body is a tiny balloon waiting for puncture. I advance, take Minnie's mug from her cool hands, and say, "I think you should go."

"*Kate.*" Her supplications are no different than James's—I wonder if she sees the irony in that. My head throbs.

"Minnie, I'm tired. Please go."

Minnie collects her things and walks to the door. I stand behind her, place my hand on her shoulder, and she's shaking. She turns and smiles, but her face is foreign to me, an archipelago of cards kept close to the chest. Not yet ready to play her hand.

"I'm considering a new bake shop," she says, after I've opened the door and our eyes are blinded by orange light. Dusk falls, and what's left of the sun tries to shine through the leaf-laden trees. "Give Bunny Blake a run for her money. They say revenge is best served cold."

"I thought you wanted beaches."

"Beaches get boring, kid. I'll be in touch."

After she's gone and I'm alone again, it occurs to me that Minnie isn't tan.

Minnie isn't tan.

His last word was *Lucia*.

TONIGHT, ELLIE SAYS, "Bake me one of your cakes. None of the fancy cartoon stuff, just something simple: two layers of vanilla cake slathered with tufts of chocolate frosting." I tell her that I ran out of baking powder and vanilla extract, to which she responds, "Improvise. That's always been your way."

"You never wanted my cakes before." I pout.

"Leave it to you to throw a tantrum when I'm dead."

We don't talk about the fact that I'm pregnant, although it's obvious she knows. James is verboten. Jonah is nonnegotiable. She'll walk out that door and never come back. Those are the rules. We stick to safe topics: local gossip and the laundry list of requests. After I bake her the cake, she cuts into it with a fork, takes a bite, and says, "You're actually good. Insanely good. It's like I'm eating a chocolate cloud or pillow. I can't decide which."

"And the dead give praise."

"Next time, get me a book. Something carnivorous

and Greek: Sophocles, Euripides, or Aeschylus—maybe *Agamemnon?*" She says, dryly.

I pull a book off the shelf: *Medea*. I recall a documentary I watched on a group of egret chicks pecking their sibling to death while the mother stood by idly, grooming her feathers. A drone voice-over stated, *In the animal kingdom, infanticide is not about pathology. It's about ensuring the strongest offspring survive.*

"You would," Ellie sighs, departing as swiftly as she entered.

Before I go to sleep, I check on Jonah. It's getting harder now because of the smell, the bloated limbs covered in ice, and his blue pallor, but I do it for the possibility that he might speak to me again. Like when we were kids and he'd crawl into my bed when he thought I was already asleep and bury his face in my hair. *You smell like milk*, he used to whisper.

Look. I did what I had to do.

"Look at you, cleaning your feathers," Ellie says. Standing behind me, she crumbles toast in her hand.

"MINNIE. I CAN'T sleep." It's four thirty in the morning and I'm standing outside Minnie's house in my pajamas. Like I'm Michael Jackson.

Minnie's groggy, startled, and her eyes are filled with

sleep. "Come in, kid. Come in." Once inside, she brews hot tea and tears mint leaves. I sit in the kitchen and the light feels medicinal, too bright for the night. Then I notice the photographs of a young man—dozens of them in frames.

"I didn't know you had a son."

"I don't."

"A lover?"

"Hardly." She slices a blueberry muffin in half, a store-bought kind with its brown wrapper and nearly plastic sheen. "That's your father when he was small."

"He died. The day he died he phoned my mother."

"Yes, I know," Minnie says. Her words create a distance between us.

"Why don't you have a tan?"

"What?"

"You went to South America and you look like you spent a month in Walmart."

"I see pregnancy's given you a sense of humor," Minnie sighs. "Is this why you drove over in the dead of night? To dissect the color of my skin? Well, my dear Kate, I'm not tan because I wore sunscreen. Last thing a woman my age needs is cancer."

"But even then . . ." I stare at her pale skin, untouched by the sun. Wouldn't she have something? Why would she lie?

Minnie's exasperated. It's the first time I've been the

recipient of her anger, an emotion once reserved for Bunny Blake and the other cinnamon-bun bakers in town. "Even what? What are you getting at, because I'd really like to go back to sleep."

"I miss Jonah," I say, realizing Minnie isn't going where I want her to go.

"He'll come back; he always does. You said so yourself." Minnie sips her tea, drinks it for real this time.

"Know what I think? I don't think he's ever coming back. I thought he would, once, but now—now I'm not so sure."

Door shut, locked, key in mouth. Choke.

As I leave I notice a photo tucked behind one of the frames. It's a faded black-and-white picture of my mother, and that boy holding a saxophone. So this is how she smiles.

I want to learn Arabic, Lucia said. Who the fuck says that before they die?

"BECAUSE A WOMAN would never go near a car, much less ride in one, if there's only a man in it. But if there's a woman in the passenger seat, she'll come closer. She'll sniff it out and if you play it just right, she's in. Another woman makes her feel safe. What woman would betray her kind? What woman would stand watch while another gets her head bashed in?" I tell Jonah that this is how we search the terrain and wait for signs of passing, of prey. We take the back roads; we chase storms. We pause in front of bus stops and say: *It's cold out. Why don't you hop on in?* I give the woman my scarf and jacket so she can feel warm, secure, and we drive for a while with the volume on the radio turned up. You play what's familiar: top-forty songs with a beat. You offer your half of a sandwich because the next diner, restaurant, rest stop, is always a million miles down the road. The moment she leans her head against the window and her body goes slack is when you climb into the backseat and say, *How about we play a game?* The belt tightens around her neck and the sandwich makes her drowsy. I tell Jonah this is how we play.

"Sometimes I think that I'm not the one they should be afraid of," Jonah says.

I laugh so hard it hurts. "There was a time when you actually thought you were someone to be feared? Silly rabbit."

Jonah pouts.

I take his hand in mine and squeeze it. One year I crashed my bike into a tree and my father raced over and held my hand. *Squeeze, I want to feel how much it hurts. I want to feel your hurt.* "Time to play the big bad brother. Time to put me in my place."

My hurt was always mine to feel. No one ever asks me about my hurt, if it exists for me. If hurt is something I can feel. No one asks me much of anything. I count my ribs with one hand.

THERE ARE MEN at the door and they're knocking. Am I dreaming? No, the pounding is persistent. I climb down the stairs and open the door and there are three men with guns and a piece of paper. Minnie stands behind them.

They say, "We have a warrant to search the premises; we have a reason to believe . . . ; are you alone in the house?"

"I'm always alone," I say. But there are others here, which I don't say. They sleep beneath the floorboards and in coolers down below. Alice lives here. Jonah lives here. Lucia lives here, not by choice. The men don't know that yet. They don't know about my doll collection, and how I've been beating Jonah at crazy eights and gin rummy because his hands are in one cooler and his head in another. Minnie is strangely quiet, like Jonah, like mice. She just stands there. I blink, thinking I saw a feather in her mouth.

Within an hour, they clasp metal around my wrists. (I don't have a taste for it.) The men in blue talk about rights, how I have them, and would I like to phone an attorney? (No.) They ask whether it's true that I'm pregnant, to which I snicker and laugh and say that this is probably the one life worth sparing. "You know, a joke," I say. "You know, ha ha."

"Funny," they say.

"I have to tell you about Jonah. What he's done. He's dangerous."

James is on the lawn, finishing a cigarette. He flicks it

in the direction of my home and comes closer. "I hope the fucking house you bought with my money burns to the ground. You don't think I know what you did to Ellie, to my *son*? The things you did to those people. I don't even know you."

"What *I* did to Ellie? I cleaned up after your slop, like I always do. And I gave the rest of them, the whole sorry lot of them, a fucking deliverance." I pucker my lips and blow kisses. I'll name my girl Ellie. I will hold her close and she will fall asleep and wake to the sound of the ocean. There are no barnacles here. They've drifted farther out, found deeper attachments.

The men lower my head into the backseat and there is Minnie, triumphant, but also sad. "I've been patient, Kate. I've lost a sister and a nephew because of your family." In a few weeks' time, I will learn that the day Tim died he phoned my mother, told her he could break free of his second wife and grown daughter (another half of me exists) and that they could finally be together. And I'll never know if it was her refusal and the soft click of the dial tone—childhood love wasn't good enough—or whether something else in his life burned the ground beneath his feet, but after Ellie hung up he put a small pistol in his mouth and pulled the trigger. Who knew in a few moments time I would be sending Ellie off into the dark to meet him? Pushing the pills into her mouth, pressing down hard on the pillow—I gave her the greatest gift and

I didn't even know it then. And all this time Minnie was playing detective, picking up clues from Jonah and meeting with the women who'd slipped away. Her job, the detectives told her, was to detect cracks along the surface and keep me from leaving.

"I knew you weren't in Cartagena. That's dramatic, even for you," I say. Then I'm ten again, with my mother and her lamb mask and our car speeding down the street, driving straight through the dark. You must know that I never followed her willingly; I was a fait accompli. In the distance, I could hear a suitcase snapping and a car, four cylinders, burning road. *I'm out*, Lionel says. *Good luck in the nut house.*

Maybe if you hadn't said *Lucia*, I would've been right behind you. I would have run barefoot into the dark alongside you. Couldn't your love have been about me?

Jonah? Can you hear me?

TELL ME ABOUT THE JOY
2014–2015

BEFORE THEY TAKE my baby girl away, I trace an outline over her tiny mouth with my finger. She smells like
cotton and clean, warm sweaters folded into drawers. Although I know they'll change her name, I end up calling
her Rebecca. I didn't have the heart to call her Ellie; I
didn't want to give her all that history. I imagine my girl
swathed in pink chiffon and having a strong affection for
owls. I picture her as tall as my knee, my hip, my shoulder, my head. Her voice will fill rooms. She will color
outside the lines and create her own books, hundreds of
them. She will raise her hand when no one else will. She
will own a Christmas tree and decorate it. She will have
nosy neighbors and a mudroom. She will live by the water
even though she's desperately afraid of it. She will wear
blue at her wedding because why not? She will have real
photos of a complete family in frames. She will never take
it all for granted. When she's older she will read the books
written about me, and watch the videos from the trial

with her husband by her side, holding her hand. *Squeeze it so hard that it hurts. I want to feel your hurt.* She will never visit me here while I'm alive, but she will stand over my grave when I'm dead. She will leave me hyacinths, because she read somewhere that those are the flowers I liked.

We will never be as close as we are now. I have five more minutes with you. I spend them imagining your whole life with me in it.

Over the past year, a man with a briefcase visits me daily. I learn that Julia Cassavetes isn't dead, not by a long shot. In fact, she's very much alive, although the clock's ticking on her cancer (tick tock, tick tock), and she, along with her sister, have identified me as one half of the Doll Collector. The other half has been cremated. At the hearings, Minnie chimes in with circumstantial evidence of seeing Jonah and me return from one of our excavations. James talks about how he wanted to change the locks and buy a gun, but Ellie laughed it off, saying, *Kate wants me to love her; she'd never hurt me.*

I shake my head. Obviously, I didn't do those monstrous things. I'm a baker; I make cakes in the shape of cartoon and sitcom characters. That was all Jonah and his friend, Lionel. (Can you give us a description of this Lionel? Do you know anything else about him? Where he lives? How your brother knew him?) In response, I tell them that everything I've done has been about protecting Jonah. Do I look like I would do those gruesome things? Sew those girls' mouths shut and bury them in the walls, all wrapped up in cellophane? The Doll Collector? Seriously?

Look at me.

"How is it then, Kate, that your brother ended up in your basement, in parts? How did his head and torso end up in one ice cooler, and the rest of his body in another?" an attorney will ask me.

"Objection," my attorney shouts.

"Well, that's complicated," I say.

"Did you murder your brother?"

"Murder? No, he was already dead."

"You found him that way."

"Not exactly."

"May we approach the bench, your honor?" my attorney implores.

After three months, they sentence me to an institution where I will live out the remainder of my days in a locked room with a tiny window. In this room there is a toilet, a sink, a mattress, and a camera that films my every movement—film my daughter will one day request and watch in her bathroom. I spend four hours a day in therapy and the rest medicated. Lately, I've been distrustful of paper so I've taken to writing on the walls. I write small so I have enough room to tell you everything.

The doctors ask me if it hurts, and how many times do I have to say yes before they hear me? How many times do I have to tell Ellie, out loud, that I love my daughter before she believes me?

Outside the room, I beg everyone to call me Rebecca but they say my first and last name, Kate Kelleher, as if it were a disease. Kate Kelleher, how are you feeling today? Kate Kelleher, we think it's time to increase your dosage. Kate Kelleher, we noticed that you haven't touched your peas. But inside, I imagine that I am Rebecca and I recreate every year of her life. It's hard being an infant and toddler with all the outbursts, tantrums, and half words spit out, but I long for childhood; I dream of swing sets, ice-cream cones, and picture books. My world is simple, clean, and large enough to fit everyone.

It's possible to live your whole life in your head.

WHEN I AM small, my mother tries to bathe me in bleach. When I am ten, she holds my head underwater as I kick and scream and choke on chlorine. *Why do you hate me?* I ask. *Oh, Kate, it's not about hate; it's about love. There's so much I don't want you to see, and you'll see all of it and hate me for not saving you from it. Children create these magical, complete worlds that adults find ways to ruin. I want to save you from ruin. Do you understand, Kate?* No, but I say I do.

THERE IS A woman on a hotel bed and her hair is on fire. I've bound my hands with ropes—you can't imagine how hard that is to do—and hold a lighter, Lionel, to the ends and feel soothed by the sour smell of hair singed from the ends. I remember burning my cheek. I remember lying down as Gillian and waking, like from a dream, as Kate. The day before my mother died my father called to give her one last chance. *Going, going, gone,* he said, trying to crack a joke, trying to bring some levity to the fact that they were no longer who they had once been. She told him that they were no longer children—their time had passed. The day my mother died she was making toast. I watched her set down the phone and move about the kitchen carrying her grief. I close my eyes and will my goodbyes, and with every want, every wish, every fare-well, I'm forced into a darkness that waits only for me. My body is a house and all of the lights flicker, fade, and burn out. I run to the bathroom and hurl myself against the shower wall. I cut the ropes. The curtains are aflame. I leave a room blazing.

What have I done?

ACKNOWLEDGMENTS

KIRA HENEHAN READ seventy pages of this book, and I'm grateful that she pressed a hot poker against my back, urging me to keep going. I'm humbled by my early readers (you know who you are!), who gave incisive and necessary feedback. I'm forever indebted to everyone who's stuck by me since my first book, patiently following my strange journey to this novel's publication.

Thank you, my tireless and wise agent, Matthew Carnicelli, for being my champion, editor, truth-teller, and cheerleader for the past decade.

If I could stretch my arms and hug you from the West Coast, Jennifer Baumgardner, I would. You saw my vision for this book, understood Kate's complexity, and I'm grateful that extraordinary risk-taking editors like you exist. The whole team at the Feminist Press has been nothing short of amazing—you have all my deepest gratitude, love, and donuts. Thank you, Jisu Kim, Alyea Canada, Drew Stevens, Lauren Hook, Lucia Brown, Suki Boynton, Hannah Goodwin, Lucy Stewart, and Nikkia Rivera—I couldn't have dreamed of a more beautiful book, from cover to cover.

My deepest gratitude to Joe McGinniss Jr., Laura van den Berg, Liza Monroy, Matthew Sharpe, and Kelly Braffet for your careful read and kind words.

Finally, thank you to my friends who are my family, for dragging me out of the darkness and into the light. Amber Katz, Lara DeSignor, Persia Tatar, Nadine Jolie Courtney, and Meaghan Cleary—your kindness during my darkest moments and friendship mean more to me than you could ever know.

The Feminist Press is a nonprofit educational organization founded to amplify feminist voices. FP publishes classic and new writing from around the world, creates cutting-edge programs, and elevates silenced and marginalized voices in order to support personal transformation and social justice for all people.

See our complete list of books at
feministpress.org